WITH BLOOD AND ASH

FEATURED AUTHORS

T.M. BROWN
DAVID GREEN
CRYSTAL LYNN HILBERT
JOEL R. HUNT
MICHAEL D. NADEAU
ROSE STRICKMAN
WYNNE F. WINTERS

AN EERIE RIVER PUBLISHING ANTHOLOGY

WITH BLOOD AND ASH

Paperback ISBN: 978-1-990245-01-5
Hardcover ISBN: 978-1-990245-02-2
Digital ISBN: 978-1-7772750-6-8

Edited by Alanna Robertson-Webb
Cover design Zoe Perdita @ Rainbow Danger Designs
Book Formatting by Michelle River

ALSO AVAILABLE FROM
EERIE RIVER PUBLISHING

NOVELS

STORMING AREA 51

HORROR ANTHOLOGIES

Don't Look: 12 Stories of Bite Sized Horror
It Calls From The Forest: Volume I
It Calls From The Forest: Volume II
It Calls From The Sky
Darkness Reclaimed
Midnight Shadow: Volume I

DARK FANTASY ANTHOLOGIES

With Blood and Ash
With Bone and Iron

DRABBLE COLLECTIONS

Forgotten Ones: Drabbles of Myth and Legend

COMING SOON

It Calls From The Sea
It Calls From the Doors
It Calls From the Veil
Dark Magic: Drabbles of Fantasy and Horror
The Sentinel
In Solitude's Shadow
The Void
A Sword Named Sorrow

This book is dedicated to our families and friends, to those who have stood by us, coffee in hand, and told us never to give up on our dreams.

In these strange times we would also like to dedicate this book to the front-line workers that fight to keep us all safe, to the parents that had to make the hard decision to stay home and the unseen and overlooked heros who make our lives possible. Thank you.

STORIES

FOREWORD

We want to take a moment and thank you for purchasing this book, for supporting Eerie River Publishing and for experiencing the talented authors we've featured.

It's in our natures to seek comfort in words, and in a world of lockdowns and change, we hope these stories guide you on a written journey into worlds filled with magic and lore.

Inside this anthology of dark fantasy, you will read original stories filled with hope and delight, despair and ruin and everything in between.

May you be forever entertained,
Eerie River Publishing.

The Spring in the Desert
Wynne F. Winters

Silas rested her back against a large rock, grateful for the little shade it offered. Red dust danced in the heated wind around her, sticking to the tan skin beneath her tattered clothes. The mountain pass walls stretched hundreds of feet high, but with midday approaching shadows were minimal. The sun beat down relentlessly, with not a single cloud to dull its might. There rarely was — it hadn't rained here for nearly 100 years.

Silas sucked on the flat stone in her mouth, trying not to think of water. That was the commodity these days — people lied for it, stole for it — even killed for it. When the drought first began no one seemed too concerned — there were water mages aplenty, enough to pull the blessed substance from the ground, and even the air. But then fewer and fewer were born every year, until mages of any kind were considered worth their weight in gold. Any water mages now living were kept under lock and key by the warlords who ruled the vast desert, forcing anyone who wanted access to bend the knee.

Or, like Silas, steal from those people.

Something stirred around the bend in the road, jolting Silas from her reverie.

She knelt, resting her fingers against the ground and closing her eyes. She detected a faint vibration, the sensation growing stronger moment by moment. Quarry.

Moving quickly Silas stood and pocketed her flat stone, already tasting the sparkling water on her tongue. The mountain pass lay between two of the largest warlord compounds, meaning anyone who wanted to travel to one or the other had to make their way through. Silas wasn't stupid enough to try robbing any of the official convoys, but unaccompanied travelers — they were ripe for the picking.

From what Silas had felt there was one on their way right now.

She waited with her eyes closed, listening to the low whistle of wind through the pass. Gradually she picked up a new sound: the shuffle of footsteps. Focusing she detected an odd rhythm — not two beats, but three. With her experience she identified the anomaly immediately: a walking staff, not uncommon for those making the journey on foot.

A solitary traveler was rare — Silas wasn't the only bandit in this desert, and bands often included five or six thugs. Still, Silas wasn't going to look a gift horse in the mouth — one would be easier to steal from than the usual caravan.

Silas waited, her body tense and ready. The steps got louder, accompanied by rustling cloth and hard, steady breathing. She waited, eyes closed, as the air vibrated with sound. Then, when the vibrations reached a crescendo, she leapt from behind the rock, dagger in hand.

A woman trod the path, a walking stick in hand. She looked a few years older than Silas — well into her twenties — but everyone looked older than their years in this place. Her dark dreads were pulled back and secured with a leather thong, and her rich skin beaded with sweat. Her eyes went wide with surprise as Silas darted forward, her small frame a blur as she attacked.

The traveler got her staff up just in time to block Silas's dagger. Gritting her teeth Silas jumped back, looking for an opening. The traveler stood with her staff in two hands, face set with determination.

Silas feinted, then dived for the traveler's stomach as she moved to block the blow. But it was Silas who had been tricked — the traveler herself had feinted, her movement bringing the staff sharply into Silas's temple.

Silas stumbled back, stars in her eyes. She'd hoped to beat the woman into submission and go through her belongings at her leisure — now she risked having the same done to her. Her eyes locked on the water skins that hung from the traveler's waist. She'd have to grab and flee if she wanted to survive another day.

Silas, still seeing stars, made to slash at the traveler's throat and force her to defend herself. With her other hand Silas grasped at the water skin, fumbling with the string that held it.

The traveler's knee slammed into Silas' stomach, knocking the air out of her.

Silas lost her grip on the skin and fell to her knees, gasping frantically as her body clamored for air. The traveler took the opportunity to retreat a few steps, her staff at the ready. Silas watched her, fingers loose on her dagger; she'd be lucky to leave with her life now. Her eyes drifted to the water skins, plump as cow udders. She could practically taste the water and feel the relief as it dampened her parched throat.

The traveler followed Silas' gaze to her own water skin, slowly taking one hand off her staff and pressing it to her belt.

"Is this what you want?" she asked. Silas, still breathless, did nothing.

The traveler seemed to consider. Then, in one smooth movement, she pulled the skin free and tossed it. It landed with a hefty thump several feet from Silas.

"There," said the traveler. "You've got what you wanted. Now leave me in peace."

Silas watched in shock as the traveler skirted around her, staff at the ready, and continued on her way. She quickly disappeared into the twists and turns of the mountain pass, leaving Silas alone.

She sat there for a long time, sweat trailing down her back. She watched the skin as if it were a snake. Who in their right mind would just *give away* water? There had to be something wrong with it — maybe poisoned, or contaminated with disease. Perhaps it wasn't even filled with water at all.

Still, she couldn't ignore her body's intrinsic scream for moisture. She crawled forward, still too weak to stand, and reached for the skin with a shaking hand. The weight and faint sloshing told her there was *something* inside, but did she dare take a drink?

With fumbling fingers she opened the cap. Water

glittered nearly to the brim, beckoning to her. Resisting the urge to drink — a compulsion so strong it was almost painful — Silas brought the skin to her nose and sniffed.

It smelled clean and damp.

Silas stared at the water, caught between instinct and intellect. In the end one truth made her decision: without hydration she would die, sooner rather than later, and if she had to die then better to do so free of thirst.

With that in mind she drank.

The water was cold and clear, the sweetest she'd ever tasted. Though she wanted desperately to chug as much as possible Silas made herself stop after a few sips. This was a blessing, but it wouldn't last forever — she would have to ration it carefully.

Replacing the cap Silas looked down the path. Who was that woman, and why would she give away perfectly good water? To someone who had *attacked* her, no less?

She has more, Silas thought, remembering the other water skins. *Perhaps I can try again, be better prepared next time.*

She started down the path, keeping to the shadows and pausing every so often to listen. Curiosity had nothing to do with it, she insisted firmly. This was about survival — why find new quarry when she had a perfectly good one right in front of her?

◇━◇──◇━◇

Silas followed the traveler through the mountain pass, taking care to stay hidden. Despite the traveler's strange actions she seemed normal enough — at least on the surface. Silas wondered if she was hiding madness beneath her calm exterior — what else could explain her throwing away perfectly good water?

She followed the traveler for two days, camping well away from the light of the traveler's fire. Days in the desert were like an oven, but the nights were teeth-chattering cold. Despite the chill Silas refused to light a fire, sure the light would give her away. Instead she wrapped herself in her bedroll as tightly as possible, catching only a few hours of sleep through her shivering.

On the second night she woke to find a figure standing over her.

"How long are you going to follow me?" the traveler asked.

Silas blinked. "I'm . . . not."

The traveler scoffed. "You know there's safety in numbers, right? Come on."

With that the traveler turned and set off toward her campfire, staff thumping against the dry ground. Silas sat up, watching her in confusion.

After a few steps the traveler paused and turned back. "You coming?"

"Uh . . ." Silas looked at the campfire, then back to the traveler, who rapped her staff on the ground impatiently. "Yes," said Silas, surprising herself. "I'm coming."

Silas lay by the fire that night, but she didn't sleep. Instead she watched the traveler, who lay peacefully in her own bedroll, seemingly deep in dreams.

Nothing about this situation made sense. Was this woman a fool? Why had she invited Silas to join her instead of slitting her throat while she slept? Silas lay wondering until the sky began to lighten, but discovered no answer.

When the traveler rose the first thing she did was offer Silas more water. "You're nearly out, aren't you?" the traveler said, nodding to the skin at Silas's waist — the one she'd previously owned.

"Uh, yeah," said Silas, taking the offered drink. She took a mouthful, but didn't swallow until the traveler took her own swill. Whatever was happening she still didn't trust it.

After a hasty breakfast they broke camp, the traveler eager to be on her way. As they finished loading up their packs the traveler asked, "What's your name?"

"What?" said Silas. She couldn't remember anyone being interested in her name — even temporary allies, or fellow thieves with whom she aligned herself to rob larger caravans, merely called her by some nickname created on the spot. It was easier not to know each other out here in the dust.

"I said, 'What's your name?' I want to know who I'm traveling with."

Silas considered whether or not to lie. "Silas," she said at last.

The traveler nodded. "Pleased to meet you, Silas. I'm Aida. Now let's get a move on."

❖━◦━━◦━◦❖

They walked through the cool part of the morning and into the heat of the day. Silas followed a few steps behind Aida, watching her strange companion. Even now she couldn't say why she was doing this — or what she was doing, exactly. While she moved around often it was always with survival in mind; if you weren't working toward food, water or a place to sleep then you weren't going to be around very long. This begged the question — what exactly was Aida about?

As temperatures reached their peak Silas and Aida settled down to rest, taking refuge beneath one of the rock overhangs. Aida provided water and some dried meat, which they ate in silence. They waited out the hottest part of the day side-by-side, watching the winds stir dust among the red rock.

"Where are you going?"

The words were out before Silas even realized she was speaking. She glanced at Aida, wondering if she would take offense. Aida simply gazed at the desert rock, undisturbed.

"Not too far from here," Aida said. "A few days at most."

"Alright." Silas traced gibberish into the dirt. "So . . . are you going to trade? Or . . . do you have someone . . . waiting for you?"

"No." Surreptitiously studying Aida's face, Silas realized her companion's eyes were blue. Blue like the sky, blue like deep water.

"Why did you give me your water skin? You could've just left me. You didn't owe me anything."

"I had it to give." Aida looked at Silas, those blue

eyes staring at something small and naked inside her. Silas would've bolted if that gaze hadn't held her frozen. "If I'd simply walked on you would've died, and I didn't want your blood on my hands."

Silas was perplexed. She'd taken lives for much less. "Why would that matter?"

Aida studied her for a moment, then sighed. "Come on," she said, rising. "I want to make good time before the sun sets."

They started off again, Silas a few feet back and more confused than ever about the strange woman she followed.

◇━◦━◦━━◦━━◦◇

"Hold up."

Aida stopped, looking back at Silas. "What is it?" she asked.

"We're almost at the end of the mountain pass," Silas said.

"And?"

"There's an ambush," Silas said. Her mouth went dry thinking about it. "The Hellion's Boys — they have an ambush set up at the end of the mountain pass. They'll take everything we have — and us, if they feel like it. Call it the 'toll' for crossing onto the Hellion's land."

Aida's eyes widened. "The Hellion?"

"The warlord who owns this territory, all the way to the East Raider's block." Despite the heat of the day Silas felt cold. She'd spent years avoiding the mere mention of the man — she felt nauseous talking about him now.

"So, what do we do?" Aida said. "Double back and

go around? That will take weeks."

"We don't have to double back." Silas looked up walls of the pass, remembering the path she'd taken so long ago. "We just have to get higher — no one ever looks up when they're the baddest bastards around."

⟡━◦━◦──◦━◦━⟡

It took the better part of the morning to find the path — it meandered, ascending in a series of dizzying switchbacks that measured a few feet at the widest and a few inches at the narrowest. Though arduous it would take them thirty or forty feet above the ambush, curving around the mountain face for several hundred feet before taking them safely to the ground. They would have to course-correct to remain on the current trajectory, but it was worth losing a day of travel to avoid the Hellion's Boys.

Progress was slow. The elements had not been kind; parts of the path had crumbled, forcing them to pause and carefully reevaluate their proceedings. And yet, even at this snail's pace, they reached the end of the mountain pass far too quickly for Silas's taste.

Positioned as they were it was easy to pick out the Hellion's Boys from among the rocks. They lounged in the shade, their weapons close but not in hand. Silas and Aida's path had allowed them to circumvent the scouts Silas knew would be on the lookout for incoming caravans. This comforted Silas somewhat — the last time she'd been this way the Boys were on high alert, making the journey more dangerous.

Silas's stomach lurched as they made their way over

the encampment. Her heart pounded in her ears, vision going in and out of focus. Her fingers were slick with sweat, the dirt caking onto her hands as she inched forward. Her body trembled, though she couldn't say if it was from nerves or the effort of moving so slowly for so long.

She forced herself not to look down, instead concentrating on each step. They were coming around the bend — the ledge would widen in a few feet, giving them sturdy footing and more cover.

Gradually the widened ledge came into view. A flicker of relief flared in Silas's chest and she hurried forward, eager for relative safety.

In her haste her boot came down on a loose stone.

Her body lurched as the ground gave way. She only just managed to catch herself, arms screaming as they took her full weight. The stone, however, fell free.

Silas and Aida watched in horror as it thudded down the mountainside, bumping and jumping before finally landing with a sickening thump on one of the Boys' heads.

The lad screamed as the stone rolled away, leaving a smear of red. The others jumped up, on the alert. Silas and Aida tried to hurry forward, Silas managing to climb back onto the narrow path through sheer willpower, but it wasn't enough. In a matter of seconds the Hellion's Boys were shouting for them to halt and pointing crossbows in their direction.

"Shit!" Silas darted along the narrow path and attempted to throw herself onto the ledge. A crossbow bolt cut across her path, barely missing her. With a cry of surprise she lost her balance and pitched sideways. She heard Aida scream her name and felt a hand grasp at her cloak, but it was too late — she was falling.

Her back hit rock as she bounced and spun her way down, a cloud of dust in her wake. She came to a painful stop about ten feet down, saved by a ledge that also knocked the wind out of her. She lay stunned in the dirt, back to the Hellion's Boys while gasping like a fish out of water.

A cry of victory erupted from below. Soon the sound of scrambling reached her ears as one of the Boys climbed up to see what they'd managed to ensnare. Still fighting for breath Silas felt for the dagger hidden beneath her cloak.

"Hey there, little chickee." A shadow loomed over her. "Let's see what we got here!"

Rough hands grabbed her shoulder, rolling her over. The Boy's grin faded as he saw her face, confusion setting in its place. "Silas?" he asked. Before she could respond, he looked over his shoulder and called to his companions below, "Hey! It's Silas! Can you believe — "

His words stopped abruptly as her dagger entered his stomach. He looked down at the blade, then up at her, his mouth moving wordlessly before she gave him a shove. In a spray of blood he went tumbling down the wall, the other Boys shouting as he hit the ground. Silas crawled to press her back against the wall, mind racing.

"Silas!" A young man with dark hair and a scar across his face came forward. She recognized him as Mica, one of the Hellion's lieutenants. "This is a surprise! Is that any way to greet one of your own? With a blade?"

"I'm not one of you!" she growled, adjusting her grip on the dagger. The hot blood made the handle slick.

"You know that's not true." Mica rested a hand on

his hip. "Why don't you come on down now? Your brother's been worried something awful about you — I'm sure he'll be right pleased to see you again."

"Fuck off!" Silas screamed, her voice ragged with rage and fear. Mica shook his head and *tsked*.

"Now, that's just not civil," he said. "Look, we're not gonna kill you — but we do need you to come back with us. If you get a little roughed up in the process I'm sure your brother will understand."

Silas fought to keep her expression fierce, to hide the terror that threatened to overtake her. "I'd rather die than go back!"

"You say that," Mica said, his brown eyes meeting hers, "but we both know you don't mean it. Just be a good girl and come down, will you? I'd really rather not hurt you worse than necessary."

Silas brandished the knife, the blade flashing in the sunlight. "You want me? Come get me!"

Mica shrugged. "Suit yourself." He gestured to the Boys around him, who grinned and raised their crossbows.

Silas gripped her dagger, but she knew it wouldn't be enough. Mica told the truth when he said they wouldn't kill her, but each of them was an expert with the crossbow; they were capable of cutting her down slice by agonizing slice. Still, she wouldn't let them see her afraid.

With a cry Silas darted forward, ready to descend the last 20 feet to her opponents, when one of the Boys shouted. He pointed at something above her. The others looked, then began to shout to one another while training their crossbows at a new target. Confused, Silas chanced a look. Her jaw dropped.

Aida stood on the ledge, hands spread before her. Between them rose an arch of water, the sunlight gleaming on the undulating liquid. Her blue eyes were resolute, her stance as solid as a mountain.

"Take her!" Mica cried as the Boys adjusted their attack. "Don't kill her — the Hellion will want her alive!" Someone fired a crossbow bolt, aiming to cripple Aida as they'd once intended to cripple Silas. Aida flicked her wrist and a tendril of water erupted from the arch, batting the bolt out of the way.

More bolts hurtled her way, but none struck home. Aida swatted the projectiles with ease, leaving the Boys cursing as they tried to reload. In the interim the water flashed and became dozens of needle-sharp ice shards.

Seeing the change, Mica shouted in panic. "What are you waiting for?! Fire! Fire! Take her down! *Now!*"

A few managed to aim their crossbows at Aida, but none got the chance to fire again. Instead several dozen slivers of ice shot into the group, piercing them through the stomach, the chest and the forehead. They dropped like sacks of potatoes. The only one left standing was Mica, panting with one hand out as his other held a flickering lighter. Water puddled around him, victim to the wall of flame he'd conjured at the last moment.

"Don't move," he said to Aida, "or I'll burn you to a crisp!"

"Stop your bluffing, Mica," Silas said. She leaned against the rock wall, holding her bruised side. "She's got you beat. We both know water mages can pull moisture from the air — but that lighter? It's gonna run out, sooner or later. Just quit while you're ahead."

Mica grit his teeth, looking from Silas to Aida. Finally he started walking backward toward the Boys' jeep, carefully hidden behind an outcropping of rock.

"This isn't over!" he shouted. "You're going to pay — both of you!"

Aida and Silas watched him start the vehicle. He fled into the distance, leaving a trail of dust in his wake.

"Well," said Aida. "At least we can take the direct way now."

"I guess."

Using her staff Aida carefully maneuvered her way down to the ledge. Silas kept her head down, watching Aida out of the corner of her eye. The knife was still clenched in her hand. "You didn't mention you were a water mage."

"You didn't mention you were associated with a warlord."

"I'm not associated, alright?" Silas snapped, looking up despite herself. Aida watched her with cool, unreadable eyes. "That was the whole point. I left — it's been years since I've seen these guys."

"We'll talk about that," said Aida. "For now, let's be on our way — I suspect our timetable has just condensed drastically."

She stretched out a hand, concentrating on the bodies below. They shook as though snakes writhed beneath their skin before water began to flow from their orifices, gathering in the air. In a matter of minutes, a sizable blue orb hung there, the corpses below shriveled husks. Silas watched, half horrified and half impressed, as Aida opened her many skins and coaxed the water inside.

"Waste not, want not," she said. She held out her

hand. "Come on — we have a lot of ground to cover."

Silas looked at the hand for a moment, wondering how she'd managed to get into this mess. Then she sheathed her dagger and clasped Aida's hand.

"Alright," she said. "Let's go."

◇━◦━━◦━◇

The pair spent the day trekking across the open desert, and while they labored under the blazing sun they talked.

"So how are you connected to the Hellion?" Aida asked.

"I'm not," said Silas, her eyes set on the horizon. "Not anymore."

"But you were."

Sweat beaded on Silas's neck, sliding down her back. Everything felt strangely dream-like, as though at any moment she might jolt awake to creeping morning light.

"I was," she said. "But not by choice.

"The Hellion — Fenrir — and I share the same mother. She died when we were young, and we were left to fend for ourselves. Fenrir has always been . . . not right, even as a kid. He was cruel and bloodthirsty. Worst of all, he was unpredictable. He'd be gone for days at a time, and when he came home I never knew if he was going to beat me or splurge on sweets for the two of us.

As terrifying as he was, I guess his temperament was exactly what we needed to survive in the Stronghold. When he got old enough to work in the warlord's gang he rose through the ranks quickly. I sort of followed along like a rat looking for scraps — trying to stay as far away from it as I could, while still enjoying the benefits. I'll admit it, there were a lot of times when I looked the other way, when I just didn't think about why there was food on the table. I was willing to turn a blind eye if it meant surviving.

Then there was the coup. It was so quick — one night of screaming and terror. Panic lit up the city like a bonfire. I hid in the cellar, listening to the chaos raging outside. In the morning the streets were bathed in blood, and Fenrir was on the throne. The other warlords were wary. There were agreements that were suddenly moot. The Stronghold was weak, with many men slaughtered from the conflict, and it would be easy to take if the others joined forces.

So Fenrir decided to make allies. His idea was that no one would dare challenge him if he forged an alliance with the biggest, baddest bastard in this desert, so he reached out to the Cannibal."

Aida's step faltered. "The *Cannibal*? That psychopath? How the Hell did he do that?"

"It wasn't easy." Silas was in a rhythm, the words flowing smoothly from her lips. Maybe she'd secretly wanted to tell this story, to unshoulder the burden of her secrets. "The Cannibal ate the first two messengers, and the third came back missing an arm, but he also had a reply. The Cannibal would consider an alliance, but only if the Hellion was willing to give him something invaluable. Something that would prove his loyalty and give the Cannibal leverage over him, if necessary."

"And what was that?" Aida asked when Silas when she went quiet.

Silas remembered that day, the exaltation in Fenrir's

voice as he claimed his victory.

The cold look in his eyes even as he grinned. "Me."

Silas felt Aida looking at her, but she didn't look back. If she stopped now she didn't think she'd have the strength to start again. The words spilled out of her, hurried and tripping over each other. "I couldn't do it. I'd heard the stories — the heads on pikes, the fields of bones, the captives strung from the walls — and I couldn't do it, so I ran.

I ran into the desert, and that's where I've been living ever since. Robbing travelers, doing what I had to, but mostly trying to stay unrecognized. There's a bounty on my head — I'm sure Fenrir wants to kill me himself. From what I hear he's barely managed to keep hold of his power without the Cannibal's help — and he's had to be ten times as brutal to do it. The moment he hears from Mica he's going to be on the warpath." Silas turned to Aida. "Your turn."

Aida laughed dryly. "Shit, you expect me to follow that?"

"You said we were going to talk."

"I'm not holding out, I'm just trying to think how to start." Aida was silent for a while, her eyes squinting as though trying to see something in the distance. "I had a vision," she said at last.

"A vision?" Silas repeated, side-eyeing her companion.

"Yes, a vision," Aida said, a little testily. "Water is a spiritual medium. When used correctly, it can be a gateway to the fifth element — spirit."

Silas laughed at that. "What the Hell? There are only

four elements! Everyone knows that."

Aida shot her a warning look. "There are five — or there were. Spirit is supposed to be the element that ties the four physical elements together, but water is the only way to interact with it directly. If you use water during meditation you can catch a glimpse into time — the future, or the past. A month ago I received a vision showing me an ancient cavern, and I realized I had to go there."

"So you've been traveling for a month," Silas said slowly, "because you had a *vision*?"

Aida's blue eyes slid to Silas, sharp as shattered ice and twice as cold. "Yes. I did, and you're lucky I listened to it by the way."

Silas snorted. "Why? I wouldn't have come this way if it weren't for you — we've got the fucking *Hellion* on our tails because of your damn vision!"

Aida ignored her. "Back when you ambushed me I could've killed you — I should have. It would've been the smart thing to do, but I'd been warned. My vision had shown me I would be given a choice: to dispense justice, or show mercy. The only way forward was to show mercy — if I didn't, my journey would be doomed.

I think I understand it, now. If you weren't with me I would've walked right into the Hellion's Boys' trap — powerful as I am, I doubt I could've taken them all unprepared. So the vision was right — I needed you to reach my goal."

" . . . I wondered why you didn't kill me." The two of them fell silent, each digesting the new information about their traveling companion.

When it got too dark to keep going they made camp.

Neither spoke as they laid down for the night, backs to each other, and tried to find rest on the rough ground.

Silas slept badly, jerking awake at the slightest sound. Her dreams were filled with half-familiar faces calling her name and snatching at her with ill-formed hands. When she finally woke sweat beaded her forehead, and the sky was beginning to lighten. At first she thought it was the light that had woken her, but then she realized it was something else: a vibration, as though the very air was shaking.

Silas sat up, scanning her surroundings for the source. After a few moments she realized it came from Aida, who sat a few feet away with her head bowed.

The air seemed to warp around her, fluctuating in ways that made it hard to breathe. The hairs on Silas' arms stood up, and a chill went down her spine. Something was happening.

"What are you doing?" she shouted.

Aida started and turned. Water splashed from her cupped hands, quickly absorbed by the thirsty earth. Immediately, the vibration vanished.

"I'm meditating!" Aida said, looking put-out. "What in Hell is wrong with you?"

"You were making things vibrate!" Silas climbed out of her bedroll and crawled over to look at the remaining water in Aida's hands. She'd never heard of water mages being able to control the air like that, but what the fuck did she know? Aida was the first one she'd ever met.

"What are you *talking* about?" Aida opened her water skin and the liquid floated into it, twisting and shimmering like silk ribbon. "I was just — I was having a vision, alright? To verify that we're on the right path."

"The air was vibrating," said Silas, now less sure. She didn't think Aida would lie — perhaps, deep in her vision, she hadn't noticed the strange occurrence. "It woke me up."

"You were dreaming." Aida picked up her staff and stood. "Come on — we need to get moving."

Silas shrugged and started packing her things. Aida was right, after all — the Hellion and his Boys gained on them every second. Silas had no doubt they would catch up eventually, but she was determined to delay the inevitable as long as possible.

It was late afternoon when they reached the caverns. They were a strange sight — rather than gently sloping into the mountainside the entrance had a near-sheer drop that went down twenty feet or so, with precarious handholds worn into the side. As they neared the entrance — a gaping hole like a monstrous mouth — Silas paused. There was something . . . *off* about this place, like an irregular pulse beating beneath the skin.

"What is this place?" she asked as Aida strapped her staff across her back, preparing to climb into the maw.

"I don't know," Aida said, turning to her. "I just know I'm meant to be here. Come — the thing we seek is — "

She stopped, her gaze moving past Silas. Silas didn't need to turn around to know what Aida saw — she could feel the faint rumbling in the ground, familiar from her years spent tracking others' movements. The Hellion was coming.

"We need to move." Aida turned away and started to ease her way down the cavern entrance, trying to move as quickly as possible. Silas waited for Aida to get a lead, then slowly started her own descent. Just before dipping out of sight she took a peek at the horizon.

A dust cloud, so small it might have been a mirage, was visible on the horizon.

Fenrir would have mages with him. Perhaps she and Aida could lose them by hiding in the caves, but . . .

With a sigh Silas continued her way down.

The cavern continued straight into the dark bowels of the mountain. Aida had lit a torch to illuminate their way, the warm crackling the only sound beyond their echoing footsteps. The flickering firelight caught images on the wall, strange carvings that Silas would've dismissed as natural wear if they weren't so regular. There was something oddly . . . familiar about them. Despite their need for haste, Silas found herself pausing along the cave wall and laying a hand against the stone.

There, so faint she might have imagined it, was vibration. The longer she kept contact with the stone the stronger it seemed to grow, until it pounded beneath her fingertips. Unlike this morning the feeling didn't frighten her — in fact it calmed her, centered her. Silas' eyes traced the strange markings, her mind trying to make sense of what her body seemed to instinctually know. What was this place?

"Silas!"

Silas turned and found Aida a few feet ahead, look-ing at her expectantly. "Sorry," said Silas, stepping away. "I'm coming."

Aida said nothing as Silas joined her, though she gave her companion a long, questioning look. Silas ig-nored it and stepped ahead, the torchlight casting her shad-ow ahead of her.

"So what are we looking for?" Silas said. "What did your vision show you?"

"Just the cave entrance," Aida said, keeping pace. "That was as far as I got before you interrupted me."

"Sorry," Silas said again. "I didn't mean to."

"I know."

They walked in silence, darkness behind and beyond their path. It was difficult to tell how long they journeyed — the hall seemed to hang suspended in time and space, as though they'd entered another world entirely.

"Hey, Aida?" Silas asked eventually, her voice echo-ing despite its softness.

"Yes?"

"What are we going to do once we get to the place we're trying to get to?"

Aida stared ahead. "I don't know. I suppose we'll figure it out once we get there."

"Okay, but what if Fenrir and the Boys get to us be-fore we figure it out?"

Aida said nothing.

Silas waited, and when there was no answer she nod-ded. "Right. Okay. Then — I know you're more powerful than I am, but Fenrir doesn't really think, he acts, so — so I can try to draw them away while you figure out what you need to do. Then we can meet up later back at — let's say back at the cave entrance. But don't wait for more than half an hour, okay? If I'm not there in half an hour, then I don't think — "

"Silas," Aida interrupted. She hadn't turned once since Silas started speaking. "Look — light."

Peering down the cavern Silas saw a patch of light in the distance. Exactly how far was impossible to tell, but it was certainly light.

"Come on," said Aida, picking up her pace. "We're almost there!"

The light was closer than it seemed — after only a few minutes the tunnel widened, and they saw the source.

The cavern was a mile high and domed. Oddly-shaped holes several feet wide allowed afternoon sunshine to filter through the ceiling, filling the air with dim, warm light. The floor of the cavern led down in shallow steps several yards wide, creating an amphitheater. At the center lay a stone. It was taller than a human and appeared to be nestled into an indention.

"This is it," Aida breathed. She hurried forward, practically leaping off each step. Silas followed more slowly. The vibration was stronger here, enough for her to recognize its source: the strange stone.

Aida circled it, running her hands along the surface and muttering to herself. "It's a spring," she said when Silas finally approached. "I've seen it in my visions — but this stone is blocking it! Why would someone block a spring?"

"Scarcity breeds power," Silas said. It was something Fenrir had said to her when he was making his empire. "Is that — is that writing?"

"Maybe." Aida wiped at the dust covering the stone, revealing glyphs carved into the surface. "Holy Hell!"

"What *is* that?" Silas said, getting closer. The two peered at the writing, which was worn down by years of wind and dust.

"I don't know," said Aida, furrowing her eyebrows. "I didn't see anything about *this* in my visions."

"Did they show you what to do now?"

"I think that's fairly obvious — we need to move this stone and free the spring." With that Aida took up her staff and began to probe at the bottom of the stone. "It's too heavy to push by ourselves, but maybe with some leverage . . ."

Silas nodded, no longer listening. The vibrations were stronger now, but muffled, like someone humming with their hand over their mouth. Curious, she rested her hand against the stone where the thrum seemed to resonate with her very bones. There was something . . . *more* to this than Aida was thinking, some piece they were missing. Closing her eyes Silas pressed her ear to the warm, dusty stone, and listened.

She heard rushing, like the roar of a mighty river crashing against the dam that held it. The sound filled her until every cell seemed to vibrate with the same frequency. With a gasp she opened her eyes and pulled away, the final piece falling into place.

"It's coming from *under* the stone," she said.

Aida looked up from trying to force her staff beneath the rounded stone edge. "What?"

"Well, look what we have here."

Aida and Silas looked up to find they were no longer alone in the cavern. At the entrance stood a young man clad in spiked leather, his face painted in streaks of red. Around him clustered two dozen men, each dressed in a hodgepodge of leather and metal armor, all wielding crossbows and spiked clubs. A few flicked lighters menacingly.

"What, exactly, was your plan?" asked Fenrir, grinning at them. "You've got no place to go! I'm starting to think you *wanted* to get caught!"

"Aida," Silas said quietly. "You keep working on the stone. Let me handle this." With that Silas stepped forward, her hands up in surrender.

"Silas! Silas, don't!" Aida's voice had a fearful tone Silas had never heard before, but she resisted the urge to look back.

"What's this?" said Fenrir, smirking. "You're really giving up this easily?"

"Like you said, we don't have anywhere to run." Silas couldn't tell if Aida was still working on the stone, but she hoped she was. "It's the only logical choice, really."

"I should've guessed," said Fenrir, victory gleaming in his eyes. "You always *were* a coward." Then he gestured to the crossbowman beside him.

The bolt took Silas in the shoulder. She cried out, her working hand going instinctively to the wound. Behind her Aida shouted her name, but Silas didn't turn. Honestly, she should've expected this — Fenrir wasn't one to forgive old grievances just because he'd won.

"Don't you move!" Fenrir ordered, pointing behind Silas. Turning her head slightly Silas could just see Aida out of the corner of her eye, two globes of water hovering over her open palms. "Or I'll fill her full of bolts! You're both coming with us, and you're not going to give us any trouble. Got it?"

Four Boys stepped forward, two of them moving toward Aida and the other two taking Silas' arms. She hissed as they jostled her wounded shoulder.

"Wait!"

Everyone stopped and turned to Aida. She'd dropped the globes, the water pooling around the stone, her hands up in surrender. The two Boys ignored her plea, still striding forward with clubs out.

"Please, just give us ten minutes! Then we'll go with you quietly," she said. It was difficult to tell, but Silas thought she saw the sheen of tears in Aida's blue eyes. "Just ten minutes, I beg you!"

"As much as I enjoy seeing you beg," Fenrir sneered. "You're not in any position to be making demands. Get her, Boys!"

The two men grabbed Aida roughly, pinning her hands behind her and frog-marching her forward. Meanwhile the spilled water seeped into the space between the stone and its seat, finding the tiniest slivers of passage to the spring below.

A thunderous boom rocked through the space, stealing Silas' breath and sending her to her knees. She struggled to breathe against the vibration — it felt like she was caught in a pounding wave, unable to surface. People were shouting, but their voices were lost in the roar. Looking up she found Aida fighting her captors and calling for her, while Fenrir shouted at the Boys to force Silas upright. All were standing.

"You don't feel that?" she asked one of the Boys as they hauled her to her feet. He sneered.

"Feel what?"

"The call," she said. That's what it was; something below the stone was calling. Calling for *her*. "It needs me. Let go."

"What are you talking about?" said the man. He jostled her on purpose, but Silas was beyond physical sensation, her whole senses taken over by the roar.

"Stop talking to her," said the other Boy. He began dragging her forward, the movement requiring very little effort due to their size difference.

"Let go. It *needs* me. Let go!"

"Shut up!" said the first man, but Silas ignored him. Instead she twisted around as best she could and reached out toward the stone, willing herself forward. She strained with every muscle and every bit of willpower.

"It needs me!"

Something caught, like a fish on a line.

The men tried to drag her forward, but found themselves fighting against an invisible force that held Silas in place.

"What's taking so long?" Fenrir snarled. "Bring her here, you idiots!"

"We're trying, boss!" said one man. He pulled at Silas with all his strength, but his feet slid against the stone. "She won't move!"

"What do you mean — "

Fenrir's angry retort was cut off as the cavern shuddered. The remaining Boys huddled around their leader, watching with fearful eyes as loose pebbles fell and dust rose.

Silas gritted her teeth, pulling with all her might. The stone trembled, though that wasn't what she was latching onto — it was something *beneath*, something that longed for freedom, that held as tightly to her as she did to it. Something familiar.

With a scream Silas threw every ounce of her will into pulling, her vision going white with the strain as joints popped and muscles bulged. The cavern shook, knocking everyone inside to the floor as dirt rained down. Still she pulled, pulled until her ears rang with the sound of her own screams, until she felt nothing but the strain.

Just when Silas thought the effort would tear her apart the stone shattered, pieces hitting the walls, ceiling and some of the prostrate Boys.

Before the dust even began to settle the spring bubbled to the surface, spilling across the tiered ground to wash the entire floor. What poured forth, however, wasn't water — it was something ethereal, a brilliant light that ebbed and flowed. It set the entire cavern aglow. As the light spilled over the walls the cavern transformed, dust dissolving to reveal white stone beneath that was carved with golden, glowing runes.

At the sight of such magic the Boys yelped and ran, leaving behind their captives. Even Fenrir fled, giving a conflicted glance back at his sister before heading down the tunnel.

Silas didn't move. At the release of the stone she'd collapsed, hardly able to breathe as the light washed over her. She was spent, her limbs useless and the taste of blood in her mouth from biting her tongue. Yet, when the light touched her, the exhaustion lifted and the pain receded.

Confused, she sat up. The crossbow bolt still protruded from her shoulder, but the pain was gone. She grasped the bolt and pulled, the weapon sliding easily from her body. There wasn't even blood on the point, and when she checked her shoulder there was a hole in the fabric of her shirt — but the skin beneath was untouched.

"Silas!"

Silas turned to see Aida wading toward her through the light, joyful tears coursing down her face. Without warning Aida flung herself on Silas, holding her close. "You did it," the water mage whispered. "You freed the spring!"

"I did," said Silas. She dropped the bolt, watching as the light consumed it. "But, um . . . what exactly is this stuff?"

Aida laughed and pulled back. "It's spirit! I never thought — you can actually *see* it! Touch it! Gods, it's like something from a legend . . ."

Silas watched as the spirit eddied around her, seeming to follow her movements. "I think — I think I've used it before. Or something."

"You're obviously a spirit mage," Aida said, as though she were the authority on this new — old? — element. "That was why the visions wanted me to show mercy — *you* were the only one who could free the spring!"

"That seems like a lot," said Silas, but a drop of something wet on the top of her head made her stop. She looked up, only to catch another drop in the eye. "What the Hell?" she said, wiping at her face.

"Silas." Aida's voice was reverent, barely more than a whisper.

"What?"

"I think . . . I think it's raining."

As she spoke more drops fell through the holes in the ceiling, until they were in the midst of a true downpour. Water soaked their clothes and hair, falling cool and refreshing on their lips. For a few moments they sat staring through the torrent at the dark clouds that cast the cavern in shadow.

"Hold on," said Aida, seeming to come back to herself. Holding up her hands she manipulated the rain into a dome above them, water running in rivulets around the sides. They grinned at each other like children, too overcome with emotion for words.

"Should we head back to the tunnel?" Silas said suddenly. "So you don't have to — you know."

"Sure," said Aida, though she seemed reluctant to move, as though fearing to break a spell. Eventually the two got up and headed back to the tunnel, where water rushed past their ankles. Aida and Silas looked at each other, wondering if the other was thinking what she was thinking.

"Do you want to look?" Silas asked.

"Do you think they'll be out there?"

"Even if they are, I'm sure they're no match for you — you could drown them where they stood in this downpour."

That settled, the two headed for the cavern entrance.

◇━◦━━◦━◇

By the time Aida and Silas reached the cavern entrance the

water was up to their knees, the sheer wall little more than mud. Silas despaired of ever climbing it, but her lament earned her a mischievous grin from Aida.

"Now that you're a mage, you've got to start thinking like one," she said, grabbing Silas by the waist. Before Silas could protest a water spout had formed under them, lifting them easily to the top of the wall.

Once there they gazed at the landscape in wonder.

Fenrir and his Boys, it seemed, had tried to flee, only for their vehicle to sink into the mud about fifty feet away. Now they knelt on the ground in amazement, staring at the water pouring down from above. Even Fenrir was staring in awe, the red paint running down his face in rivulets. Silas knew what he was thinking — that this changed everything.

She thought so too.

Lightning forked in the distance, and thunder rumbled so loudly that Silas felt it in her chest. Her eyes traced the desert landscape, made unfamiliar by the storm, and in the midst of the chaos Aida's hand found hers.

They stood together for a long time, fingers entwined, watching the world's rebirth.

Wynne F. Winters
About the Author

Wynne F. Winters has been known to dabble in the fantastic and the macabre, sometimes at the same time. She's been published in several horror anthologies, including Daughters of Darkness, Black Rainbow, and Mother Ghost's Grimm. She's also been known to post stories online under the Reddit username u/firesidechats451.

If you're interested in hearing her controversial tea opinions, being regaled with grisly true crime details, or finding out when a new story of hers is up, you can follow her on Twitter @WintersWynne or check out her Facebook page at https://www.facebook.com/WynneFWinters.

MASTER AND APPRENTICE

DAVID GREEN

PART ONE - THE CITADEL

Takar Bane believed what he needed to do was right, and that it would be done alone. No one else possessed the strength, or will. Bane was the only Redan prepared to act for the greater good of mankind.

The time for action drew near.

Bane strode through the corridors of the Citadel. A massive fortification that loomed on the outskirts of Sanisco City, the building served as the training grounds and base for the entire continent's Redan Monks. They were peacekeepers, men and women who guarded society and those who couldn't protect themselves. Four percent of the entire population could bend the elements - Earth, Wind, Fire, Water and Spirit - to their will, but of this number only half passed the trials to take their place among the Redan. Takar Bane was their best. Unlike most he'd mastered control of all the elements to the highest level; this included spirit, which was the rarest and most obscure of magics.

His steps drew him closer to the council chamber, and though resolved that his task would be one of solitude it didn't mean he wouldn't give his fellow Redan's one last chance to help him. *Plus*, he thought, *my brethren can assist in other ways. I wonder if that is their purpose for living*?

"You know," someone muttered breathlessly at his side, "you'd be the head of the council if you weren't so… contrary, Master."

Bane blinked away his thoughts and looked down at his apprentice. He had forgotten she was there, but felt a swell of pride and sadness as he regarded her. Sabea Crow was the most talented apprentice the council had come across since himself. *How I wish I could count on you in this*, he thought, *but I know you wouldn't understand. And I can't bring myself to make you, not yet.*

"You're probably right," Bane said instead, laying a dark-skinned hand on her shoulder and slowing his step a little. "Could you imagine me being cooped up on the council, though? I'd have gone mad."

"Master," Sabea replied, rolling her eyes, "people think you're crazy anyway," she laughed. "I suppose I should be thankful. I much prefer it out in the frontiers with all its shit, piss and death than hanging around San-isco."

A Redan's main duty was to protect. The city of Sanisco had mostly embraced civility, with the population finding it a safe place to live, but crossing the mangled, rusted bridge into Arin, or anywhere out of city limits, was a different matter entirely. Beasts, outlaws and the Sickness festered amongst the plains. The few cities left had become overcrowded, and many lived in villages and towns of the frontier. Adventurous folk who had wanted to take their chances in the wilderness, to delve into the secrets of their ancestors known as 'the civilization that came before', could possibly find their fortunes. It was a Redan's task to protect the way of life of the families and communities that had sprung up around these initial explorers.

Bane knew Sabea lived for the thrill of battle. At only seventeen she'd become more adept than most with the four elements. Her inability to manipulate Spirit seemed to be her only blemish, a failing becoming increasingly more common among the Redan. Takar Bane knew the truth, though. He could sense her natural affinity in that field; it just hadn't awakened yet. That was the secret of Spirit; the element was alive, and to use it a sacrifice was needed. Weaving meant a small part of the magic user traded away. It fed on souls, because of its very nature, and that aspect of the element was central for why he approached the council now.

"If you're lucky enough to see my age," Bane told her, "you'll appreciate a more sedate way of life, though that's not for me either. Look, we're at the chambers."

The doors were pieces of art, ornate and gleaming, weaved with all five elements by Redan of ages past. Bane could see the faint glow of the magic used, and it was also emanating from the rest of the Citadel. Elemental magic left an imprint that adepts could see, like a trace memory, and the civilization that came before seemed to have lacked the talent. Their ruins, built without sorcery, were like a twisted bridge that would collapse after time. The legends spoke of fires raining from the heavens that destroyed them, making humanity take centuries to rebuild.

Whatever had happened to their ancestors meant the ruin created such a collapse that it had opened the way for the rise of elemental magic. The Redan had harnessed it to repair the disaster, leaving the work of the early magicians unmatched while the talent of using the elements had diminished with time.

I know why our power is waning, he thought, *and how to put a stop to it.*

"Why did you call me here anyway, Takar?" Sabea asked, arms crossed beneath her breasts and she threw a glare at the chamber doors, "It's not like you need me with you."

"I have a task for you," Bane replied, "it needs carrying out immediately."

"Anything Master, you know that," Sabea replied immediately, a slight frown on her forehead, "I thought… no, it doesn't matter."

"You guessed today was when you'd become a full Redan in your own right?" Bane asked gently.

"Yes," she answered, eyes fixed on the marble floor.

"Sabea, look at me," Bane said, placing two fingers under her chin, titling it upwards. He stared into her remarkable, orange-hued eyes; they never failed to take his breath away, such was their intensity, "you are ready. It won't be long. Sadly, today is not that day. I need you to take a message into Arin Town where Hexan Ashes will be waiting."

"What shall I tell him, Master?" Sabea answered.

"Contact me when you arrive," Bane answered, placing his palm on her cheek, "I would not write this down. Go."

"Yes, Master," Sabea said, before grinning and flicking her head towards the council chambers, "good luck in there. You're not the most popular of people, you know?"

They'll think even less of me after today, Bane thought, watching her walk away. She was a daughter to him in so many ways, especially since he lost his own.

He called upon Spirit and pushed the doors open, striding through them. Adepts could see when another called upon the elements, but holding Spirit masked it. Bane drew as much of the five elements as he could call upon, safe in the knowledge the others would be unaware. *Not a single Spirit user among them*, he thought to himself, keeping the sneer from his face. The Redan in the chamber had been talking amongst themselves, but a hush descended as Bane marched to the dais in the centre of the circular room. The council, comprising an even split of twenty-four men and women, wore multi-colored robes as a representation of their elements. Average Redan would wear garments in the color which signified the strand of magic they associated with most closely. Bane wore black, and had done so since the Sickness claimed his family.

"Takar Bane seeks approval to address the council of the Redan," he called, weaving in a slither of Spirit to raise his voice. The others had always resented him for how easy he made such a difficult task as amplification look.

"Takar Bane," Rikken Hessam, a woman sitting in the centre of the raised semi-circular seating, spoke. There was no official council head, but if there was it would have been her. "The council of the Redan recognizes you, and grants you the freedom of speech. Use it wisely."

Bane inclined his head in response, then swept his

gaze across those gathered in front of him, dark eyes twinkling. He felt a rush of power; holding all five elements made him feel invincible. Exceeding the limits of what he could draw was dangerous, but Bane had always been a risk taker. He had to push past his barriers this time. *Gently does it though,* he told himself.

"Fellow Redan," he said, focusing on Rikken Hessam, her watery, blue eyes seeming to shine brighter from the amounts of the Water element he held, "I come to you to seek your help. Possibly the most important undertaking since this building, and our order, came into being."

"So lucky you came to us," Hessam replied, a mocking smile on her lips. Some council members laughed, others appeared bored, "Enlighten us, please."

Fools, Bane thought, the Fire at his command making his blood run hotter than normal. He tried to force the reckless emotion away; his ability to focus was of paramount importance.

"I have discovered why our command of the elements diminishes," he paused, expecting a reaction from the council. There wasn't one. Bane seethed at their lazy ignorance. "I have traveled further than most, seeking answers about the civilization that came before. Perhaps the dead could tell stories on why we fail? I found those reasons."

"Where?" Hessam asked, leaning forward slightly in her chair. "We know of every relic within five hundred miles of Sanisco."

"Far to the north, where ice smothers all life into a slow death. Yet it does not destroy, it preserves." Bane held up a single finger, the black flame of Spirit hovering above it, "We know our ancestors did not control the elements as we do, because magic is not of this reality. The element we call Spirit exists as another realm, the domain of death, our afterlife; the same place we pull our magic from. When the skies spat flames, scorching the earth and destroying the civilization before us, so much death weakened the walls between our dimensions. Now that seal is closing again, and soon our magic will disappear forever."

Silence followed Bane's proclamation. Hessam's mouth opened and closed mutely, like a marooned fish gasping for air.

"Ghoul's shit!" a man cried, breaking the uneasy stillness.

"You've finally snapped," Hessam muttered. Bane looked into her eyes to see truth there, and the possibility he was correct terrified her.

"Think," Bane replied, pouring passion in his voice, one last attempt to change his plans to something less... absolute, "we've all seen the records left from our ancestors. They proved their gods false, the afterlife revealed to be a myth, yet we *know* it exists now. Who among you hasn't seen a specter?" Suppressing the memory of his wife and children, Bane continued, "Who hasn't felt the extra strength required to call upon an element, even for such a simple task as lighting a candle? How many new apprentices did we enroll this year? A quarter of the previous intake. Our magic is failing, but, my friends, there is a way to stop that."

"How?" a shout came from a council member, a woman with a wild look in her eyes.

Takar Bane paused, starting at his feet. *Here it is,* he

thought, *one last roll of the dice.*

"The barrier between the Spirit realm and ours is strengthening," he said, looking up and staring into Rikken Hessam's eyes, "I propose we destroy it."

"You're a lunatic," Hessam whispered, "a fucking madman. Your grief has unhinged you, but even if you're correct that would mean living among the dead."

"Yes," Bane answered softly, "we spend our lives fearing death, but those such as we should not dread the end. We should embrace it; only then can we master it."

"Enough," Hessam snapped, "this is preposterous. We have listened to you long…"

Bane stopped listening, instead thinking of his apprentice. *If she'd used Wind, she would arrive in Arin Town at any moment,* the thought, *and then...*

"I demand a vote," Bane cut in, his amplified voice drowning Hessam's, "as is my right."

"Fine," Hessam spluttered, gathering herself, "Takar Bane wishes the council of Redan to vote," she shook her head, "on the following motion: 'To destroy the barrier between our world and the afterlife.' Is such a feat even possible?"

'*Master,* Sabea Crow's voice echoed in Bane's mind, *I'm in Arin Town, but there's no sign of this Hexan Ashes. Are you sure this is the right place?*'

'*He'll be there eventually, you are the message to him,* Bane replied, smiling sadly. *I am sorry, Sabea. Please remember, what I do is for the greater good. I've always been proud of you.*'

'*Master…*' Bane blocked the connection between himself and Sabea. He could feel her battering away at his subconscious in an attempt to contact him. He knew he had to act fast, as she would attempt a return to Sanisco immediately; he could not have that.

As Bane spoke inwardly to his apprentice, the vote had reached its conclusion. All had cast against his plan. *Just as I expected,* Bane thought. *I must continue alone.*

"To answer your question, Hessam," Bane said, holding five fingers out in front of him, "collapsing the barrier between our realms is possible. All it requires is the use of all five elements."

One by one different colored flames appeared above Bane's fingertips. Red for Fire, green for Water, blue for Wind, brown for Earth and, finally, black for Spirit.

"And the help of twenty-four adepts, willingly or not."

Bane brought his hand down to the ground, weaving together the full power of the elements he'd gathered into his fist. A multi-colored conflagration exploded as he slammed into the marble floor, the spectrum rushing outwards and washing over the council.

Silence.

Nothing seemed to have happened. Bane straightened as the other Redan patted themselves down in relief, expecting the worse but finding nothing untoward had happened. Rikken Hessam laughed.

"You've done it this time, Bane. Using magic against the council? We'll have you quartered for this. It will be my pleasure, they will do it in front…"

She coughed suddenly, water spilling from her mouth. She raised her hand to her jaw, but her fingers passed straight through the flesh and out the other side, her lower face disintegrating into red slime. Her skin seemed to turn pinker, steam oozing from her ears and nostrils. Her eyeballs popped, viscera sliding down her face. Rikken Hessam, and the other council members, were being cooked from the inside. Bane's control of the elements had turned their blood to fire and set the water inside them to boil, steaming them alive. His power melted their flesh and weakened their bones; those still with tongues screamed as they liquified on the spot.

That wasn't all Bane had weaved. Earth and Wind had created a barrier outside the Citadel, one that only he, and those he allowed, could cross. Then there was Spirit, the element cast to control what came after.

As the council perished their souls became trapped while they attempted to cross into the afterlife. Bane saw them forming, green-hued specters with faces locked in the anguish of their deaths, longing for the peace death was so cruelly denying them.

"Twenty-four adept souls," Bane said, pulling in almost more Spirit than he could handle, "enough for what I need."

He sucked on Spirit, not just on the element that came from that foreign place, but from the specters hovering in front of him. Just as he felt he could hold on for no longer Bane unleashed his power. The specters screamed as one, drained into nothing and cast into oblivion. A black dome cascaded outwards, encasing the Citadel and all of those who remained inside.

PART TWO - THE FRONTIER

Sabea Crow slid face-first through the mud, coming to a stop as she crashed into a stack of crates.

"Fuck," she grunted, pushing herself up to all fours and shaking the filth out of her eyes, "the bastard's an Earth elemental. Shit."

She spun on to her back and looked across the hundred metres the demon had flung her; the fact that she'd weaved a little Wind as she twisted through the air like a rag doll saved her from any real damage. Creatures aligned with Earth were the trickiest to deal with, though, Sabea reflected, they weren't the most intelligent. She was the only soul left alive in the village, as the demon had obliterated the town before Sabea arrived, and her desire to limit its rampage was becoming redundant. All she could do now was kill it. The elemental had decided that she was no threat, instead busying itself by tearing the limbs from the discarded creatures, blood spurting across its face and beady, purple eyes.

Redan training focused heavily on dealing with creatures such as these. Monsters were a regular menace in the frontier, be it elemental or the mutants and ghouls that roamed the wastelands, but magical brutes had been on the rise in the five years since Takar Bane had taken control of the Citadel. *Whatever he's doing in there has really sent this world to shit*, Sabea thought, climbing gingerly to her feet, *as if it wasn't bad enough before*.

Sabea probed the part of her mind that felt numb, the section she would use to speak to Bane. All masters and apprentices shared a link, but now it felt like she was flicking her tongue across an old wound on the inside of her cheek. Occasionally she felt a faint stirring, as if Bane was doing the same thing. It meant he was still alive, and she didn't know if that made her more happy or livid.

Bane trapped every person who had been in the Citadel that day, and the midnight barrier her former master had constructed around it was impenetrable. The entire council had been lost.

The Redan now numbered less than two hundred, which wasn't enough to protect the Continent, and there were too few to test for new recruits. They were dying out, all because of Takar Bane. '*Please remember, what I do is for the greater good...*' he had told her, before raising the walls in between their link. The might of the elements he'd unleashed at the Citadel had knocked her senseless, even though she'd been miles away in Arin Town. Sabea had been in denial at first, insistent that the council must have turned on Bane and he defended himself. Until she returned to Sanisco, and saw the obsidian dome; she recognized the trace of her master's magic.

Shaking her head clear of old worries she could do nothing about, Sabea returned her attention to the Earth elemental. It was now beating an already deceased villager headfirst into the ground, the body disintegrating into a bloodier stump with each plunge.

Mindless beast, she thought, constructing a way to defeat it. Other elementals were easy, as each aspect had its opposite that acted as an Achilles heel. Fire didn't do too well against Water and so on, but Earth wasn't as easy since it resisted the other elements. *Still*, Sabea thought, *I have a way.*

She watched while the creature busied itself further with the remains of the town. Sabea hadn't gotten a good look at the beast before, the elemental capable of silent and quick movements despite its size. Hairless, with a hide thick than a leather cuirass, the creature matched the size and width of a one-floor house. The brute had a flat, stunted nose, thick lips and eyes that seemed too small for the massive head. Each finger and toe ended in claws as long as a human hand and, from the way it tore through the corpses, they were as sharp as daggers.

Sabea strode towards it, arms down by her sides and fingers splayed. Black flames appeared above each digit as she walked, Spirit responding to her command. It was something that had unlocked within her shortly after the incident at the Citadel, and Sabea found she was a fast learner. She harnessed that most rare of elements to lift the demon into the air, holding it with invisible strands above the ground. Some flames on her right hand switched color, brown this time, and a hole appeared in the ground wide enough for the creature. She slammed it inside as her flames turned green; water filled the hole, quickly rising above the trapped monster's head. The beast raged and lashed out, the hole not large enough for it to stretch its arms enough to gain a purchase for climbing.

Sabea didn't take any chances, quickly placing a shield of Spirit across the top of the makeshift pit. Arriving at the edge of the breach she watched as the Earth elemental drowned, a grim frown on her face. Before she was adept with Spirit witnessing any creature die, even by her own hand, would have hurt her. Now she was almost indifferent to it. Her new talent had fractured her soul, and each time she used it she lost a part of herself.

The creature knew it was about to die; it stopped thrashing, instead looking up at Sabea as it pleaded with her to set it free. Then purple orbs glazed over, the stare turning lifeless.

"I need a drink," Sabea muttered, weaving Wind and lifting herself from the ground.

◇━○━◇━○━━○━○◇━◇

"Where the fuck have you been?" Sabea growled, stomping into the only bar in Tijua village. The day was hot, her red, fitted garments dripped with filth and her patience had worn thin. Now it had broken. Her peer, Hexan Ashes, sat at a table with a flagon of ale in front of him, his green clothes as pristine as the day he had them made.

"I knew you could handle it alone," Hexan replied, his emerald eyes twinkling. The man was handsome, though age had caught up with him. His smooth, raven hair held the beginnings of white at his temples, and his beard was flecked with grey. Fresh wrinkles etched their way into his face on an almost weekly basis. His warm, welcoming laugh still boomed, full of pleasure at seeing his friend. "Come, sit. Tell me of your day."

"Fuck off," Sabea replied, thumping into the chair opposite him. The drinking hole was busy, but she tried to get the attention of a serving man anyway. She was too weary to stand at the counter like everyone else, "Supposedly you were my backup. An Earth elemental massacred an entire village not ten miles from here!"

"Well," Hexan replied, wiping foam away from the hairs around his mouth, "I had a Fire demon to deal with that had attracted Ghouls. Nasty business."

"But you don't have a mark on you," Sabea replied, narrowing her eyes in suspicion, "Look at me; this is what you look like after a fight."

"No," he replied, weaving a slither of Fire and lighting a bacco tube, "that is what you look like when you blunder your way into things without thinking."

"Fine," Sabea snapped, not wanting to argue. Hexan had been there for her after the incident at the Citadel, and he was the one to help her through the trials of becoming a Redan Monk. He'd been her shoulder to cry on after losing her master and father figure. Originally Hexan finished her teaching after Bane, but now they saw each other as equals. Sabea had the greater power, Hexan the experience. "Is the barman blind? I'm dying of thirst."

"All right," Hexan replied, blowing smoke across the table. Sabea inhaled deeply. She didn't smoke herself, but enjoyed the dusty smell bacco produced, "Did you hear? The Council wants to see us. Well, you. At your earliest convenience."

"Pah," Sabea spat, "the Council. The real one is dead. These're just the cowards left standing that didn't want to fight anymore."

"So you won't go?"

"I'll bleeding go," she muttered. "Have to, don't I? Now, stop talking about those fools. I've had enough of Redan business for one day."

"So, what are you going to do now?" Hexan asked, making eye contact with a serving man just out of his teens, flicking a finger towards their table.

"I want to get drunk and fuck something," Sabea answered, the young bar attendant's eyebrows shooting up as he heard her words, "but I'll take the ale if it's all I can get."

"I can help you with both," the man said with a confident grin. Sabea leaned back, looking him up and down.

"Do you have a cock?" she asked, nodding towards his groin.

"Well…yeah," he answered. He glanced at Hexan who stared at the table, his face still as stone.

"Then I'm not interested, sweetheart," Sabea answered, grabbing Hexan Ashes's tankard and taking a long pull from it. "Another couple of these, and keep them coming. I don't want to see the bottom of one until tomorrow."

PART THREE - SANISCO CITY

"Why do I do this to myself?" Sabea groaned, sitting on the steps leading to the tavern she'd spent the night drinking in before passing out on the floor. "All this magic, and I can't cure a fucking hangover."

Hexan Ashes shrugged, looking a little worse for wear with crumpled robes and pronounced bags under his eyes.

"Not talking?" Sabea asked, swilling her mouth out by channeling Water and spitting into the mud. "Couldn't stop you last night. 'The Redan' this and 'the Council' that, even when I asked you not to."

Hexan just shook his head, before widening his eyes in alarm. Without warning he shot to his feet and staggered off to the side of the building. The sounds of him heaving his guts up made Sabea chortle darkly.

"Bless," she shouted to him, "just take your time. You'll think twice before trying to drink me under the table again."

It was already growing hot. Most days were like this, until suddenly it wasn't. Freak snowstorms, deluges of rain, thunder and lightning could, and would, appear without warning. *Wouldn't mind a little rain*, Sabea sighed, sweating under her robes and the leather armor pieces that covered it, *or at least a bit of air*.

She called on Wind, making it circulate in front of her a little, before pulling on Water and refilling her cup. Sabea had attempted making rain fall occasionally; a big mistake she finally gave up on. It always worked, only too well, and the last time had caused floods. She'd had to use all the elements to clear that one up, an experience she didn't want to repeat while soothing a sour stomach and pounding head.

"Will we leave then?" Hexan asked, coming back from around the corner. He'd produced soft paper from somewhere and dabbed his mouth delicately with it. "The Council expects you."

"Not yet," Sabea replied. "Let's just sit and take the air for a while longer."

They sat together on the steps, Sabea leaning on her friend's shoulder.

"Do you ever think about how we use the elements to kill creatures made from them?" Hexan asked after a spell.

"No," Sabea answered quietly, "I try not to. Can't be a good thing though, right? It's the ghouls I feel sorry for. Poor bastards."

"Why?" he asked. "We're putting them out of their misery, whatever they are."

"I know what they are," she murmured, idly producing elemental flames above her fingertips and making them dance, "They used to be like us, except from the civilization that came before. Not the ones who got underground and hid from the fires, these were the ones who were too close to the surface, these avoided getting killed but bore the full brunt of the fallout. It's what the Sickness is, you know. If we didn't euthanize anyone who caught it that's what would happen to them."

Hexan pulled her around to face him.

"Who told you this? Why did you never tell me? This is dangerous talk."

"My old master said not to tell anyone, but what's the point in not telling you? He found things during his journeys to the North. It set him on the path to do what he did, I reckon. Watching his own family put to death. He didn't tell me everything, but whatever Takar Bane…"

Sabea's head rang like a bell as she spoke Bane's name out loud. She hadn't uttered it for years, and now the words knocked all sense from her. Sabea collapsed, sliding wordlessly down the steps and into the mud. A part of her mind still worked; the block that kept her from communicating with Bane seemed to tremble, as if speaking his name had weakened it. Instinctively she poured all five elements into it, screaming in her mind.

'*TAKAR BANE.*'

Sabea blinked at the bright, blue sky above her. She vaguely heard Hexan calling to her, his hands on her shoulders as he shook her.

"I'm all right," she croaked. "Get off me."

The bell rang again, and with it came a feeling of vulnerability she hadn't felt in five years: the awareness of someone else sharing her thoughts.

'*I was wondering when you'd figure that out,*' Takar Bane whispered in her mind, '*You've grown strong, apprentice.*'

'*How…why…*' Sabea struggled. The things she'd wanted to say to her master fumbled away from her like grain falling through outstretched fingers, '*What did you do? Why did you block me out?*'

'*Come to me,*' he answered, '*I've taken steps to bring you here, anyway. The time is right. I have missed you, Sabea.*'

Bane speaking her name jolted her into action. Intuitively she flung up a barrier in her mind. She felt a probing presence against it and strengthened the block further, confident it would hold Bane out now that she was in control.

"Come on," Sabea said to Hexan, climbing to her feet, "we need to leave. Now."

She called upon Wind and rose into the air, moving quickly towards Sanisco City, Hexan following her lead without asking questions.

◇━◦━◇━◦━◇━◦━◇

Sabea Crow hadn't stepped foot in Sanisco City since the incident. She tried to avoid the obsidian dome looming over the city's horizon, but her eyes kept being pulled back to it against her will. It had grown larger, its circumference now smothering more than just the Citadel. The mood of the place had changed too. Folk shuffled around the streets, eyes cast downwards. She'd never liked the city, a place built on the ruins of a society wiped away. The new buildings made to fit into the plans of a dead civilization, but now an unnatural quiet hung about the avenues and parks. Businesses were shuttered and homes had fallen into disrepair. *It's like people have lost the will to live,* Sabea thought. She looked at Bane's bubble again without thinking, then returned her eyes to Hexan Ashes immediately. Whenever she glanced in the Citadel's direction she felt the barrier in her mind bulge, as if Takar Bane sought her attention.

'Are you happy with what you did to the world?' she asked, lowering the wall standing between their communication.

'*No,*' came Bane's immediate reply, '*but, as I told you, it is necessary.*'

'*Fuck you,*' Sabea snarled, '*I looked up to you, and you betrayed us all. What did you do to the Redan inside the Citadel? Are they still alive?*'

A moment's hesitation answered her question.

'*They were essential sacrifices,*' Bane whispered, '*Come to me, you will see. Sabea…*'

The walls slammed into place again as she suppressed a shiver.

"I feel sick," she said out loud to no one in particular.

"Drinking will do that to you," Hexan answered over his shoulder. "Are you going to tell me what happened back there?"

"No," Sabea replied. "Where are we meeting the council?"

"We're close," he replied, pointing to a triangular building perched atop a hill. Sanisco was a town of rises and dips. Looking around at the horizon, and trying to avoid Bane's imposing black dome, Sabea reckoned the spot where the Council had rebuilt was the highest peak in the city.

They made their way into the building, the lone guard recognizing Hexan on sight. The men nodded to each other as they strode passed.

"Light security," Sabea murmured, glancing around at the building. She sensed no magic from it, built the old-fashioned way by wood and sweat.

"We don't have enough people to spare for guard duty," Hexan replied. "Anyway, since Bane, and before him for that matter, who would attack the Council? I'll wait for you here."

They stood in a small room, a set of plain, wooden double doors ahead of them.

"You're not coming in?" Sabea asked, annoyed at the gentle fluttering she felt in her stomach.

"They just want you," he said, sending a draft of Wind towards the doors to push them open. "Good luck. Try not to piss them off."

"No promises," she grinned, gripping Hexan's shoulder before striding into the council chambers.

The room was functional, with a single chair sitting in the center of a rectangular room. Beyond it was a raised platform, on which sat the six Redan that made up the current Council. Three women, with a matching number of men, their reduction in number painting a stark picture of where Bane's treachery had left them.

"Sabea Crow," a man spoke in a dusty, creaking voice, "we have summoned you before the Council of the Redan because of a matter of the greatest importance."

"Why have you tarried?" a woman asked, her tone weak and willowy. "We expected you at first light."

"Well, you know, it's always good to let off a bit of steam after you've seen a village of innocents torn apart by an Earth elemental." Sabea snapped, her promise to Hexan on the verge of being broken already. "Oh, wait. You wouldn't know, would you? You're all too busy hiding in this place, rather than doing what it means to be a Redan. Or have you forgotten?"

"That's enough," another woman spoke. Sabea thought she should have remembered the council members' names, she'd heard them at one point, but she had never seen the reason in committing them to memory. The cravens weren't worth her time. "You forget your place."

"Do I?" Sabea laughed, thumping down into the chair reserved for her. "Perhaps I do. Cowards don't like to be told they're yellow, do they?"

The council descended into angry mutters and curses. Sabea sneered back. *They're all at it,* she thought, *acting high and mighty. Except that one.* She noticed one of the Council members looking back, a smile on her one-eyed face. The woman raised a single finger. Slowly the other Redan noticed her gesture and fell silent.

"Do you know who I am?" she asked, her voice sounding like iron striking steel.

"Yes," Sabea replied. The Redan was Stenus Lagrim. A renowned warrior, she had earned her stripes in the frontier. She must have been almost ninety years old, and had only moved to the Council when its lack of leadership and wisdom became apparent in the months after the incident.

"And will you speak with me? It's clear you think the others aren't worthy of your respect."

"I will, Master Lagrim. What do you need from me?"

Stenus Lagrim nodded, her smile growing wider and eyes twinkling with fondness.

"I'll cut right to it. I see, like me, you aren't one for wasting time," the Redan glanced at the other council members and winked. "We called you here because, for the first time in five years, Takar Bane has contacted us."

"He...has?" Sabea responded, her hand rubbing at her temple as she felt a large pulse against the barrier in her mind. It was like her master knew he was being spoken of and wanted to listen in on the conversation.

"Do you know of this already?" Stenus asked, her eyes narrowing shrewdly.

"No," Sabea said, not wanting to divulge in her contact with Bane. It couldn't be a coincidence. The disgraced Redan planned something, he said he'd taken steps. "I'm just surprised, that's all. I try not to think about him anymore."

"I understand," Stenus replied, a look of compassion on her face. "He was like a father to you, and he betrayed us all. Tell me, what would you do if he was in front of you?"

"I'd want to know why," Sabea answered immediately. "I'd want answers."

"And if you didn't like them? Could you kill him?"

Sabea looked at the six Redan. With Stenus Lagrim being the exception they were all hale and hardy enough to be out making a difference in the frontier, not spending their time playing Council. They were incapable of the mental strength needed to protect the world. *I have it*, she thought.

Sabea desired answers; she needed to know why Bane had turned traitor. She wanted so badly to understand why he had abandoned her, the apprentice he'd had since she was five years old after the Sickness had taken her family. Hers and Bane's bond had grown closer when his family had succumbed to the same terrible fate, and Sabea had thought they'd make the world a better place together.

"Takar Bane needs to pay for what he's done," she answered, suppressing the clanging of the bell in her mind at the mention of his name, "and if none of you can do it then I will."

"Good," Stenus answered. "Bane sent something through the barrier. It looked human, but by the time the sentries found it the body had disintegrated into a pool of slime and bones. It wrote a message in blood on the ground in front of it."

"What did the writing say?" Sabea asked, leaning forward in her chair.

"A simple directive. 'Send my apprentice, or see our world die.'"

PART FOUR - THE DOME

Sabea and Hexan stood side-by-side at the edge of the onyx dome. A bridge built by the early Redan linked the Citadel on Catraz Island with the mainland city, and at first the magical barrier Bane had created covered just the island. It had slowly expanded over the years, taking over the bridge and encroaching upon the township. The boundary was opaque, though the darkness seemed to shift across its surface.

This was the closest Sabea had ever come to the dome. She could feel the elements pulsing from it as Spirit whispered to her from within, her soul aching to respond to the call.

"So, what do we do now?" Hexan muttered, pulling at his collar as he sweated. The heat was sweltering and, despite being close to the ocean, the air was unnaturally still.

"I don't know," Sabea answered, shaking her head. "Has anyone tried to just walk through?"

"At first," Hexan shuddered, "but they didn't return. He wants you; it'll be safe."

"There were about five hundred Redan in there," Sabea said, turning to look at her friend. "Do you think they're all dead?"

"Yes," Hexan nodded grimly, "or at least I hope so. There are worse things than death, and who knows what else Takar Bane has done to them?"

"We're about to find out," Sabea said, working her shoulders and breathing in deeply. "You sure you want to do this? It was only me he asked for."

Hexan glanced at the dome and grimaced.

"I wouldn't see you go in there alone."

"You always were soft," Sabea laughed, holding out her hand to him, "but I appreciate it. Take my hand."

As Hexan did as he was told Sabea opened her mind to communicate with Bane. It was becoming easier to do; she felt his presence immediately, as if he stood in an adjacent room to her.

'*Bane,*' she said, '*You wanted me, I'm here. How do I get through?*'

'*Just walk, my apprentice,*' his voice reverberated in her head. '*The way has always been open to you. You're surprised? Don't be. My intention was for you to be a part of this before the end. This task benefits everyone, you most of all.*'

'*Hexan Ashes is with me, he won't let me come alone.*'

'*Prudent, I suppose,*' Bane replied, '*though I mean you no harm. I'd planned on his presence, and I sent you to him for a reason. There is nothing anyone can do to stop what is to come, the work is almost complete. You both have a part to play.*'

Sabea pulled her mind away from Bane's, but didn't sever their bond. *What's the point now I'm on his fucking doorstep?* she thought, steeling herself for coming face-to-face with her teacher. He'd planned this from the start, and the notion worried her. She meant what she said to the Council; Sabea would kill him if she had to. She had to hope Bane didn't expect that she could.

"Come on," she said to Hexan, "he's expecting us. Count of three?"

Hexan nodded and counted. As they hit their mark they strode forward as one, passing through the dome.

◇━━◦━━━◦━━◇

Sabea thought she was blind, the darkness was so thick and impenetrable. She raised an arm in front of her, then realized she was on her own.

"Hexan?" she called, her voice echoing.

She didn't feel alone. It was like all that lived in the past or present, and those yet born, watched her as one. They could see through her, pick at her memories, judge her actions.

Sabea.

A faint whisper caught her attention. Unsure of which direction it came from she spun in a tight circle, becoming dizzy from the lack of orientation.

"Who are you?"

Sabea, the voice called louder this time, *come to us. We've missed you.*

"No!" she screamed, recognizing who the words belonged to. "You're dead. This can't be real."

Two green-hued specters materialized ahead of her, their features ill-defined, but Sabea knew who they were. It seemed they held out their arms to her.

We've always been here, the larger shape said, *waiting for this time to come.*

"Father," Sabea whimpered, tears rolling down her face, "Mother, what has Bane done to you?"

He is setting us free, the ghost of her mother answered. *We will be together again soon.*

Instinctively Sabea drew on Spirit and pushed out-wards. They weren't real, just mockeries conjured by Bane. The phantoms screamed as thunder clapped and lightning flashed inside them, growing brighter and moving outwards. Sabea covered her eyes and turned away as the light swallowed her.

She felt like she was floating. Opening her eyes she saw stars twinkling all around her as she slowly journeyed through them. A crimson cloud stood out in the far distance.

We have been here for thousands of years, and hopefully will be for thousands more. Takar Bane's voice said, a memory from her first day of apprenticeship with him. The stars vibrated in time with his words. *In the past humanity sought to control us, their drive destroyed us. We should be humble, use our gifts and work with the elements, not seek dominion of them. To protect is our purpose. Our time is short, so we must seek to leave the world a better place than how we found it.*

"What changed, Master?" Sabea cried, moving closer to the ominous, rouge veil. One-by-one the surrounding stars blinked out and disappeared, leaving Sabea alone in the darkness with the red portal.

Death, came a whisper. It was not a memory this time, but words cold and emotionless, as if the universe itself spoke to her. *Death is the only inevitability, the way it has to be.*

The portal flickered, images flashing upon it and seeping directly into Sabea's mind. Large, triangular buildings buried under sand. Wooden ships sinking at sea. Millions dying through sickness and poverty. Priests dressed all in crimson torturing men, women and children with hundreds more burned at the stake. Uniformed men crouching in narrow tunnels dug into the earth, cowering together as the land exploded around them. Thousands cheering and saluting a mustached man speaking at a podium, then images of mistreated families entering dirty little buildings filled with poison, never to return.

Sabea saw the richer becoming wealthier and the poor being driven into destitution. She saw violent storms, floods, plagues and fires ravage their homes.

Then she witnessed the fires from heaven, the ground erupting into mushroomed flames. The seas boiled, the earth cracked, and people died by the millions.

From the ashes five flames appeared. Elemental magic, a gift to rebuild. They moved in a circle, increasing their speed until they collided together. The world healed.

Death doesn't have to mean the end, Takar Bane's voice, clear and strong. *Come to me.*

Sabea tried to resist, but felt as though countless hands grabbed her, their fingers pulling her closer to the crimson portal. She screamed as she passed through it, the sorrow of all that had died cascading on her until her senses fled.

PART FIVE - THE MASTER

"Sabea!" Hexan shouted urgently, grabbing her shoulder and shaking her roughly. "Wake up."

"Get the fuck off me," she shouted, leaping to her feet and intuitively calling on all five elements, the flames dancing above her fingertips.

"No!" Hexan cried, quickly raising a shield of Wind around himself in case Sabea attacked. "It's me. Your friend, remember?"

Sabea stood panting, arms held out at her sides, ready to unleash the full might of her power. Memories began flooding back in. The dome, her task, Hexan. Her knees sagged a little as she let go of the elements.

"I'm sorry," she muttered, holding her face in her hands. "I…what happened?"

Hexan drew her into an embrace.

"We stepped through the barrier," he said, stroking her hair, "and you collapsed. You were only out for a few seconds, but you had me worried."

"It felt like hours," Sabea whispered, pulling away from him. "You didn't see or hear anything?"

"No," Hexan said, looking around, "there's no sign of anyone else. This place has changed since I saw it last."

Sabea shook her head quickly, trying to dispel the horror she had just witnessed. *The whole history of humanity has been death and destruction,* she thought. *Is that what Bane wants to stop?* She looked at her surroundings. They stood on the bridge leading to the Citadel, the imposing building looming ahead of them on Catraz Island. The colors seemed drained out of the place, the sea below them grey and the bridge a dull brown. The sky above was dark; not black, but gloomy and inhospitable. Again Sabea felt she was being watched, whispers lingering at the edge of her hearing. Spirit seemed to be on the air. She opened herself to it and it filled her, easier than ever before. She didn't even need to try, it was as if it flowed naturally through her.

"Only one place for us to go," Sabea said, looking at Hexan. "Are you ready?"

He nodded in reply, then walked towards the Citadel. Sabea followed.

"I saw them," she said, keen to break the silence. "My parents, but it wasn't really them. Other things too. Hexan, I think we're *in* Spirit."

"What do you mean?" Hexan asked over his shoulder. "Spirit is an element, not a place."

"Maybe," she replied, "but it's everywhere here. It's like oxygen."

Hexan paused, and with a look of concentration held a hand up to his face. Suddenly five black flames appeared above his fingers.

"Spirit," he laughed in disbelief, looking at Sabea with wide eyes. "I've never been able to call upon it before. It feels different from I thought it would, colder."

"Lifeless," Sabea answered, the whispers growing louder.

"Yes," Hexan replied, looking around. "Do you hear that muttering?"

Sabea nodded and sent out a gentle ripple of Spirit around them.

Green-hued phantoms filled the bridge, each one

turned towards the Redan making their way towards the Citadel. Sabea could make out the features on the faces closest her, the pain and hunger in their eyes stark. The whispers had increased in volume, and though the specters spoke in hushed, incoherent tones their voices merged to create a roar. Sabea strained to listen to the apparition of a young girl an arm's reach away who stared lifelessly at her, muttering without pause.

In the night they came, killing my father, my mother, my brothers. Left me till last. I can't stop seeing their dead eyes over and again. There is no rest, no escape. In the night they came, killing…

Sabea channeled a trickle of Spirit into the ghost-child. She seemed to respond immediately, the green color fading into blue as her form became more full. Awareness sparked in the specter's grey eyes.

"Why do you all look at me?" Sabea asked.

The child glanced around at the crowded bridge, then back at the Citadel, cowering at its intimidating presence.

"This is what he wants for us all," she replied, her voice like a breath of stale air.

"Who?"

"The one in the Citadel," the ghost said. "He draws us near, your world and mine, until they're one like this place."

"And what do you want?" Sabea asked, casting her gaze across the colorless, dead vista.

"Oblivion."

Sabea felt Hexan draw upon the other elements, having let go of Spirit. He fired a jet of Fire into the sky, lacing it with Wind so it spread. The flames spluttered out after travelling a short distance, its glare not affecting the gloom.

"Sabea," he muttered, "that's the strongest thread of Fire I've ever pulled. I think you're right, this is where we draw on our power, but Spirit utterly dominates this place."

"This place is death," Sabea responded, turning back towards the Citadel and letting the phantom fade to its previous state. "I know what Bane wants. We have to stop him," she pointed at the ghosts, "otherwise that will be us when we die, and we're fucked for all eternity."

"What's your plan?" Hexan asked.

"I'll try to talk to him," she replied as they reached the Citadel's entrance, "and if that doesn't work I'll destroy the bastard."

Sabea used Wind to push the doors open and strode into the place that had been her home for most of her childhood. The building wasn't the same though, not in the way it once was. It felt wrong. *If this is how Bane thinks the world should be*, Sabea thought, *then I don't want any part of it.*

"Where do you think he'll be?" Hexan asked, scanning their surroundings.

"There," she replied, pointing in the council chamber's direction, "he'll be right where this all started."

Their destination was at the very center of the Citadel, a straight path down the long corridor from the entrance. As they walked they moved past fallen Redan. Sabea inspected one, and there were no signs of violent death. The body seemed bizarrely preserved, as if it were only sleeping, though it was drained of all color and emaciated. She moved to another close to it, discovering it in the same state.

"Garrett," Hexan whispered up ahead, crouching in front of a corpse. "At least now I know."

"Who was he?" Sabea asked, kneeling next to her friend.

"My love," he replied, cheeks wet with tears. "Few knew about us, but he was the only one for me."

Hexan pressed his palm against Garrett's forehead. Sabea felt him pull on Fire, turning the body into ashes. He shook his head slowly and looked at her.

"I couldn't leave him like that," he said, "he deserved more than to be some husk in a lifeless mausoleum."

"I understand," Sabea replied, gripping his forearm and squeezing it. "Let's finish this."

Hexan nodded before she pulled him to his feet.

"Hold on to Spirit," she said, "it hides what you do with the other elements. It will be the same for him, but it might give us the edge."

Following her own advice Sabea let Spirit flood into her before drawing on Earth, Wind, Fire and Water. She'd never held so much in her life, and didn't think she could draw so much outside of this place. The sensation was intoxicating, but she recognized its danger and, in these circumstances, necessity of it. Takar Bane was the strongest Redan in centuries. *We'll need a miracle to defeat him if it comes down to a fair fight,* she thought. *It's a good job I don't believe in those.*

They pushed through the council chamber door's. Inside, facing away from them, was Takar Bane. He kneeled before a crimson portal, like the one Sabea saw in her vision. Her master seemed transfixed on the image reflected in it. His wife and children, looking alive but distant, like puppets made of flesh.

"They're here somewhere," Bane said without turning. "I haven't merged the realities enough yet, but once I do I'll find them again. You'll find your family too, Sabea."

"You became mine," she said, stepping cautiously towards him, Hexan at her side. "Everybody dies. The others keep going, trying to make this world a better place than they found it. Remember?"

Bane climbed to his feet and faced them. Sabea's breath caught in her chest. His dark skin had turned grey, almost the same shade as the husks outside the chambers, his eyes as black as midnight. His cheek bones poked against his flesh, so sharp they seemed to be on the verge of piercing through. The Redan's black robes hung from him and he swayed slightly on the spot, as if the effort of standing was almost too much.

"How are you alive?" Sabea asked, sensing no elemental power from him.

"Spirit," he answered, holding up his shaking hands. Ten black flames hovered above his fingertips. "I haven't let go of it since I started this. I feed from it, and it draws from me."

"What did you do to Garrett?" Hexan demanded, as Sabea felt him pull on the elements. Unused to using Spirit, he'd let go of it.

"Hexan," Bane nodded to him, "I'm sorry for his part in this, and yours. Allow me to show you."

With stunning speed Bane hurled a black tunnel of Spirit at Hexan that latched on to him before he or Sabea could react, and a rush of noise followed as the magic link-ing the two Redan pulsed backwards towards its creator. Hexan convulsed, his eyes rolling. His skin lost its color, growing grey and thin as blood dripped out of his mouth and ears. Sabea could hear him choke and gargle on it. She fired Spirit towards Bane and felt a wave of lethargy, as if a piece of her life force departed her. Halting her weave she turned to look at Hexan, watching helplessly as the magic ripped his life from him.

Finally the onyx tunnel disappeared. Hexan dropped to the ground, like a marionette with cut strings. He looked just like the corpses outside. Sabea kneeled in front of him, attempting to send Spirit into him. Fire. Water, Wind, Earth. He didn't respond. It was as if he had never existed, like the elements couldn't recognize him.

"You fucking bastard," she screamed through tears, looking at Bane and shrinking backwards. He was whole again, just as she remembered him from five years ago, his appearance matching the kindly, powerful figure she knew.

"I'm sorry for that," he said, walking towards the blood-red portal in the center of the room, situated where the Council used to convene, "but that, too, was necessary. I needed more strength for this last task."

"I'll kill you, Takar Bane!" Sabea shouted, surging to her feet. She quivered with the power of all five elements pulsating through her body. "This isn't life. You want us to live alongside the dead? Why? It's madness!"

Bane looked at her sadly. He took a step towards her, then shook his head, changing his mind.

"It is the only way," he replied quietly, "the only way to preserve our magic. See how strong you are now? Think of the things humanity could do. We could defeat death."

"Takar," Sabea pleaded, "death is a part of life. Is controlling the elements in this way right? They were a gift, and we used them. Nothing lasts forever. Does the world seem healthy to you since this madness began? Demons are everywhere, more succumb to the Sickness than ever. We've seen the mistakes mankind has made, so why not teach them a better way instead?"

"You think they'll listen?" Bane snapped angrily, flicking a finger at the portal. The images of war, annihilation and destruction from Sabea's visions appeared again. "People elected some of these monsters that sowed so much hate and slaughter! Humankind courts its end. The only way to counter that is to bring death to them, to master it ourselves. We'll never die, and our loved ones will never suffer again. Think of what we could accomplish with the full power of the elements at our fingertips."

"We'll never live either," Sabea replied, "not really."

They stared at each other across the chamber. A flicker of pride crossed Bane's face, replaced quickly by sadness.

"It doesn't matter," he said, turning back to the portal. He motioned again, and the crimson ingress reverted to the image of his family. "You cannot stop what has begun. That last soul was all I needed."

Bane channeled a colossal volume of Spirit into the doorway. It seemed to vibrate and grow wider as he poured his power into it. *This is it*, Sabea thought, *I can stand by and watch, or I can stop him*.

She closed her eyes and took a deep breath. Takar Bane had taught and raised her since the age of five, but the world was on a precipice. Sabea looked down at Hexan's lifeless body and willed the elements together, pulling on every drop she could. She gasped, the energies lifting her off her feet. Hovering a foot above the floor she opened her eyes, unleashing all five elements at Takar Bane's back.

They collided into him in a multitude of colors, temporarily blinding Sabea. She dropped to the floor, holding herself on all fours.

Silence.

Blinking her way back to sight, Sabea discovered that the crimson doorway had vanished. Bane lay on his back in the center of the room. He stared upwards towards the ceiling, clinging to life. She crawled to him, his eyes shifting to hers as he clasped her hand, his skin pulsing with the shifting shades of the elements.

Sabea gasped with shock.

"You've absorbed everything I threw at you," she said, "it should have killed you."

"It will," he whispered, a tear leaking from his eye. "Thank you for everything, and for playing your part."

Without warning the flames of the elements surged from his fingertips. A wave of cacophony and color erupted from him, tearing his body to pieces and throwing Sabea across the room. The whispers of millions blended into a bloody roar as she landed, covering her ears with her hands and squeezing her eyes shut. Fire seemed to burn at her as Water cooled her down, and it felt as though the Earth weighed heavy upon her as Wind attempted to lift her up. Spirit watched without judgement.

Finally, it was over.

Silence descended on the council chambers. Sabea

rolled to where Hexan's body lay, hoping that what she'd done had somehow reversed his death. There was no sign of him or Bane, their bodies obliterated by the elemental blast.

Listlessly she climbed to her feet, making her way back to the bridge. *Heroes in stories always feel triumphant after saving the day,* she thought. She moved automatically back the way she came, unaware of what was around her she walked into the Citadel's doors. Sabea sent a slither of Wind into them, squinting her eyes in preparation of the daylight outside.

She didn't need to. The gloom she witnessed under Bane's dome had spread as far as she could see. The air felt cold, flat and lifeless. On the bridge green-hued specters drifted aimlessly, while bells rang across the city on the mainland.

Sabea, someone whispered in her ear, *what did you do?*

She turned to see the phantoms of her parents by her side, a haunted look in their ethereal eyes. Her senses returned to her. She felt the elements alive in the air like she'd never experienced before, all dominated by Spirit. Sabea sank to her knees. Takar Bane had won, the volume of their vast power combining to tear down the walls between realities, and there was no way back.

DAVID GREEN
ABOUT THE AUTHOR

David Green writes dark fiction, usually of the fantasy and horror variety.

Growing up in Manchester, UK and now living in Galway, Ireland, David has never seen the sun. Instead, he's lived under a perpetual sheet of rainfall, which has no doubt influenced his dark writings. Published in a number of anthologies in 2020, David is the author of the upcoming dark fantasy series Empire of Ruin. Book one, In Solitude's Shadow, published by Eerie River Publishing, is releasing in June 2021.

Midnight Shadows, Eerie River Publishing, 2021
It Calls From the Sea, Eerie River Publishing, 2021
Dark Magic, Eerie River Publishing, 2021
In Solitude's Shadow, Eerie River Publishing, 2021

Website: www.davidgreenwriter.com
Amazon: https://www.amazon.co.uk/~/e/B0867VRV91
Newsletter: tinyurl.com/y92ly355
Twitter: https://twitter.com/DavidGreenWrite
Facebook: https://www.facebook.com/davidgreenwriter

THE MONSTER OF CARROCH

ROSE STRICKMAN

W hen the sweating, anxious servant finally found Callum McRathray, his master was cutting the throat of a red deer. The animal let out a long moan as its blood welled up. Crimson spilled onto the fallen leaves and its eyes rolled, revealing rings of white, as its tongue lolled from its mouth. Callum watched it die, his face unsmiling.

"Mr. McRathray," the servant panted, hands on his knees. "Mr. McRathray!"

"Yes, Angus, what is it?" Callum cleaned his knife on a convenient tuft of moss.

"Alastair…The housekeeper's son…"

Callum didn't look up, but he stiffened. "What about him?"

"He's missing. He disappeared after breakfast, and now no one can find him."

Callum went very still, and it seemed the summer forest went still with him. Around them a pool of quiet welled up, then spread out. Not a single leaf stirred.

At last Callum stood. He loomed over Angus, a tall,

dark hulk of a man wearing the plaid of the McRathray clan. Leaves clung to the wool, and his face was as impassively grim as ever. Only his eyes flashed, strange fires alight within.

"Help me with this deer," he said at last, and together the two men manhandled the dead animal down the hill to where their horses waited.

"Mr. McRathray?" Angus said at last, when they had slung the deer over the back of Callum's mount. "Should we alert the Watch, sir?"

Callum snorted, and not gently. "What good would those cloth-headed idiots do? No. I will find the lad, but I will have to stop by the house first."

He mounted up and clucked to his horse. Angus did the same, and soon the men were trotting away down through the forested hills, under the purple shadows of the mountains.

❖━●━○━━○━●━❖

Callum McRathray's home, Rathray House, was the grandest in the neighborhood. It was a two-story stone building at the top of a hill, which overlooked the valley whereof he was landlord. It was surrounded by stables, cow byres and vegetable gardens.

Callum left his horse with the stable hand and strode into the house. There he found his housekeeper, Caitlin, sobbing in the kitchen while the kitchen maid, her niece, hovered uselessly. Callum scowled when he saw the village Magister was in attendance, holding Caitlin's hands and murmuring holy platitudes.

"Out," Callum ordered the maid, who scurried away immediately. "Magister Siddons," Callum said, only somewhat more politely, "I need to speak with my house-keeper."

Magister Siddons looked up at the larger man with no great warmth. He disapproved of Callum McRathray, who avoided holy services like the plague and gave the Magister only the bare minimum of respect. It was technically Siddons's duty to report his landlord's absences from services to the church authorities, but Siddons couldn't bring himself to do it. Callum frightened him as he frightened everyone, and on those rare occasions when the landlord did attend services he sat and stared without breathing a single word of prayer. It was like having a piece of a darker, wilder world in his clean, tidy church, and Siddons didn't like it.

"Mistress Caitlin's son is missing," Siddons announced. "I was giving her some comfort."

Callum barked a laugh and threw his hunting knife, still somewhat bloody, onto the table. Both Siddons and Caitlin jumped at the clatter. "Muttering holy verses won't bring her son back," Callum sneered. "Allow me to speak with her privately."

Siddons flushed, but bowed his head. He murmured one last phrase to Caitlin and left the house, muttering under his breath, "Yes, we all know how *private* you have been with Caitlin Matheson…"

Back in the kitchen Callum knelt before Caitlin, taking her hands in his. "What happened?" he asked, far more gently than was his usual wont.

Caitlin wiped her eyes and sniffed. "We were out in

the garden," she said. "I was harvesting vegetables, and he was larking about…Then I turned around and he was gone."

"You're sure he's not just out playing somewhere?"

"We looked everywhere…Asked all the neighbors. He's nowhere!" Caitlin looked up, eyes bright with a new and fearful thought. "Mr. McRathray…you don't think it was the Monster of Carroch, do you?"

"That's a story, Caitlin," Callum said gently, though his eyes darkened.

"He steals children, they say," Caitlin whispered. "He lives in the mountains, and comes down to steal children to eat."

Callum said nothing, but patted her hand soothingly. Then he stood and went to throw the kitchen door open.

Light flooded the stone-flagged room. A swirl of wind blew in, sending straw and dried leaves skittering across the floor as it fluttered Caitlin's skirts. Callum stood in the doorway, blocking the light, letting the wind whirl around him. He remained there for a long time.

"Sir?" Caitlin said at last, softly. "Callum…"

"Pack me some food, Caitlin, and a change of clothes." The wind whistled around him in the doorway. It carried the first breath of autumn, the first distant hint of frost. It blew chill, with the scent of snow on Carroch Peak. "Don't worry, I will find Alastair."

Caitlin gave a gulping sob. "You will?"

"Depend upon it." Still Callum didn't turn away from the sun, from the wind. "I will find him. Now do as I say."

That afternoon saw Callum McRathray walk away from the house with food, medical supplies and a change of clothes packed away. His knife was in his belt, and pistol at his hip. His household, all red-eyed with worry, watched him stride away. He had explained himself to none of them, but no one dared to question him. Caitlin leaned heavily against her niece, watching her master leave with a mixture of desperate hope and deep apprehension.

Callum walked beneath the forested hills. Below him the fertile valley spread, patched with farms and grazed by cattle. Beyond the valley the moors stretched, empty and desolate, overlooked by the mountains. Above all the other mountains loomed snowbound Carroch Peak, huge and brooding.

Callum paused suddenly. He bent to pull leaves off a heather plant. He stood a moment, feeling the plant fragments in his palm buzzing with power. With a single puff he blew them into the air.

They whirled up in a column, flying above his head. For a moment they hovered, twirling, before they fell limply to the ground. Callum sighed, then he rolled up his sleeve and drew his knife. He traced the blade across his skin, blood welling up in a thin, red line.

He gathered blood droplets into his fingers, then tossed them into the air. Like the leaves they whirled in a miniature cyclone for a moment before falling to earth, the dust absorbing them immediately.

Callum's jaw tightened. "So it's like that, is it?" he murmured.

The wind played around him, tugging at his clothes and lifting his hair. He could hear a far-off echo of laughter.

Jaw still clenched, Callum McRathray bandaged his arm and continued on across the moors, following the line of the hills.

The summer night took a long time to settle completely over the land. Even after night had fallen some light remained in the sky, the sun refusing to utterly set. Callum cooked his oats on a fire and slept out in the open, unaffected by the cold wind blowing down from Carroch. Yet he slept badly, tormented by anxious dreams.

He awoke surrounded by bandits.

Callum lay blinking in the clear morning light, looking up at the ring of thin, filthy men surrounding him. One gave him a kick, and he grunted in pain.

"Well, take a look, boys," the bandit said in a southern Albionese accent. "Looks like we've got some Callie gent here."

The other men gave sniggers. Callum remained on the ground, silent, but he tensed. These men looked like decommissioned royal Albionese soldiers—he could tell from their ragged, stained blue uniforms. Such men, hungry and unpaid for too long, made for vicious brigands with little respect for the local Caledonians.

"You got a voice, Callie-man?" The first soldier kicked Callum again. "You talk?"

Callum stood quickly and smoothly, and the strangers faltered a little; Callum was considerably taller and wider than any of them. "I've a name," Callum ground out, "not that I'll tell it to you."

"Big words, Callie-dog," sneered one of the other soldiers. His cohorts fanned out, swinging rusted muskets from their backs, drawing notched knives. "We've got you outnumbered, so just hand over your valuables and — "

The soldier suddenly broke off as he began choking. He bent over, hands going to his throat, face already purpling. Callum stood still, fist clenched.

"Thomas?" The other brigands stared in fear and consternation. "What — ?"

More chokes, and the other robbers sank down, hands going to their throats, lungs struggling to pull in air. Soon all lay purple-faced, eyes bulging, writhing on the ground.

"You…witch…" one managed to gasp.

Callum's eyes flashed and he tightened his grip, yanking the last breath of air from the soldier's lungs. The man gasped soundlessly and soon his eyes glazed over, face dead and eyes still wide in desperation.

Callum stood in the northerly wind as it blew the heather around him. Then he opened his fist, and the imprisoned air rose around him in a momentary whirlwind before escaping into the sky.

Slowly Callum made his way around the soldiers. Most of them lay dead, but one still lived; unconscious, but alive. Callum gave a slow half-smile.

Drawing his knife he yanked the soldier's head back and slashed across his throat. The soldier gave a moan as he died, blood spilling out. Callum caught the blood in his palm and stood, letting out a sharp whistle. The wind responded by blowing harder around him, the echoes of laughter and far-off voices sounding once again.

Callum tossed the soldier's lifeblood into the air. It whirled around him as the leaves and the shallow blood had before, but did not fall to earth like those. Instead the blood droplets swirled and rose, until a puff of wind blew them northward toward the forested hills and the mountains beyond.

Callum sighed. It was good to finally have a direction, but he wished it was not this one.

He looked at the ring of dead bodies, then he spoke.

"Ones of Earth," he said, and the ground gave a shiver beneath his boots. Callum could not communicate with the Earth elementals as readily as the Air, but today they were in a receptive mood. "Here's a feast for you. Leave nothing behind."

The ground shivered again. Roots started crawling out of it like worms, roping around the corpses and pulling them downward as the earth enveloped them like water. Callum did not stay to watch. He strode on, climbing uphill toward the forests and the mountains.

◈━◇━━◇━◈

Callum passed few other people on his journey into the hills, but he stopped at a woodsman's cottage where he shared whiskey and oatcakes with the woodsman and his wife. He asked if they had seen a little boy, about four years old, with dark, curly hair.

"Your son, is it?" The woodsman, a garrulous man insensitive to the eldritch, frowned in concern. "He's missing?"

"Yes." Callum sipped whiskey. "I'm afraid so. He's somewhere in these hills though, I know it."

The woodsman's wife, a black-haired woman with eyes like deep dark wells, spoke then. "We haven't seen any missing boys, Mr. McRathray, but be careful in these hills. There's more than just animals in the trees."

"That's my Fiona!" The woodsman slapped her affectionately on the behind. "She thinks there's spirits behind every rock."

"The Monster of Carroch Peak is real," Fiona insisted. The wind lifted up her dark hair, strands waving in the breeze. "Shaped like a man, he is, but nothing human about him, not anymore. He sold his soul to the demon who lives in the mountains, and now he's madder and more evil with every passing year. He gets his power by killing children." She shivered. "He took Mrs. Ross's youngest last year. They never found that little girl again."

"Nonsense!" her husband said roundly. "Utter rubbish. The Rosses' youngest just wandered off. I've lived all my life in these hills, and I can tell you there is nothing more dangerous than the occasional bear or adder. Would you like me to go with you, Mr. McRathray? Help you look for your lad?"

"No, thank you." Callum handed back the whiskey bottle. "I could not keep you from your work, but I would be grateful if you keep an eye out."

"Of course, of course, and we'll tell everyone else to keep a watch too." The woodsman shook his head in concern. "Such a little lad, all alone in these hills…Anything could happen. Even if there is no Monster," he couldn't help adding, glancing at his wife. She just shook her head and said nothing.

Callum nodded. "Indeed. I thank you for your kindness."

⟨━◆━◇━━◇━◆◇⟩

After he left the cottage Callum pressed deeper into the forest, heavy with summer growth. The leaves muttered and whispered against one another. The streams, still icy even at this time of year, chuckled and murmured over black rocks. Callum hiked along one such stream, leaping from rock to rock as he stretched out all his senses.

He wasn't sure when he realized that he was being followed; the awareness of inhuman eyes upon him crept like a cold finger up his spine. The quick, insubstantial figures darted in the corners of his eyes as the creatures fled his gaze.

Callum thought briefly of the woodsman's wife, but dismissed the idea; she was not nearly powerful enough to send elementals after him, even if she'd had reason to. No, this was some game of the elementals themselves. The Air had demanded a blood sacrifice before it would reveal Alastair's location, and now the Earth darted and flitted after him. The elementals were at some design, perhaps one of their random games…and perhaps not.

Finally Callum came to a halt, balanced on a boulder in the stream. "Enough!" Around him, the water continued to chatter and flow, but silence fell on the rest of the woods, with even the birds ceasing their song. "Where is Alastair? What have you done with him?"

Silence a moment longer, then the wind blew down a long, cold sigh from the snowy mountains, clearing a path through the woods. It led away from the stream, uphill.

Callum grunted. He crossed the stream, jumping from boulder to boulder, until he hopped onto the shore, where he hiked uphill to the high stone cliff.

It jutted out from the earthy mountainside, over-grown but not so camouflaged that Callum could not see the jagged cave mouth high overhead. A trickle of water dribbled out, falling in a shining stream down the cliff face.

Callum studied the cave grimly. Not only was it diffi-cult to reach, but the elements in there would be Earth and Water. Cut off from the sky, he would be under a severe disadvantage, but the wind hissed behind him. It urged him into the cave, and he could see the frog-leaps of the Earth elementals. Though shadowy and peripheral they were heading toward the cave mouth, and he knew that was where he must go.

Callum remained where he was a moment longer, thinking. Then he hunted around for a suitable branch, get-ting out his roll of bandages.

Having prepared his torch and packed it away Cal-lum started climbing the cliff, hauling himself up by grasp-ing saplings, his fingers finding every crevice. It was a long, painful, exhausting journey, and Callum was panting by the time he hauled himself over the lip into the cave. He rested a moment beside the cold trickle of the stream before getting out his makeshift torch, striking his flint and steel together until it lit. Then, holding his flaming torch high, he walked forward into the darkness, boots splashing through the icy water.

⟡━◈━◇━━━━◈━◇⟡

Inside, the daylight died quickly. Callum climbed awk-wardly along a slanting floor carved out by the stream. The water's voice echoed in the cavern, and the torchlight flickered and played on the walls. Even Callum couldn't tell, in that wavering light, what was shadow-flicker and what was elemental play.

"Alastair? Alastair!" Callum's voice echoed off the cave walls, fading away, transfiguring into something like deep laughter, a malicious cackle, before dying in the dark heart of the mountain.

Callum drew his knife; blade at the ready and torch in hand, he pressed deeper into the darkness.

Twice he slipped and nearly fell, only just recovering himself. A roar began to build, the sound of torrential waters pounding around him. Callum grimaced, feet already soaked from the cave's stream, but kept going. His senses, sharpened by the darkness and stillness of the cavern, told him that there was another human presence here, and not far away. His heart hammered, loud enough, it seemed, to echo against the stone.

The passageway squeezed tightly around him, narrowing until he was wriggling more than walking. He was crawling through the cracks until, with one final struggle, he pushed through the passageway, buttons scraping off as he stumbled into a wide, open chamber.

The cave stretched away, far beyond the reach of his torch. The waterfall's sound was deafening here, thundering into deep water. Callum stepped forward, feet splashing, and saw the waterfall at last.

What had sounded like a huge cataract was only a foot high. The water foamed over a shallow shelf of stone, the cave's acoustics making it sound like a vast fall, but Callum had no eyes for the waterfall. For there, curled up on a stone island in the middle of the pool, lay Alastair.

The boy lay asleep or unconscious, dark curls tumbling down, face thin and strained even while unconscious. He stirred, murmuring, and Callum nearly collapsed in relief. "Alastair," he called, but the boy didn't stir.

Callum started forward, wading into the pool only to freeze as dim forms emerged from the depths. They curled around him, fish-like and serpentine. The elementals of Water bared their fangs at him, scales flashing in their own weird, eldritch light. On the stone island, Earth elementals gathered around the boy, teeth sharp and wet as they snarled at Callum.

He retreated, splashing back out of the pool onto the narrow shore. For a moment he regarded the scene: shallow waterfall, sleeping boy, vicious elementals. Then he let out a barking, humorless laugh.

"Oh, really, brother? Is this the best you can do?"

"It's stymied you, hasn't it?" The voice slithered out of the shadows, slid around the cavern, and the Earth elementals shivered. "You can't reach the boy."

"Give him back to me, and we will leave in peace," Callum growled. "If not…"

He whistled sharply, and a wind blasted through the cavern where no wind had ever flown before. It whirled around the island, sending the Earth elementals cowering down. Even the Water elementals retreated, flashing back into the depths.

But the wind died too soon, fading quickly away; the air returned to its fetid stillness. The Earth elementals straightened again, capering around Alastair's unconscious body.

The dark voice cackled. "You have no power here,"

it taunted. "Not within my domain. Go now, little brother. What I want your son alone can give me."

The speaker stepped out now, and Callum blinked. He had expected some transformation, but nothing like this. His older brother was barely himself anymore. Clad in rags, skin pallid as a cave fish's from long years underground, black eyes showing no whites at all. His hair hung in stringy, dark folds, and his ears were pointed like daggers—like an Earth elemental's.

Truly he was now the Monster of Carroch.

Duncan McRathray grinned at his brother, and his teeth were a ranked series of fangs gleaming in the torchlight. "Did you think I wouldn't know, that I wouldn't see our blood shining through him? He's another one like us. The power is strong in him, though he's too young still to guess where his allegiance lies. So…" Duncan's fangs snapped like a deep-sea fish's, "I will drain the power from him and add it to my own."

"As you did all those other children?" Callum said softly. "All those children you stole…They all had some of the power, didn't they?"

"Indeed," said the Monster of Carroch, "but power like young Alastair's is rare. All the others had only a dollop of strength, a dram of magic, while Alastair's is a mighty brew." He shot a covetous look at his unconscious nephew. "I will take his power and add it to my own, then I will be the greatest of our kind in these hills. My domain will be unlimited!"

"Domain?" Callum spat contemptuously. "Oh, aye, a grand domain. More like a filthy hole in the ground with a trickle of water running through!"

"You always were too human, Callum," Duncan said. "Land, money, livestock — what do these matter? Yet you always wanted them, always wanted to be part of a world where you don't belong. The lad doesn't belong there either; it was easy to lure him away. Leave him be. Go on your way, and perhaps I won't kill you."

"Oh, you'll kill me," Callum said calmly. "Killing is all you know anymore, isn't it? You left your humanity behind long ago, after you disappeared into these hills. You're not a person anymore. You're not my brother, you're just a monster. The Monster of Carroch."

Callum McRathray pursed his lips and whistled.

The gale that tore through the cavern whipped the waterfall apart, sending water droplets spraying. The Earth elementals cowered once more, and Duncan ducked back, snarling. The wind tore at him with iron fangs, and thin strips of blood appeared on his pallid frog-flesh. But again the wind died too soon, and Duncan was able to snarl out a command in speech like the grinding of rocks.

A nearby stalagmite came to sudden, hideous life, snatching at Callum with ropy arms. He dodged, but stumbled into the pool. The Water elementals swarmed around him like sharks to blood, tearing at his flesh with knife-sharp fangs. Callum cursed and nearly lost his grip on his torch, but firming his grasp he hissed into the flames. The Fire elementals dancing there responded, spitting gouts of flame down to hiss upon the surface of the water. The fires died quickly, but still sent the Water elementals swimming for cover. Callum was able to splash through the shallows, away from the stalagmite now uprooting itself from the floor as it grew stubby legs to pursue him.

On the far side of the pool Duncan gave a mad laugh, the sound echoing crazily in the chamber. "What use are Fire and Air against Earth and Water, little brother? Give up, before you are crushed and drowned!"

In response Callum clenched his fist.

Duncan broke off, gasping like a fish. For a moment he staggered, swaying, before straightening up with a grinding laugh. "If you think I need air in my lungs any-more — "

Callum shot him.

He had thrown down the torch, still burning on the stone, and taken advantage of Duncan's momentary dis-traction to load and sight his pistol. Now the bang echoed deafeningly in the cave as the gunpowder, still miraculous-ly dry, ignited. The bullet slammed into Duncan's shoul-der; he shrieked, and the stone itself rippled in response to its master's cry. Callum's brother staggered, clutching his wounded shoulder in pain and disbelief.

Callum had reloaded his pistol and was aiming again, this time meaning to meet his target in his broth-er's heart. But Duncan straightened — his inhuman face pinched — and snarled out another command in the lan-guage of stones.

The cave erupted into life once again, rocking around Callum like the waves of the sea, rippling the pool and sending the Water elementals diving down. A vine of stone ripped Callum's pistol out of his hands, and two great hands pinned him back; he was immobilized. In the tumult the torch went out, leaving the cave in utter darkness.

For a moment the only sound was the waterfall, until Callum's breath rasped in his throat. He did not struggle;

there was no struggling against the grasp of the earth.

The crunch of feet on grimy stone resounded, and the Monster chuckled. "You're no match for me, little brother." His voice drifted nearer. "You never were. Now I shall kill you, then drain the power from your son, and none in these hills shall ever match me again."

Duncan said something else in the Earth language, in the grind of rocks and fall of soil, and the stone hands began to tighten around Callum. They squeezed him, tighter and tighter, until Callum gasped for breath and a ringing built in his ears. How ironic, he spared the energy to think, that one so powerful in Air was about to die for want of air —

Callum thought it was his dying imagination when the whistle sounded, but then the wind blew into the cave. It flew in through the passageway, skipped into the dark cave and filled it with the freshness of scented trees, loam, heather and the open sky —

And Callum McRathray found one last scrap of strength, enough to fill his lungs and let out a bellow. A rough, gruff, wordless shout was coughed up from his dying throat, bringing a blast of air not from the cave mouth, but deep from the cave's depths. It came from deep underground, from the hollow chambers far below.

The creature that was Duncan McRathray shrieked. He fell back, arms going over his head, as the two winds smashed over him. Each was filled with teeth that tore at him, stripping the flesh from his bones in bloody rags. The enchanted stone relaxed, letting Callum free, and he fell, collapsing at the lake's edge as his lungs squealed for air. The Monster screamed, his shrieks filling the cavern even as the scent of his blood filled the air.

The screams stopped at last, and there came a soft thud from the far side of the lake. The two winds died away, fading to mere breezes, before falling still.

When he could move Callum felt around. He found his pistol, but it had fallen into the lake and was now soaked. He groped around some more, his fingers finally closing on the torch. It was out now, of course, but it had only recently been aflame and still remembered the sensation.

Callum made a spitting noise, like flame, and the torch leaped alight again. Callum held it up, surveying the cave. The elementals had all disappeared, and Alastair still lay asleep on the island. And, across the lake where a pile of wet bones glistened, a pool of blood was slowly draining into the water.

Callum remained still for a moment, staring at the gruesome sight. Then he moved, pulling himself slowly to his feet. His lungs still hurt.

He waded into the lake, unafraid of the Water elementals. They would not challenge him now; in all likelihood they had already forgotten all about the magical battle. The Earth elementals might remember, but they would hold no grudge; unlike humans, elementals were incapable of loyalty, and respected only power.

Callum McRathray therefore waded unhesitatingly across the lake and hauled himself out onto the island. Alastair was already stirring, moaning as his eyelids fluttered open. He squinted up at Callum in the torchlight. "Mr. McRathray?" he whispered.

"Yes," Callum said gently. "It's me, lad." He helped

the whimpering boy sit up. "How are you feeling?"

"Strange." Alastair looked around fearfully. "Where are we?...I want to go home." He began to cry.

"Ah, don't weep, lad." Callum held his son close, rocking him against the dark. "You're safe now, and we'll go home together."

⟨⟩━◦━◦━━◦━◦━⟨⟩

Fiona, the woodsman's wife, was out doing the evening milking. She looked up fearfully at movement from the forest, but when she saw who it was she stood up hastily. "Mr. McRathray, Mr. McRathray! You found him!"

"I did indeed." Callum came to a weary halt by the woodpile. In his arms he held a sleeping child. Both man and boy were scratched, worn and exhausted, their clothes torn and faces filthy — but in Callum's eyes shone the light of triumph, and the boy slumbered peacefully in his arms.

"Come in, come in," Fiona said, guiding them into the cottage. "It's getting dark, you can't go any further to-night. I will tell my husband."

That night the woodsman and his wife held a cele-bratory feast for Callum McRathray and the lost boy, now found. Man and child spoke little, but the woodsman gath-ered that Callum had found the boy trapped in a cave, and only with difficulty had he pulled him out. "There now!" said the woodsman. "I knew there was some logical expla-nation. Don't you go wandering off again, young man," he said to Alastair severely.

"No, sir," Alastair said meekly.

Callum found himself catching Fiona's eye. It

gleamed knowingly, but she said nothing.

Callum shifted on the bench. "Indeed," he said. "No one need worry over the Monster of Carroch, now or ever again."

Fiona raised her mug. "I will drink to that fine news, sir!"

"Yes, indeed!" said her husband, and they all drank heartily to the death of the Monster.

Callum and Alastair slept the night by the woodsman's fire, Callum holding the boy securely under his arm. He woke only once, to the gentle, silvery music of Air elementals dancing over their heads in the dark cottage. Alastair awoke too. The boy watched the elementals silently, their dance reflected in his eyes, and, across the cottage, Callum thought he saw Fiona's eyes gleam too.

Eventually the Air elementals disappeared, and the three of them drifted back to sleep again.

The next morning Callum and Alastair prepared to set out once more. "Please come to Rathray House, next time you're in that country," Callum said. "You will both find a warm welcome there."

"Thank you, sir," the woodsman said heartily. "Though, truth be told, we hardly ever leave the hills."

"Our lives are here," his wife agreed.

"Still, thank you for your aid and hospitality." Callum gave Fiona the briefest flicker of a glance. "Thank you both for all your aid."

A slight smile tugged Fiona's lips, but she merely inclined her head as her husband bid their guests a cheerful farewell.

She stood back and watched as they set off down the slope: a great, tall bear of a man leading his little son by the hand, heading home to the boy's mother, to their lives beneath the open sky. Then she pursed her lips and blew them a warm, gentle breeze to keep them safe on their journey home.

Rose Strickman
About the Author

Rose Strickman is a fantasy, science fiction and horror writer living in Seattle, Washington. Her work has appeared in anthologies such as *Sword and Sorceress 32, Air: Sylphs, Spirits & Swan Maidens* and *UnCommon Evil*, as well as online e-zines such as *Feed Your Monster, Enchanted Conversation* and *Luna Station Quarterly.*

Connect at https://www.facebook.com/rose.strickman.3 or see her Amazon page at amazon.com/author/rosestrickman

Fire and Wisdom
Joel R. Hunt

As he reclined in his armchair and listened to the cauldron bubbling in the fireplace, Wisdom Lorus reflected on how tedious travel was. For two weeks he had been confined to this carriage - a miserable, single-story, four-room affair with a cramped bedchamber and no servants. How the Grand College expected him to fulfil his duty in these pitiful conditions, Lorus would never understand.

At least he had books to keep him company. Wisdom Wilifur's latest treatise on potion-craft was nothing short of revolutionary, with a captivating chapter on boiled mandrakes. The man had a way of turning strict formulas into a literary delight. It was a shame he was such a bore in person.

Without taking his eyes off the page, Lorus jotted down another note.

"The mandrake's ready," said a voice from the fireplace.

Lorus read to the end of his page, then closed the book around his finger and turned to address the flames.

"I beg your pardon?"

"The mandrake, master," repeated the fire. "It's boiled. It'll be soft if it's left much longer."

Lorus arched his eyebrows.

"Remind me, Red; are you an ordained wisdom of the Grand College?"

"No, master," said the fire.

"Have you ever been distinguished with honours for your potion-craft?"

"No, master."

"Have you ever concocted the elixir of life?"

"No, master."

"Do you know who has done all of those things?"

"Wisdom Wilifur, master."

"Correct. And if Wisdom Wilifur recommends we cook the mandrake for one hour, we cook it for *precisely* one hour."

"Yes, master."

Lorus settled back in his chair and flicked open Wilifur's book. The next page was a simple list of toxic nightshades and their various interactions with boiled mandrake. However, Lorus' eyes glazed over the information. With each word he tried to read, his mind became more focused on the incessant bubbling of the cauldron, until it was all he could think about.

He drew a string across the page, set the book aside and rubbed the bridge of his nose. As casually as his pride allowed him he rose from his chair and sauntered across to the cauldron. He took a set of prongs and slid them into the boiled root. The mandrake held its form but had lost its toughness, exactly as described by Wilifur. The fire gave a smug crackle as Lorus lifted out the root and placed it in a hemlock infusion to soak overnight.

"Keep any more lucky guesses to yourself," said Lorus. "We're following the rest of the recipe *as it's written*."

Before Red could reply the door to the driver's platform opened, and a heavy-set face peered inside.

"Sorry to intrude, m'wisdom, but -"

Red yelped. He whipped from beneath the cauldron and coiled around Lorus' arm, the fire of his body condensing and reshaping. When he reached Lorus' shoulder, he had taken the form of a small porcupine with flaming quills. Lorus shielded him from view.

"Get *out!*" he snapped. The driver jumped and slammed the door.

Lorus' face flushed with a heat that had nothing to do with Red's fire. He glared at the door, listening out for any sign of disobedience, but heard nothing. He rested a hand on Red's back. With the familiar now in his restrained form the warmth of his flickering quills merely tickled Lorus' fingers.

"Are you alright?" Lorus asked.

"Yes, master."

Lorus marched to the driver's door and wrenched it open, stepping out onto the platform beyond. The driver had returned to his seat, face drained of color, his eyes locked onto the floor. Lorus was short, even for a Grand College wisdom, yet with how the driver cowered under his cold fury he may as well have been a giant.

"Who do you think you are?" Lorus snarled. "You have the audacity to look upon a wisdom's unrestrained familiar? His pure form? I could have you lashed!"

The driver sank to the floor in supplication, scraping at Lorus' boots.

"Mercy, m'wisdom," he said, "Please have mercy. I didn't mean to, I didn't realize."

Lorus grimaced at the display. He would have let the man continue to cower and tremble, but Red nuzzled his neck before giving it a sharp nip. The pinching burn was one thing; Red's imploring eyes were another entirely. Lorus sighed.

"Fine," he said, "but don't let it happen again, or I'll get myself a new driver and you can *walk* back to the Grand College."

"Bless you, m'wisdom," said the driver. "It won't happen again, I swear it."

"For your sake I hope not. Now, what was so important for you to barge in on us like that?"

The driver wiped his brow and rose back to his seat, but he kept his eyes firmly on Lorus' ankles.

"It's the runes of binding on our wheels, m'wisdom. Some of them are wearing away."

"Is there any chance of the spirits getting out?"

"No, m'wisdom. They're bound tight, but they might get free enough to change our course."

Lorus peered at the horizon. Even from the vantage point of the driver's platform there was nothing but road ahead, with endless farmland on either side. Not a college in sight, or even an inn, so stopping the carriage out here would mean yet another night spent in his unbearably cramped bedchamber.

"We've been travelling long enough already," said Lorus, "I won't have any more delays. Do whatever you must to keep them under control until we arrive, and you can reapply the runes while I'm attending to my business in town."

Whether or not it was what the driver wanted to hear, he gave a vigorous nod.

"Right you are, m'wisdom."

"Good man."

Lorus spun on his heel and returned to the study, slamming the door behind him as a reminder that the barrier existed for a reason. Then, sinking into his armchair, he pressed a finger to his neck where Red had nipped him. A burning blister was already rising there, and Red nuzzled his hand by way of apology.

"You're too soft for our own good," Lorus huffed.

"He didn't mean any harm," said Red.

"Hm."

The remainder of their journey was pleasantly brief. Whether the driver had been spurred to action by Lorus' threat, or they were simply closer to their destination than Lorus had realized, he had barely finished his chapter when he felt the carriage rumble to a halt. Red, who after the earlier interruption had remained in his porcupine form, clambered from Lorus' lap back up to his shoulder. The pair approached the outer door, where the childlike amazement of the crowd outside filtered through.

"Look at them wheels!"

"No horses."

"How does it move?"

Lorus shook his head. Such wonders filled the world, with new discoveries coming from the Grand College each and every day, yet these peasants were excited by something as simple as a spirit-driven carriage. It was no surprise they needed his help.

A heavy clank announced the descending of the outer steps. As Lorus emerged into the town beyond, the crowd that was waiting for him took a collective breath. No doubt he was the first wisdom that many of them had ever seen, and in their excitement some of them even forgot to bow. The driver made no such mistake, sinking so low that his nose almost brushed the carriage steps. Lorus waved him away.

As Lorus stepped onto the cobbles of the town square – if the rabble of houses and store fronts could even be called as such – the commonfolk surged inwards, entreating his wards and blessings. Most had the mud-coated hands of farmers, though a few looked to be tanners and smiths. Lorus muttered a few cursory incantations before gesturing for the peasants to give him space, though it took Red whipping in a circle around his shoulders for them to oblige. Gasps and applause rippled along the crowd, and as Red settled next to Lorus' cheek the commonfolk fell to whispering amongst themselves.

A voice barked over the murmuring, and the crowd parted to reveal a ruddy-faced tower of a woman. From the mud that caked her boots and splattered her cheeks it was clear that she was another farmer, no doubt fresh from working the fields. However, adorning her soiled clothes was the intricate robe of a town elder. Unlike the rest of her the robe was immaculately clean, evidently having been put on just for Lorus' arrival. There wasn't a single crease spoiling the fabric; it might have been the first time she'd ever worn it.

The woman approached and bowed.

"Elder Meril, I presume?" said Lorus.

"Aye, my wisdom, that's me," she said with a beaming smile, "May I say it's an honor to have ye in our humble town."

She thrust her hand out to shake his, but not before wiping it along her robe and smearing field dirt across her otherwise spotless garment. Somehow it left her skin no cleaner. Lorus swallowed back his disgust and accepted her filthy hand. Her grip was crushing, and he slipped his fingers out of her palm before she snapped them off.

"I'd like to get straight to business," said Lorus. "One of your townsfolk reported witnessing a demon."

Meril's smile dropped in an instant. She nodded.

"Aye, that's right. Old Tom. If ye'll forgive him he don't dare return to the barn where it happened, but he's happy to speak to ye if ye'd like."

"Please," said Lorus.

Lorus gestured for her to lead the way, and as she turned he beckoned Red down his arm. The familiar got to work lapping away the grime that had rubbed off of Meril's hand onto Lorus' skin. If the woman noticed the faint scent of burning dirt she had sense enough to stay quiet.

She led him to a small shack at the edge of the town, where a wizened man waited for them. As the pair approached him he and Meril exchanged pleasantries, and the man gave Lorus a perfunctory bow.

"Are you the farmer who encountered the demon?" asked Lorus.

The man wrung his cap between white knuckles.

"I… I am, m'wisdom."

"What can you tell me about it?"

"Beggin' yer pardon, m'wisdom, but very little. Took one look at it and locked up me barn. I were lucky to get me Dolly out, it happened so fast."

"Your dolly?"

"His cow, my wisdom," Meril explained. Old Tom gave an earnest nod.

"I see," said Lorus, "And this Dolly, did she show any signs of attack? Bite wounds, claw marks? Any unusual behaviours?"

The man's face crumpled in thought.

"None, m'wisdom, as I can recall. Checked her over meself."

"Is there anything else you can tell me? What you saw, for example, when you looked upon this demon?"

A haunted sheen flashed across the farmer's furtive eyes. He lowered his voice, leaning in so that only Lorus could hear.

"*Claws*, m'wisdom. Claws as like I've never seen before, long as yer arm."

"You're certain it was a demon?" asked Lorus.

Old Tom blinked in confusion.

"What else would have claws like that, m'wisdom?" he asked.

"I see," said Lorus, nodding to the farmer and turning to Meril. "Well, please excuse me; I must prepare before I approach this entity."

"O'course, my wisdom."

Lorus turned on his heel and marched back to the carriage, beckoning Red to his shoulder.

"Damned fools," he hissed, "I thought they'd at least

know what we were dealing with."

"A vampire, perhaps?" asked Red.

"With no bite marks on the cow? I doubt it."

"A spectre then?"

"He didn't mention any light or noise, just the claws. Odd way to describe a spectre."

Lorus fell quiet as he moved through the dispersing crowd, ignoring their looks and whispers. Mounting the steps to his study he held his palm beneath the lock, and Red flowed down his arm and slipped through the keyhole. The door opened with a soft click. Lorus stepped inside, Red hopping back onto his shoulder.

"He said it was a demon, didn't he?" Red asked.

"It's not a demon."

"I know that, but what if he did *see* a demon?"

Lorus paused, frowning.

"An illusion?" he asked.

"Could be."

"Hm. Unlikely, but possible."

Heading to the corner of the study, Lorus opened the cabinet that stored his travel arsenal. Given the uncertainty he opted to prepare for as many scenarios as he could. After putting on his armour plate he hooked a dozen satchels and vials to his belt, alongside a silver-bladed dagger that had saved his life more times than he cared to count. Having all but ruled out vampires he decided not to burden himself with stakes, but in their place he equipped his bandolier. Each of the seven compartments held a spell scroll, and he took his time considering which he might need in the upcoming confrontation. Here, for the first time, Lorus was grateful for the mundanity of his journey, as the lack of activity had left his scroll store fully stocked.

All the while Red watched him like an excited toddler, bouncing back and forth along the nearby shelves.

"Ready?" he asked as Lorus loaded the final scroll into his bandolier.

"As much as one can be for an unknown foe," said the wisdom.

Returning to the town square Lorus found Elder Meril and his driver in deep discussion about the workings of his carriage. That was good; it was fitting that a town elder showed some intellectual curiosity regarding college matters, though if he waited around until the peasants educated themselves he'd never leave. He strode over and placed himself between the pair. The driver sank into a silent bow and wisely excused himself, leaving Lorus with the elder.

"Take me to the demon," he told her.

"O'course, my wisdom."

This time no farmers flocked to his side. Though the entire town had come out to witness his arrival, none were as eager to accompany him to the barn and the beast that supposedly lurked there. That suited Lorus, as a crowd of frightened peasants would only get in his way.

He let Meril take the lead. The paths she took him down were paved with nothing more than dirt, barely wide enough for a horse and rider, and on either side bushes and stone walls marked the edges of an ocean of farmland. The town itself had disappeared behind waves of hedgerows by the time Meril announced their arrival, opening a gate into one of the fields.

"This is Old Tom's land," she said. "The demon's

trapped in his barn two fields over."

"Thank you for your assistance, elder."

Lorus set off into the field. Meril hesitated by the gate.

"Would ye like me to come with ye?" she asked.

"That won't be necessary," said Lorus, "The fewer humans exposed to my magics the better."

Meril hid her relief well; a peasant might not have noticed.

"Right ye are, my wisdom," she said, giving a firm nod, "I'll be here if ye need anythin', and I'll keep the rest of the village out of ye way."

"See that you do."

Lorus followed the fence that ran along the field's edge, where a footpath had been worked into the earth by generations of farmers. The next field was masked behind hedgerows, with a narrow stile for travellers to pass over. Waiting for him there, hidden from the view of the gate, was an old, wooden barn.

Lorus had no doubt that this was where the entity was trapped. A heavy wooden beam had been nailed across both doors, and throughout the field stood hastily erected straw figures bearing the basic runes of protection that most peasants were familiar with.

As Lorus stepped closer to the barn a scuffle of movement echoed within. He waited for it to fall silent again before turning to his familiar.

"Alright, Red, let's see what we're dealing with."

Red shot from Lorus' fingers and landed around the hinges of the barn door. Latching himself there the familiar drew in his flames and wrapped them around the metal, reducing the surrounding wood to cinders. Once the fire reached a self-sustaining heat Red lashed across the beam and engulfed the second set of hinges, and soon the doors were held to the rest of the barn by nothing more than flaking char. Across the field where Lorus was standing the caustic scent of burning was followed by the creaking of old wood. He raised a hand.

"That will suffice, Red."

The familiar flickered, then leapt from the hinges and scurried back to Lorus' boot. The embers that Red left behind continued to glow and crackle, and before long the barn doors let out a mournful groan as they tore away from the building. Lorus narrowed his eyes against the ash and dust that was kicked up by the collapse, tensing himself for whatever might leap at him or seek to make its escape.

Nothing emerged. Daylight now pierced the small barn, laying bare its meagre contents. Tools and troughs and a number of haystacks, but no monster.

"We heard something in there," said Red.

"I know."

Lorus flicked open a container on his bandolier, drawing out a scroll and reciting its incantation from memory. As he completed the spell the parchment crumbled away, and a blue haze fell across Lorus' vision. Floating wisps materialised across the fields, the runes on the straw figures rippled like water, and in the distance a hill erupted with the light of a powerful ley line. When Lorus turned his second sight towards the barn it was bathed in an otherworldly glow, yet appeared as empty as before.

"What do you see?" asked Red.

"Just the usual. We'll need to get closer."

They approached with caution, each scanning the interior of the barn as if searching for a fly in a fog cloud. Red flared with a fierce energy. Lorus rested a palm on his dagger's hilt and let his fingers brush the satchels of salt and wolfsbane at his belt, ready for whatever threat might emerge. Lorus reached the centre of the barn, his every sense on high alert. He turned in slow circles, but nothing else moved in the flicker of Red's flame.

Then, in the darkest corner of the barn, wood scraped on wood. Something shifted, rising up. Lorus knocked open the next container of his bandolier and beckoned Red to his finger. He thrust his familiar's light forward, banishing the shadows to reveal their foe. What he had at first taken to be a bundle of sticks leaning against the wall was now stretching and growing. Roots crept along the ground, twigs flexing out like claws as bark split into a jagged maw.

It was no wonder Lorus' second sight had found nothing in the barn; the so-called demon was no illusion or magical beast.

It was a wood elemental.

Lorus spat out a chuckle. While they might frighten a gaggle of peasants an elemental posed little threat to a trained wisdom, and this particular specimen was laughably pitiful. Despite its sharp extremities it was frail enough to be knocked down by a breeze. Lorus was surprised it could carry its own weight, starved as it was. With a shaking head he replaced the catch on his bandolier.

"Waste of our time," he said. "Sort it out, Red."

"Yes master."

The elemental took its first shaky step towards

them, but Red closed the gap in less than a blink. Too late it sensed the danger, rearing away from the familiar and swatting at him with razor-like branches. Red weaved through them with ease and latched onto the dry, wooden legs. His flames engulfed the creature in an instant. The shriek it let out was that of a tree being twisted in two, a vine stretched to its breaking point.

With its echo trembling through the barn Lorus almost didn't hear the creak behind his shoulder.

He twisted aside just as a thorn-covered claw raked the air where his head had been. The shock knocked him off balance, and he stumbled away from the next assault. A second elemental must have been pressed into the opposite corner, only coming to life as it heard the death-cries of its fellow.

Lorus barely had time to find his footing before the second elemental's thorns were launched at his face again. He drew his dagger and slashed it in a wide arc. The thorns were faster, retracting and lashing out again. Lorus only just stepped aside in time, but with each attack he became more familiar with its movements. When the next strike came he slammed down his elbow, catching the thorns with his armour and trapping them against his breastplate. He severed the spiked limb and tossed it aside.

The elemental staggered in confusion. It lashed out with its stunted claws, then roared like a tree in the wind and thrust its fist to the ground. A tremor ran under Lorus' feet. Ashen vines pierced the dirt and latched onto his boots. He tried to step away, but he was shackled to the earth. The elemental readied its remaining thorns and shambled towards him.

Lorus raised his blade.

A blaze streaked across his vision. The creature screamed as Red pierced its wooden chest, sending plumes of smoke coiling to the ceiling. It staggered away, trying to wrench the familiar from its insides and forgetting Lorus entirely.

The roots tightened around Lorus' ankle. He dropped to one knee and began slicing himself free, but as soon as one root was cut another grew in its place. He worked with growing frustration, getting no closer to freedom, until a shuffling movement drew his attention.

A third elemental clawed its way from the barn's largest haystack. The wisdom jumped upright and made to back away, but his boot remained fastened to the ground. The creature turned a featureless face towards him.

"Red?" Lorus called over his shoulder.

"I'm a little busy, master!"

With a desperate grunt Lorus reached out towards his familiar. He clicked his fingers, and a section of flame tore away from Red and darted towards Lorus' hand. The moment the fire reached his palm Lorus thrust it down to the roots, splashing it over the bindings. The roots began to wither as fire licked around them.

The third elemental loomed closer. It was thinner than the others, but wiry, with long, sturdy arms and a rib-cage of twisted branches. At the end of each limb hung thorns the length of Lorus' spine. It studied him for a moment, then flexed its thorns and raked for his throat. Only a desperate parry saved him from being impaled. His knife cracked against the wooden claws and sent splinters clattering to the ground.

By now the heat was baking Lorus' foot, and with a twisting wrench he pulled his boot free from the dying roots and staggered away. Beside him the second elemental was screeching, lashing at itself over and over to remove the growing flames, while the third was readying its claws for another assault.

It was time to end this.

The elemental lunged, but Lorus was ready. He spun aside and swung out with his knife. More splinters rained down. It turned, raking its claws, which he let clatter off of his shoulder plate. He severed one of its central vines, vegetation sloughing away. As it reared back Lorus reached into his pouch and pulled out a vial. He flicked off its lid and waited for the elemental's next attack. When it advanced he matched its step, jumping close enough to pour the vial's contents onto the trunk running up the creature's middle. The wood hissed, turned white and then flaked away. He finished the job with a heavy slash from his dagger, snapping the trunk in half. The lifeless branches fell to the floor.

Almost in tandem Red's elemental finally succumbed to the flames, staggering to the ground and writhing. The familiar hopped away to clamber back onto Lorus' shoulder, and they both watched until the last elemental stopped moving for good. Inspecting the three corpses Lorus sighed, rubbing the bridge of his nose.

"Someone needs to teach those peasants to count," he said.

As they made their way back to the gate Meril ran up to meet them.

"Is the demon gone?" she asked.

"Yes," said Lorus, "All three of them."

The elder's face turned pale.

"They were elementals," Lorus explained. "I'll have the College send a junior wisdom in the coming weeks to inform your townsfolk how to identify basic entities. Then, perhaps next time a wisdom has to aid you, they'll know what they're dealing with."

"Tha's very kind, my wisdom."

They didn't speak again until they had returned to the town square. The crowd must have dissipated while he worked, but voices called out the moment he stepped onto the cobblestones as townsfolk swarmed in from every doorway. Old Tom took the lead, his face awash with hope and admiration.

"Is it done, m'wisdom?" he croaked.

"It is."

A cheer filled the square. They pressed in to give their thanks and Meril sprung back to life, jumping in to keep them from getting too close.

"Get back, give our wisdom space!" she bellowed. To her credit, the townsfolk listened, forming a ring around Lorus which they seemed, by their own volition, unable to cross.

"Bless ye, m'wisdom," said Old Tom, bowing low to the cobblestones, "and bless the Grand College."

Lorus nodded, then pressed on through the crowd towards his carriage. Meril appeared over his shoulder, keeping pace.

"I presume there's a matter of payment?" she asked.

"No need," said Lorus. "It is a wisdom's duty to protect all in the College's domain. We require no payment for that."

"Ye too kind, my wisdom! Truly ye are."

Lorus waved her away. Reaching the other end of the square and finding it empty, he peered along the main road. His driver had moved the carriage a distance away from the crowds, no doubt to attend to the wheels in peace. Spotting him sat at his platform Lorus beckoned the man over.

"Have you reapplied the runes?" he asked.

"Yes, m'wisdom," said the driver with a bow. "We're ready to set off as soon as you command it."

"Good. We'll go momentarily, but first I want you to catch up to Elder Meril and inform her of the College's suggested donation."

"Yes, m'wisdom."

The driver trotted off and Lorus strolled up the road towards the carriage, eager to leave this meagre town behind. As he walked a gentle gust wafted his hair and caused Red's spines to flicker. Strange; the trees dotting the roadside were motionless. Lorus raised his eyes to the sky. It took him a moment, but he found the gust's source perched on his carriage. Its talons were as sharp as the breeze, eyes roiling like mist. Nothing else of the bird was visible, so he took a few steps closer to frame her against a cloud so that her shimmering outline could be seen.

"Wisest Emerel sends her regards," said the familiar, her voice an echo in the wind.

Lorus bowed. Red flared up, bathing his master's face with prickly heat.

"It is a pleasure to see you again, Venta," he said. "I would be grateful if you could inform my wisest that the reported demon has been dealt with. As it transpires, the threat was nothing more than some lost elementals."

Venta appeared, for the briefest moment, to smirk.

"The word of peasants is rarely blessed with insight. However, before you return from today's…" the bird paused, sampling the next words in her beak, "*great victory*, another matter requires your attention. Gennonbar has seen a significant rise in fae activity. You are to travel there immediately and connect with the territory's resident wisdom, Shureek. She will aid your investigations. Deal with what threats you can, and inform the college of those you cannot."

A bead of sweat rolled into Lorus' eye. He shuffled Red further down his shoulder to escape some of the excess heat.

"I have been traveling for some weeks, Venta," he said.

"And this has placed you close to Gennonbar. Do you take issue with your instructions?"

Lorus bowed again.

"I act at the command of my wisest," he said.

"Very good. Wisest Emerel wishes you safe travels, and a triumphant return to the Grand College."

"Safe travels to you also, Venta."

"Goodbye, Venta!" chirped Red.

The bird considered him with a fierce, misty glare, then spread her wings and flapped. She rose faster than Lorus' eye could follow, and when he again tried to catch sight of her against the clear blue sky he saw only a formless ripple that spread into nothingness. Lorus pursed his lips.

"Don't do that again," he said.

"Do what?" asked Red.

"Spread your flames. Every time we encounter Venta, you puff yourself up and give off more heat."

"Oh. Do I?"

"Yes. It's embarrassing. They'll think we're trying too hard to impress them."

Red's flame shrank back down.

"Sorry, master."

They settled back into Lorus' study, and the wisdom prepared one of the three meals that he could put together without a servant. The driver, who now had sense enough to knock first, interrupted while it was cooking to hand over a sizeable coin pouch that had been donated by the town. Lorus dismissed him and tossed the coins into a nearby drawer. With that the carriage began its gentle rumbling, and they were on their way to Gennonbar. For the remainder of the evening Lorus bathed, then changed into his study robes and read more from Wisdom Wilifur.

When night fell the pair retired to their bedchamber. Lorus settled into his four-poster bed while, on the nearby table, Red climbed into his glass lantern. The familiar's porcupine form dissipated as he relaxed into his unrestrained state.

"Goodnight, master," said Red.

"Goodnight."

Lorus pressed against his pillow, wishing he were in the more comfortable bed of his college chambers. This one barely gave him room to spread out; it was like a quilted coffin.

"We want to impress them, though, don't we master?" asked Red.

Lorus rubbed the bridge of his nose before glancing at Red's lantern.

"I beg your pardon?"

"Venta," said Red, "and Wisest Emerel."

"You're still thinking about earlier?"

"Yes. Well, we *do* want to impress them, don't we?"

Lorus rolled onto his side and watched his shadow flicker in the lantern's glare. As Red's flames billowed back and forth Lorus' shadow shrank and grew. Shrank and grew. When the light caught his back, it filled the entire wall with his image.

"We will," he said.

<hr />

Lorus woke to the caustic stench of smoke.

"Red!" he shouted, bolting upright and scanning the room. Red peered out of his lantern.

"Is everything alright, master?"

"I… I thought…" Lorus trailed off, sniffing the air. The scent of burning still lingered in the room, but it wasn't coming from Red. Lorus followed his nose to the door.

"I smell it too," said Red, thrusting up his glowing snout. "A fire, a big one. Wood and vegetation. Open air. Burning stone. It smells man-made."

"You have a good nose for fire."

"Thank you, master."

Lorus threw on his clothes and plucked Red out of the lantern. Jogging through the study he emerged onto the carriage's outer platform, ignoring the driver's timid greeting. The walls of Gennon loomed on the horizon, and from outside the city thick plumes of smoke choked the sky. Even at a distance Lorus could taste the burning in the air. A gust of wind cleared away the smoke long enough for Lorus to spot an enormous bonfire by the roadside. A dozen figures patrolled its edges, with a steady stream of fresh fuel being brought over from the walls and hurled into the blazing pit. They seemed almost like a trail of ants.

As the carriage approached, some of the figures took notice, turning to salute the arriving wisdom. Each of them wore the uniforms of city guards, even those bringing additional wood. The blackened heart of the bonfire was twice the height of the tallest man, and from the look of it had been burning all morning, yet still more fuel was being added. Branches, vines and all manner of vegetation were hurled into the flames.

The source of this fuel appeared to be the city walls. Several sections were utterly overgrown, with choking plant life reaching up like a hand to tear the stone down, and a small army was at work cutting it back. Most coated the outer layer of the wall, but near the merchant's gate an enormous tree had pierced through cracks in the stone. Lorus grimaced. The guards' effort to remove the vegetation was admirable, but it should never have been permitted to reach this point in the first place.

Drawing closer to the city another feature caught Lorus' attention. Along the top of each wall, in a solid line that encircled the city, were hundreds of heavy troughs. They looked to be attached to hinges, with runes just visible along each surface, but at such a distance it was impossible for Lorus to work out what the runes were for.

He finally turned to the driver.

"Knock when we've reached the wisdom's tower," he said.

"Yes, m'wisdom," the man muttered. Lorus noticed then how stooped the driver was, and how his eyes seemed intent on closing, despite clear effort. They had been on the road all night, and the driver hadn't slept since the previous morning.

"Make sure to get plenty of rest while I'm attending my business," said Lorus.

The driver looked up, too tired to hide his surprise.

"I will," he said. "Thank you, m'wisdom."

Some minutes later Lorus was dutifully alerted by a knock at the study door. He emerged in the heart of Gennon on a busy city street at the foot of the wisdom's tower. The reception wasn't as warm as that which he had received at the previous town; several passing merchants watched him with curiosity, but a wisdom's carriage was a more common sight here.

The tower guard's face tightened as Lorus approached. He saluted, but the gesture seemed strangely forced.

"Welcome to Gennon, Wisdom Lorus."

"I am here to speak to Wisdom Shureek," said Lorus.

"Of course, please follow me."

The tower had, naturally, been styled after those from the Grand College, which meant that Lorus could have found his way unguided. The spiral stairs and room distribution was nearly identical to what Lorus was used to, and he could navigate every tower in the Grand College blindfolded.

"Interesting contraptions on the battlements," said

Lorus. "I presume the runes will tip the troughs if they detect smoke?"

"That's right, my wisdom."

"Get a lot of fires in Gennon, do you?"

The man glanced across, but it was Red that his eyes landed on.

"Yes, my wisdom. We do."

They climbed the remaining stairs in silence. It was something of a relief when they arrived at the top floor and Lorus was gestured towards Wisdom Shureek's quarters. He waited for the guard to open the door for him, but the young man appeared to be in the throes of some internal battle.

"Your familiar will have to remain here, my wisdom," he said at last.

"For what purpose?"

"It's simply how we do things here," the young man said.

"Hm. A strange custom," said Lorus. "Very well."

With an uncertain glance Red hopped onto a nearby sconce. Once he had made himself comfortable the guard knocked on the door, then waited for confirmation from the other side before letting Lorus into Wisdom Shureek's chambers.

It was strange to walk into a room without Red coming with him. Lorus felt half naked. He entered into a library of sorts, with shelves adorning each wall and armchairs set out around a fireplace. In the far corner a young lady, barely a woman, was sorting through the books on one shelf. She nodded to Lorus as he passed. Through the next doorway was evidently Wisdom Shureek's study, and

Lorus was intrigued by the state of it; half-finished mech-
anisms covered every table, with more nuts and screws
than notes and scrolls. That line of study had never been of
interest to Lorus, but he admired anyone dedicated to the
pursuit of their craft. Shureek, however, was not present.
He returned to the library and checked the other rooms
it opened into, but none were of interest and none were
occupied. He approached the young woman by the book-
shelf, who continued to work as if he weren't even present.
Lorus gave a pointed cough.

"Girl," he said, "fetch Wisdom Shureek."

She turned and regarded him with narrow eyes.

"Excuse me?"

"Wisdom Shureek," Lorus repeated. "She was supposed to meet me here."

"She did," said the woman. "I *am* Wisdom Shureek."

Lorus' mouth ran dry, and a bloom flushed into his
cheeks which he tried to hide with a curt bow.

"My sincere apologies, Wisdom Shureek," he said,
"With your familiar not being present, I didn't realize..."

"My familiar isn't 'not present'," said Shureek, "It
doesn't exist."

Lorus paused. His brow creased in thought.

"I see. When were you ordained?"

"Last winter."

"You should have received your familiar by now. I
apologize, the Grand College can lose track of matters in
the border territories. When I return I shall inform them
of this oversight, and make sure a senior wisdom is dispatched here to complete the ceremony."

"You misunderstand me, Wisdom Lorus. I have already completed the ceremony, and I have already been offered a familiar. I told the senior wisdom that I had no wish for one, not now or ever."

Lorus studied her face, waiting for her to reveal the jest. Her eyes, however, held nothing but sincerity.

"Why would you turn down your familiar?" Lorus asked.

"I have seen countless deaths at the hands of elementals. Dwellings demolished, our city walls besieged. What would possibly drive me to want one perched on my shoulder?"

"But familiars aren't elementals," said Lorus, "Not anymore. Everything that made them wild is extracted long before the ceremony."

"Is that so?" asked Shureek, "My sentries tell me your familiar is made of fire. Does it ever revert to its unrestrained form?"

"Of course, but there's no harm in that."

"Would you thrust your hand into its unrestrained flames?"

Lorus scowled. A question that foolish deserved no response. Shureek seated herself and gestured for Lorus to take the seat opposite.

"Whatever you may claim about your familiar, the truth of the matter is that the element remains. And, while ever it does, the *elemental* remains. Will you take refreshments?"

Lorus sat and watched her select a tart from a tray of sweets. She passed it to him on a plate, which he took with a nod of gratitude.

"I must say, you have some strange notions in the

border territories," he said.

"One might say the same of your central territories," said Shureek. "Besides, we have a lot to offer here. The frequent conflict with the faefolk leads to a lot of first-hand experience, the sort that can't be gained from lectures. Would you like our healer to look into your injuries?"

"My injuries?"

"Your neck," she said.

Lorus raised his hand and felt the splattering of blisters there.

"Ah, I see. That's nothing. Red nips me from time to time."

Shureek's face tightened.

"Your familiar *nips* you?"

"Only if he needs to bring something to my attention. He can't very well speak in the presence of commonfolk, can he? What would the College think?"

Lorus chuckled at the thought, but Shureek remained unamused. She refilled her cup and took a thoughtful sip.

"Are you its master, or its horse?" she asked.

Lorus blinked.

"I beg your pardon?"

"It rides you," Shureek said, "and it communicates its wishes by inflicting pain. You might as well hand it a whip. If this is the experience of bending an elemental to one's will, I am pleased to have no part of it."

Lorus' face flushed with heat. If anyone but a wisdom had said such a thing he would have struck them on the spot, and likely far worse. Only the thought of losing his position prevented him from a furious retort. With an enormous effort of will he forced his face to neutrality, standing with hands half-clenched by his side, and gave a stiff bow.

"Evidently you have no need of my services here," he said. "Shall I rebuke our Wisest Emerel for sending a beast of burden in place of a wisdom, or would you like the honor yourself?"

For the first time since he had stepped into the room Shureek's mouth twisted into a smile.

"You take umbrage too easily, Wisdom Lorus," she said, pouring him a cup and sliding it across the table. She waited for him to retake his seat before continuing. "I apologise for the...*character* of my observations. I am not known for my discretion. However, regardless of your relationship with that pet elemental of yours, I have no doubt regarding your capacity as a wisdom. Wisest Emerel was, naturally, not wrong to send you. Gennonbar needs your help."

Lorus picked up the cup he had been offered and took his time in bringing it to his lips, sipping it and returning it to the table. He leaned back in his chair and scratched his chin. When it became apparent that Shureek was comfortable with his extended silence, he nodded.

"I am not a petty man," he said. "I will not shirk my duty based on some personal slight, but know that I come to your aid as a representative of the Grand College. I will not have that institution insulted by way of my own position being disrespected."

"I understand."

"I will overlook this initial... misunderstanding, but further instances will be reported for review."

"Of course."

Lorus waited until he had fully cooled before he continued.

"I understand you are having particular trouble with faefolk currently."

"That's correct," said Shureek. "There's a village in the forest about an hour's ride from here. We were expecting a messenger from there several days ago, but none ever arrived. We believe they may have been attacked. We want to investigate and, if possible, locate and destroy the faefolk's grove."

"That sounds simple enough."

"I'm pleased you think so. I trust the college sent you with an arsenal?" asked Shureek.

"Of course."

"Good," said Shureek. She drained her cup and slammed it onto the table. "Then prepare yourself for the dangers of the forest. We set out on the hour."

<hr>

When Lorus and Red arrived in the clearing beyond the main gate they found a squadron of soldiers waiting, saddled up and ready. Each wore the sleek, functional armour of the border territories, unburdened by the ceremonial pomp of the Grand College guardians. Their weaponry was formidable; two of the men hefted fierce halberds with blades of pure silver coated in runes. The weapons thrummed with violent potential, capable of dispatching both mortal and magical creatures with ease. Four others had crossbows slung across their backs, with runes etched into the wood. The rest were equipped with longswords, and though they were sheathed Lorus had no doubt that their blades were equal to that of the halberds gleaming in the morning sun.

They hailed his approach with appropriate formality, though their wariness around Red was evident from their tense muscles and poorly-hidden glances. Lorus had no time for such irrational attitudes. He busied himself with readying his own horse, filling its saddle bags with supplies and hooking on Red's lantern. He had loaded his bandolier carefully, attempting to predict the spells that he might need while tracking and fighting the faefolk, and he was checking the catches of each compartment when Shureek arrived.

The guards saluted in unison and lined up for inspection, and Lorus watched her with interest. Shureek's travel gear had transformed her entirely; gone was the young librarian, and in her place stood a squat, armoured soldier. Strange embellishments adorned her limbs, and beneath her helmet she might have been a man.

As she saddled up on the neighbouring horse Lorus nodded to the tubes running the underside of her arms.

"Is that the fashion in Gennonbar?" he asked.

Shureek regarded him with a hint of amusement, putting him in mind of a bored feline. As he watched she extended her arm and flexed her wrist. A spring released near her elbow, and a scroll fired into her waiting palm. With a click the now-empty tube jolted to one side, being replaced by another that was ready to fire.

"My own design," said Shureek, reloading the first tube and resetting her device.

"Impressive," admitted Lorus. She shrugged off his

compliment and trotted to the head of the squadron.

"We all know what the faefolk are capable of," she said. "We have faced them on our walls, and each time we've forced them back, but there are settlements in these forests that have no walls and no armouries. We journey today to offer them aid, but we may well be on a mission of vengeance. Hope for survivors, but prepare for none."

She didn't wait for a response. Turning her horse she took the lead down the eastern road, towards the forests that bloomed on the horizon. Lorus fell in beside her, and the rest of the squadron eased into formation behind.

The initial stretch of the journey was easy-going; the road was wide and well-paved, except for the odd shrub or sapling pushing up through cracks in the surface. However, as the farmland around them gave way to trees the cohort passed a number of silent hamlets, little more than cottages for woodsmen or herbalists. Most of the houses were in serious disrepair, and if anyone was home they didn't emerge to greet the group.

A further half-hour's ride led them deeper into the forest. Here the road gave way to dirt trails, and while the trees were wide enough apart to allow the passage of carts and wagons they passed no travellers in the other direction. Lorus was almost surprised when a cluster of dilapidated houses appeared through the trees.

Shureek raised a hand, and the cohort halted.

"We come from Gennon," she called towards the buildings. "If anyone is present make yourselves known."

Above them, disturbed by the noise, birds jumped into flight. Unseen creatures rustled through the undergrowth, but otherwise the only response was silence.

"I am Wisdom Shureek," she bellowed, "and I order all loyal subjects to announce themselves now."

Nothing moved. No one spoke. A wary anticipation gripped Lorus' stomach as he peered through the broken windows and empty doorways. Shureek shifted in her saddle and flicked the reins.

"Come on," she said.

The forest had already begun to reclaim the quiet settlement. Vines coated what was left of the houses, and paths were choked with weeds. In the heart of the village a water well crumbled around a tree sprouting through its stone, yet these warranted barely a glance. Instead, Lorus' attention was taken by the corpses. Throughout the village, on display like the work of an artisan, a dozen or more villagers were skewered on branches and sharpened tree trunks. Their faces were twisted in agony, even under the pall of death. Lorus swallowed back bile.

"Do the fae always do this to their victims?" he asked.

Shureek trotted to his side.

"Look closer," she said.

Lorus dismounted and approached the corpses. One particular body stood out to him, impaled so thoroughly on a small tree that one of the branches emerged from his gaping mouth and forced him into a permanent scream. It was a grisly sight. Red gave a quiet whimper and hopped into his lantern. Lorus, however, leaned closer. Something about this didn't fit. His eyes were drawn to the corpse's face, and he ran over every detail of the awful sight with an insatiable curiosity.

At last he saw it. A ring of bark bulged over the dead

man's lips. Lorus had seen that type of growth before; when a tree grew too close to a wire fence it swallowed the wire beneath a ripple of bark. This dead man had suffered the same fate. He hadn't been forced onto the branch, the branch had *grown through him*.

Lorus lurched away.

"How is that possible?" he hissed. In truth he knew the answer the moment he had spoken, and Shureek's pointed silence only confirmed his suspicion. He turned to her, pale-faced and grim. "This was a wood elemental."

She gave a curt nod before turning to address the squadron.

"Spread out," said Shureek, "Find the tracks."

It didn't take them long. After only a few minutes a cry from one of the soldiers drew them all to the outskirts of the village, where the earth was scarred with deep pits. The holes were jagged and uneven, as if trees had been uprooted by a storm that left the rest of the forest untouched.

"This is it," said Shureek. "These tracks will lead us to the monsters responsible. Be on your guard."

She didn't need to tell them twice. A change had come over the cohort since discovering the bodies of the villagers. This was no longer a matter of duty, it was a mission of revenge.

The tracks were scattered and haphazard, but their size made them easy to follow. Red took the lead, darting through the bushes like a hunting hound while the cohort remained riding, even going as far as eating in the saddle. As the day went on they met no resistance, but Lorus' hand never left the hilt of his dagger.

Late in the evening they emerged into a wide clearing. Shadows from the setting sun crossed the earth like prison bars, but Red flared up to allow a better inspection of the place. It had evidently been used by others before them, with the remnants of old campfires dotting the earth and faint trails beaten down by footfalls. Shureek trotted around the treeline, examining the space from every angle.

"This clearing's as good as any," she said when she had finished. "We'll set up here."

She gestured to the rearguard, who unloaded bags from several of the horses before getting off of her own and tying its reins to a nearby tree.

"We're going to stay the night here?" Lorus asked.

"Don't want to lose our trail," said Shureek. "It's the best chance we've had in months to find the ones responsible for all of this."

Lorus watched the men unloading tents.

"We don't even have a carriage," he said.

Shureek walked over and took the reins of his horse. She regarded him like a cat trying to decide whether a mouse was worth the effort.

"Carriages can't reach this far into the forest," she said, "and it'll only get wilder from here. We'll need to leave the horses and continue by foot before we reach the fae."

Lorus bristled.

"I wasn't suggesting we take a carriage to the grove itself," he said. "I simply feel we should be well-rested before we confront them."

"A sound strategy," said Shureek. "I will ensure your tent is located on the softest patch of ground in the clearing."

As the tents were being erected and a campfire set up

Shureek sent out some of the cohort to scout the surrounding area. Most returned with nothing to report, but shortly after nightfall Red nipped Lorus' neck and gestured to a pair of soldiers who had just reappeared at the edge of camp. Their faces were pale and drawn tight.

"What did you find?" asked Lorus.

They glanced to one another, each hesitant to speak.

"A mine, my wisdom," said the woman at last. "Looks like they'd only just started working it. A few shacks and carts, nothing more, but the fae got to them."

"Like the village?" Lorus asked.

The soldiers nodded.

"Is it recent? Might they still be in the area?"

"The bodies were...*off*, my wisdom."

"I see," said Lorus. The soldiers' pale complexion made sense then. It couldn't have been a pleasant find. "Make your report to Wisdom Shureek, but it sounds like there's nothing we can do for them now."

"Yes, my wisdom."

When the camp was fully set up Lorus and Shureek took the two largest tents, with the soldiers being split among the smaller three. Lorus' tent, he found, was predictably worse than the carriage's bedchamber, barely more than a sleeping roll spread out on bare dirt and surrounded by canvas. It would provide little safety, either from the elements or the forest creatures, and even less comfort.

"Well," he said to Red, "I suppose we should make ourselves at home."

Where the canvas met the ground Lorus carved a series of protective runes, each baked solid by Red to ensure they would last the night. As the final rune was added to the circle it let off a pulse of power. The tent wouldn't have the comfort of a proper bedchamber, but at least it would be just as safe.

Laying Red's lantern within the circle and letting the familiar clamber inside, Lorus removed his armour and bandolier. He placed his silver dagger within easy reach, just in case, but dumped the rest in a pile before the tent flap; perhaps it would keep out the night's chill. With that done he climbed into his sleeping roll and rested his head on a pillow made from his rolled-up shirt.

Sleep wouldn't come. His ears twitched at every noise from beyond the tent, and he found himself repeatedly reaching out for the hilt of his dagger simply to assure himself that it was still there.

"Are you awake, master?"

Lorus eased open his eyes.

"Yes," he said, "I've not been able to sleep. I keep picturing those impaled villagers."

"Me too," said Red. "I can see their faces as clearly as yours."

"It's a rotten way to go. It's not only our duty now, but our moral responsibility to track down the fae responsible and eliminate them."

"Yes."

The pair lay in silence, staring at the top of the tent.

"Master?"

"What is it?"

"Did a wood elemental really do all of that? The ones we fought in the barn seemed…weaker."

"The elementals we encountered were starving,"

said Lorus. "They need wild nature to sustain themselves. Streets, towns and even farmland is a desert to them, but out here they have everything they need. I should have anticipated it. I knew that they'd be more powerful than the elementals near the Grand College, but I never imagined how *much* more powerful."

Red pressed a flaming paw against the curved lantern glass.

"And…I used to be like them?" he asked.

Lorus paused, considering his words carefully.

"You were once an elemental, yes," said Lorus, "but you were never like *them*."

"So I never killed people?"

"No elemental would, at least no more than any other wild beast. These have been manipulated by the fae, turned into vile weapons to butcher the innocent. You wouldn't ever have done what they did to those villagers."

Red was silent for some time, his flame flickering in deep thought.

"Thank you, master," he said at last.

"Goodnight, Red."

"Goodnight, master."

Lorus lay back down and closed his eyes. Images of the dead villagers haunted the darkness, but he pushed them back and strained to clear his mind. It was a difficult task. In all directions the tent was pierced by the shrill chirps and incessant rustling of forest creatures, a stark reminder of how far they were from civilization.

Lorus reached out and drew Red's lantern close. Slow hours dragged by, but in the warmth of his familiar's glow he finally drifted to sleep.

⬦━◦━━◦━◦⬦

Camp was struck earlier in the morning than Lorus would have liked. Fitful dreams of branches growing through flesh had left his mind sluggish and his eyes heavy, but he refreshed himself with a cooked breakfast while the soldiers worked. As he turned over a rasher of bacon he spotted the two scouts from the night before dragging a bag between them with all the energy of geriatric zombies.

"Looks like they didn't sleep any better than we did," Red whispered from beneath the frying pan.

Lorus shuffled where he sat, suddenly aware that he was the only one in the camp not hard at work. It was his right as a visiting wisdom, of course, but he felt strangely out of place. He waited until the scouts lumbered past and then called them over.

"Yes, my wisdom?" they asked in dreary unison.

"I was just wondering whether you might like some bacon?" Lorus asked. Their tired eyes widened, and for a moment Red stopped crackling.

"I… er… yes, my wisdom. Thank you!" said the woman.

"That's very kind of you," said her companion.

They each took a rasher in gloved hands, and Lorus watched them tear into the meat before continuing their work with renewed vigour. He smiled to himself, throwing on another rasher. From beneath the pan Red was staring at him.

"Shut up," said Lorus.

He had hardly finished his breakfast when the cohort

were on the move again. For most of the morning they followed the elemental's trail deeper into the forest, but lost it in a particularly dense patch of brambles.

"They can't have disappeared," said Shureek. "Fan out. I want us back on that elemental's trail."

"Wait," said Lorus. He steered his horse towards the trees, stood in his saddle and reached for a low-hanging branch. Testing it with his weight, and finding it sturdy enough to hold him, he clambered up.

"What are you doing?" asked Shureek.

"Getting to a vantage point," said Lorus. "Fae establish their groves where ley lines converge, and now that we're on the trail all we need to do is find the nearest ley line and follow it deeper into the forest. It'll take us right to them."

Shureek came dangerously close to grinning at him.

"Good plan," she said. "Try not to break your neck while you're up there."

He climbed as high as he dared until the branches were groaning beneath his weight, and then pressed his back to the tree trunk and pulled a scroll from his bandolier. Inciting its words the parchment crumbled, carried away in the breeze.

The familiar glow of second sight settled on his eyes, and through it the forest thrummed with energy. Wards and glyphs of the faefolk shone from every other tree, circling the bottom of their trunks. However, their light paled in comparison to the gleaming fissure in the earth that split the forest in two.

"I see the ley line!" he called down. "About a quarter mile to the north of us."

"You heard the wisdom," Shureek said to the soldiers. "Let's go."

Lorus rushed down the tree, not wanting to be left behind. When he got to the bottom he found Shureek waiting for him, holding his reins as he slipped back into the saddle.

"Good work," she said. He only had time to nod back before she was trotting away to the head of the formation.

It was harder to locate the ley line from the ground with vegetation masking its glow. However, as they drew closer its flickering light filled Lorus' vision.

"This is it," he said. For the others, who saw nothing, Lorus traced his finger along its length, pointing them deeper into the forest. "At some point it'll cross a second line. That's where we'll find the grove."

They marched parallel to the line, following it as closely as possible without blinding Lorus. Their progress halted when the front row of horses froze in place. The riders, Shureek included, did everything to urge the animals on, but the horses only whinnied and tossed their heads. Something was holding them back.

A ripple ran along the cohort. Spotting no immediate danger Lorus trotted next to Shureek, following her eyeline past a stream and onto the trees beyond. They appeared for the most part to be natural, and were nearly identical to the hundreds of others that the group had passed since entering the forest. What set these apart, however, were the shapes formed by the knots and whirls of the tree trunks.

Each one bore a face.

"Fae territory," said Shureek.

The guard nearest to Lorus spat, then traced a rune

in the air. Shureek drew her horse around and addressed the group.

"We walk from here. Belvin, Graz; you two guard the horses. If we aren't back in two days return to Gennon and contact the Grand College. The rest of you will follow Wisdom Lorus and I into the very clutches of the faefolk. Do not lower your guard for even a moment. There will be bloodshed before we are done."

Perhaps it was the behaviour of the horses, or perhaps the faces disturbed Lorus more than he realized, but as he crossed into the faefolk's territory a chill ran down his spine. Red's quills flickered, and he could tell that his familiar felt it too. Lorus had expected the tree-faces to merely mark the boundary of the faefolk's forest, but as they delved deeper inside the unsettling features only became more common. Almost every tree was embellished with a face, sometimes several, positioned so as to watch the group pass. With each passing tree the faces became sharper, more realistic, until they were so human that they might have been carved in place, if faefolk used such craft.

The group progressed in silence; even the birds were quieter here.

Lorus grimaced as a sharp flame nipped his neck.

"Master," hissed Red, "the faces in the trees are watching us."

"The eyes are designed to follow passers-by," said Lorus. "You recall the portrait in Wisest Emerel's study? These faces are no different."

"But master…that one just *blinked*."

Red's words ran down Lorus' spine like ice. He took in a sharp breath as he reached for his dagger.

"Ambush!"

The guards nearest the treeline fell before they could flinch. Out of the trees a dozen shrieking fae descended, lashing out with daggers of flint and weaving between the armoured soldiers. They struck from all directions, but Shureek was ready for them. She flicked her wrist and a scroll appeared in her hand. With a word it flaked into dust, and in its place grew a gleaming, silver spear. She turned and braced herself, a fae already mid-leap impaling itself on the newly-forged weapon.

"Master!" cried Red. "Behind you!"

Lorus turned to find three fae charging towards him. His hands moved almost without thought, plucking a bag of black powder from his belt and hurling it into their midst. Before the creatures could change course Lorus reached towards Red and snapped his fingers. A spark tore towards his fingers, and Lorus tossed it at the bag. The detonation swallowed the fae in a ball of fire, leaving only chunks behind.

With the blast still ringing in his ears Lorus drew his dagger and a scroll of binding, but already the fae were falling back into the undergrowth. A soldier charged in pursuit. He cornered one of the fae in the crook of a tree and bore down on it, sword at the ready.

"Stay away from the trees!" barked Shureek.

The soldier had already swung his blade. At the last second the fae melted through the bark as if it were mist, and his weapon struck the wood. The moment it took him to dislodge his sword was all they needed. Hands emerged from the tree and grasped his arm, pulling him in as if it were syrup. He cried out as the bark hardened around him, until a flint blade flashed through the bark and opened his throat. His cries rattled into silence.

The cohort drew tighter together, weapons levelled at the undergrowth. Lorus kept his eyes moving in all directions, a frightened bird just before flight. Minutes crawled by, and it seemed the fae may have retreated for good. Then he spotted movement in the branches.

"Above us!" he cried.

A soldier collapsed to his side. Red darted from Lorus' shoulder and engulfed the fae on her back, causing it to scream as it clawed at both Red and the soldier. More fae dropped down from the trees, and Lorus ran to help another fallen soldier when a sudden weight collapsed onto his shoulders. He hit the earth, only just managing to twist and face his attacker.

It was the first time Lorus had seen a fae up close. It had the face of a screeching baby, with bark-like skin and eyes of pure amber. Its mouth was lined with splinters of bone, and it gnashed and spat in desperation to tear his flesh away. Its dagger swung for his neck. Lorus caught the creature's wrist, but its strength outmatched its size. His muscles burned with the effort of keeping the jagged flint from his throat. His scroll had slipped from his grasp, and he couldn't reach his bandolier without letting the fae's blade plunge down.

It brought its free hand down to bear on his face, needle-like claws sinking into his cheek. The flint dagger scraped his flesh.

Lorus reached out to Red and clicked. Flame whipped from Red and he slammed it into the fae's screeching mouth. The creature reeled back with a splutter, clawing at its glowing throat. Its amber eyes bulged, discoloured smoke drifting from its nostrils. It writhed, spasmed and then collapsed.

As Lorus staggered to his feet he found that the soldiers had turned the ambush in their favour. Fae bodies littered the forest floor, and the soldier who Red had leapt over to save was now clambering free from the burning corpse that he had left behind. When Red laid eyes on Lorus' bleeding neck he darted up and pressed himself against the wound.

"Master, you're hurt!" he whimpered. "I'm sorry, I shouldn't have left you!"

Lorus placed a hand on Red's flickering quills.

"No, you did well."

Shureek watched them with a curious expression before turning her eyes to the dead.

"Our friends fought valiantly," she said. "If we succeed in eliminating the fae we'll recover their bodies on our return, and see to it that they get a fitting burial. For now, we must leave them here. Our task is too important to delay."

The surviving soldiers gave weary nods, and after a brief rest to drink and tend to wounds they continued their journey. Lorus noticed that far fewer of the trees bore faces now, and whenever the cohort passed one Red would leap over and scorch out its eyes. None, it seemed, were faefolk.

After some time Shureek made her way to Lorus' side.

"When we were fighting you wielded your familiar's element with your own hands," she said. "How?"

"After years of being bonded it comes naturally," said Lorus. "I know the weaves of Red's flame as well as he does."

"But doesn't it -" Shureek began, before thinking better of the comment and starting again, "Doesn't he become weaker each time you take part of his form?"

"It does him no harm in moderation," said Lorus. "With enough time he grows it back."

"Fascinating," she said. Lorus searched her face for signs of mockery, but found none. He smiled.

"You know, if you ever changed your mind it would be a rather simple matter to get your own familiar," said Lorus. Her face twisted into a grimace, but he pressed on; "With your experience at tracking elementals the College might even let you catch your own. That would be something special, particularly at your age."

The corners of her mouth twitched.

"I suppose it would," she said.

They walked on together, until a soldier called Shureek over to inspect a potential elemental footprint. When she was gone Red pawed at his neck.

"Master," said the familiar. "Why did you lie to Wisdom Shureek?"

"I beg your pardon?"

"You told her that taking my flame does me no harm."

"Yes."

"Why did you say that?"

Lorus hesitated. There was something in Red's tone that he had never heard before.

"What do you mean?" Lorus asked.

"Well, when you take flame from me, it *does* hurt."

Lorus halted mid-step. A cold shiver ran through his chest.

"You've never told me that before."

Red's quills sank and dimmed, as if he had forgotten how to burn.

"I thought you knew," he muttered.

A lump squeezed Lorus' throat. He tried several times to respond, but the words wouldn't come. He raised a hand to Red's cheek and swallowed back the lump.

"Red…" said Lorus, "I never…"

A hiss from Shureek silenced him. She crouched by a bush ahead of the squadron, beckoning them all closer and pointing with her spear. Another elemental footprint, and this one looked fresh. She gestured for the soldiers to ready themselves for combat, then slipped through the bush to follow the trail.

This time the tracks were easier to follow. They were deeper and more frequent than before, and led the group into a clearing that had been utterly torn, as though it had been host to a localized stampede. Shureek faltered.

"Do you think the grove is here?" she whispered.

A low, earth-shaking tremor replied. The very forest bent and swayed, and a wood elemental burst into the clearing like a hill come to life. It was easily the mass of a hundred trees wound together into a living tapestry, and its every step shook the ground. As the sun disappeared behind its writhing body Lorus' chest pounded, his fingers trembling across his bandolier. There was no way they could defeat such a creature.

As if reading his thoughts Shureek barked out a single order.

"Hold!"

The elemental raised a dozen trunks and slammed them down. Lorus leapt back, but instead of the sickening crunch he was expecting the elemental pulled away at the last moment. Each of the soldiers had brought their weapons up in defense, and the elemental twisted itself to avoid their blades.

The true impact of the weapons' runes finally became clear. From the beginning Shureek had prepared for this conflict. Whenever questing vines or lashing branches came too close one of the silver blades cut through them with ease, leaving a scorched scar as if they were bolts of lightning. So long as the soldiers remained armed the elemental couldn't touch them.

The same could not be said for the faefolk hiding within. Having learned from the earlier ambush they kept their distance, melting through the vegetation to fire volleys of blowdarts before sinking away to reload. The first darts clattered harmlessly on armour, but Lorus knew it was only a matter of time before they found their mark. He reached into his bandolier and called out an incantation. The scroll in his hand crumbled away, and in its place burst a flock of bats the colour of parchment. As the next volley of darts rained down the bats flew to intercept the projectiles; not a single dart made it through.

The elemental bristled in fury. It drew itself high, then slammed down and sank its roots into the ground. The dirt around the soldiers bulged and rippled. Branches and vines lashed out, knocking soldiers off their feet and gripping them like snakes. Red burned away the roots that were climbing up Lorus' leg, then jumped away to aid one of the constricted soldiers while Lorus searched for others to free. He found a soldier clasping at a vine around his throat. The man's face was purple with the pressure, but Lorus didn't dare use his knife in case he cut too far. He reached his hand out to his familiar, but faltered. His fingers twitched.

"Red!" he called.

The familiar's face appeared through the flames. He spotted Lorus' hand, and his features sharpened in resolve.

"Do it!" Red shouted.

Lorus snapped. A shard of flame tore away from Red and leapt to his palm, and Lorus flung it at the vine around the soldier's throat. It seared the thing to ash, and the man wrestled himself free. Driven by fury he grasped his fallen halberd and charged. The elemental flinched from his blade, and he buried the halberd into a central trunk. It cracked, then split open, and with a groan that shook Lorus' skull the great beast tore in two.

Shock gripped the clearing. Then, as each half of the elemental crashed into the ground, a cheer erupted among the soldiers.

"Wait!" cried Lorus. "Stay on guard!"

Even as the soldiers celebrated the two halves of the beast remained in motion. Questing branches reached out across the split. Vines lashed from both sides, fastening to every surface they touched. With an effort that shook the ground the two halves wrenched themselves back together, wood coiling around wood, trunk binding to trunk. The soldiers fell silent. They didn't understand what they were seeing.

Lorus did.

This wasn't one elemental, it was an entire cluster of them.

"We have to find the grove!" cried Shureek.

Lorus' second sight was fading now, but he could just make out the ley line they had been following. He pointed to where it disappeared in the undergrowth.

"Red, scout ahead!"

"Yes, master!"

As his familiar darted away the fae emerged for their next volley of darts. Shureek's crossbowmen were ready. Bolts poured into the elementals, one striking its mark as it pierced a fae between the eyes. The moment the body slumped down a great shudder ran through the cluster. It let out the shriek of a dying forest; a hundred falling trees, a thousand crackling leaves. One of the elementals peeled away from the cluster and slumped to the ground, dropping the body of the fae alongside it. It withered, shrivelled and brown, until it stopped moving for good.

"That's it!" cried Shureek. "Kill the fae and we kill their elementals!"

Whether the fae understood her or not, the elementals responded with another pounding of the ground and a burst of savage branches that knocked Shureek to the ground. Lorus ran to help her, but Red burst from the depths of a thicket, quills flashing in urgency.

"Master!" he cried. "The grove is through here!"

Shureek was back on her feet in an instant. She deflected another branch and gave Lorus a steely nod.

"We'll deal with the elemental!" she shouted. "Go!"

Lorus charged after Red. As he ploughed into the thicket a hundred brambles sought to push him back, gouging scars into his armour and clawing at the seams. He lost count of how many thorns pierced his skin, splattering the forest floor with his blood. Undeterred, he swam through the dense vegetation, eyes locked on Red like the lighthouse that would lead him to shore. The sky disappeared behind an endless canopy. The sounds of battle faded from behind. The silence of the forest was disturbed only by the crunching of leaves and his own laboured breathing. He could almost believe he'd waded into another world, yet still the bushes and brambles continued.

Then, as he thrust out his hand to sweep aside the next branch, Lorus found himself grasping air. The resistance of the thicket fell away, and he staggered free.

No daylight pierced the grove's heavy canopy, instead it was lit with the gentle glow of a dozen floating wisps. A perfect circle of trees walled off the clearing, each lending its roots to a dense, interwoven carpet that covered the earth. In the centre of the intricate pattern a ring of stone opened into the darkness below, and even the wisps couldn't pierce its depths.

Lorus' chest tightened, and he realized, with some surprise, that he had been holding his breath. He should have been unaffected by fae charms, but the urge to maintain the grove's silence was almost overpowering. He clenched the hilt of his dagger and focused his mind on the sensation of the grip beneath his fingers, the sound it made as he drew it and the dancing of his own shadow as Red prowled the clearing.

"No one here," he whispered. Red looked over and nodded.

It couldn't be this simple. Even with the fight they

were having beyond the thicket the faefolk surely wouldn't have left their sacred grove unprotected. Lorus peered at the trees that surrounded them, each one perfectly shaped, not a single one showing any sign of damage; no broken branches, discoloured bark or even the marks and scratches of forest life.

He gestured to the nearest tree.

"Red, burn it down."

The familiar squirmed.

"Master, do we need to do this?" he asked.

"We destroy them, or they destroy us," said Lorus.

With great reluctance, as if Lorus might change his mind if only Red took too long, the familiar pawed his way over to the tree. He hesitated, then pressed himself against it and let unrestrained flames lick against the bark of the tree.

Nothing happened.

Lorus approached and pressed his dagger against the wood. He scored a slow, deliberate line across its surface, but the blade didn't leave a scratch.

"I thought so," said Lorus. "We can't destroy them, at least not by simple means. We need to find the heart of the grove."

Red met Lorus' gaze, and they both turned to the stone ring in the centre of the clearing. Whatever was hidden in the dark bowels beneath it must be the key to destroying this place. Lorus took a deep breath and approached. The shadows within the ring should have revealed something of its mysteries, yet even as he stood at its very edge Lorus couldn't discern a single feature within.

"Master!"

Lorus spun, dagger thrust out and bandolier open. Across the clearing, as if it were no less a part of the grove than the trees, stood the oldest fae that Lorus had ever seen. It didn't have the shrieking baby-face of its fellows. Instead, this creature had shrunken, wizened features, with antlers emerging from its skull and a cloak of leaves obscuring its body.

The fae stared at them, and they stared back. For a long time no one moved.

Then the fae muttered a single, incomprehensible word.

The ground trembled. The roots shook. The wisps sought shelter in the canopy above.

Lorus leapt aside as a river of fire burst from the stone ring. It spilled out until it filled a third of the clearing, and only then did it take form. The flames stood on legs as thick as tree trunks and threw back a head that could swallow Lorus whole. Its eyes blazed as bright as the sun, and those eyes turned on him with a burning fury. Its flaming limb lashed out, catching him square in the chest. The protective runes on his armour prevented him from being seared right through, yet even with them the intense heat stabbed at Lorus' skin. He needed to end this quick, before his runes burned away.

Rolling away from the flames, Lorus plucked a scroll from his bandolier and began a hurried incantation. A whip of fire caught his hand. The scroll flashed and fizzled, burning into embers before the spell was complete. Lorus flinched back and cursed.

"Master!" cried Red. "Take the fae!"

As he spoke the familiar condensed into a burning

bolt and shot, as if from a crossbow. He pierced the elemental's flames and was lost within the roiling light, but
emerged in a burst of smoke on the other side. The elemental reared up and roared, like a bear trying to swat a wasp.
Again and again Red darted through the beast, tearing
away slivers of fire each time he pierced its body. Lorus
knew it wouldn't be enough – Red would tire long before
the elemental was defeated – but it served as the perfect
distraction.

Lorus turned his attention to the fae. It must be the
chief of the grove, and it watched him with its emotionless, amber eyes as though all was proceeding as planned.
Lorus charged, thrusting his knife at its midriff. Suddenly
he was striking thin air, and the creature stood behind him.
Lorus reached into his pouch and flung a red powder at the
fae's eyes. The creature responded with a powder of its
own, not so much as flinching as the cloud between them
dissipated. Lorus lunged again, once more finding the fae
behind him unharmed. The fire elemental roared, shaking
the grove. Red was still darting through its body, but with
each attack the familiar was slowing.

Lorus recoiled as the fae appeared inches from his
face. Its eyes bore into him, and its ancient mouth split
open.

"Fire returns to fire. Destruction is undone."

The creature's voice was as old as the earth, spoken
by a tongue never meant to taste human speech. Lorus
stabbed at its throat and hit nothing. The fae, appearing
over his shoulder, gestured towards the elemental where it
had cornered Red against the edge of the grove. With one
last look towards Lorus Red kicked off of the ground and

ploughed into the beast.

He never emerged from the other side.

"*Red!*"

The burning coal of the elemental's eyes fixed on Lorus. A hand clamped to his waist, and needle-like claws sank between the seams of his armour. Lorus felt nothing but pulsing fury. He clamped onto the fae's wrist, squeezing until it snapped. As fire bore down on him Lorus turned, smashing the hilt of his dagger into the fae's nose. The creature collapsed and Lorus fell with it, pinning it to the ground. Lorus jammed his silver dagger against the fae's exposed throat.

"Release him!" he screamed.

In spite of its injuries the fae was impassive.

"*There is no 'him',*" it said. "*There never was. Only fire that you had stolen and broken.*"

The elemental halted inches from Lorus' back. The heat scorched his skin, but his anger burned greater. He pressed his blade down until sap-like blood pooled along its edge.

"You want broken fire?" he growled. "What happens to your elemental when I slit your throat?"

"*It will die,*" said the fae, "*and you will be responsible for destroying the last of its kind.*"

"There are more."

"*More, yes. Weak. Trapped. Dying. Only here do they live true to their nature. When the remaining wilds of this world are destroyed, the beings that embody them will vanish, along with the elements stolen by humanity.*"

Lorus clenched his jaw until his teeth were close to shattering. His anger wanted to sever the arrogant creature's windpipe, but his hand refused to comply. He found himself reflected in those deep, amber eyes – a tiny human surrounded by a titan of flame. For the first time in his life Lorus imagined the wild elemental that had been distilled to produce Red. It must have been a creature like the one now towering over him, full of life and raw power. The fae was right. Those pitiful creatures that Lorus had dispatched in the barn, those tame and starving elementals, weren't strong enough to produce a familiar. Without truly wild elementals, there could be no Red, and without Red...

Lorus' chest tightened and his eyes misted over.

Without Red...

The dagger dropped from Lorus' trembling hand. As soon as it hit the ground he knew he was dead. Nothing was stopping the fire elemental from consuming him now. He clamped his eyes shut and tensed for burning pain.

None came.

"*Your mercy is meaningless,*" said the fae. "*As humans invade our forest, the fae will cease to be. Elementals will cease to be.*"

Lorus tried to respond, but his throat wouldn't function. His lips wouldn't part.

"*Spare us and die,*" the creature continued, "*or destroy us and leave. The future holds only one outcome.*"

The world blurred as Lorus blinked away tears. He looked to the motionless fire elemental and searched through its flames, hoping – praying – to find Red in there. He saw only endless flames.

"It doesn't have to," he said.

The fae shifted. Without ever seeming to rise it was standing between Lorus and the elemental. For the first time it appeared uncertain.

"Lorus!"

Shureek's voice broke into the grove. As he turned the forest came to life. Branches and vines wove between the circle of trees, reaching out for the ground before re-forming into giants. Even standing apart the wood elementals were mighty creatures. Without the protective runes that Shureek's squadron were equipped with these beings would have torn them apart with ease. Yet without the forest they would dwindle away, until they were little more than dry sticks hiding in a barn.

Shureek's voice called out again, closer this time, and moments later she burst into the grove.

"They got past us, we couldn't stop them!" she cried, clutching the remains of a broken spear.

"Stand down, Shureek," said Lorus, raising his hands and gesturing to the other soldiers who filtered through the trees. "The battle is over."

"What are you talking about?" Shureek took in the clearing, her eyes snapping from the wood elementals to the mountain of fire looming behind the chief fae. "We've lost?"

"No," said Lorus. "We'll only lose if we keep fighting. All of us."

The chief fae regarded him with impassive eyes. A flicker of curiosity flashed along them as more fae drifted into the grove. The soldiers bristled, but none of the creatures bore weapons. They gathered around their chief.

"You are arrogant, human," it said.

"Perhaps," said Lorus.

"You believe you can change what is certain to be."

Lorus looked from the chief to the elementals, then to Shureek. She met his gaze, confused but trusting.

"I do," said Lorus.

The faefolk chittered amongst themselves. At some unseen signal they fell silent in unison.

"*Despoil our forests no longer*," said the chief fae.

"Then leave our cities in peace."

The chief held his gaze for what seemed an eternity. It nodded.

Behind Shureek the brambles rustled and twisted. They slid aside, revealing a clear passage out of the grove. The soldiers hesitated, but as Lorus made his way towards them Shureek drew herself up and turned to them.

"Come, we have a long march back to Gennon," she said. "There is no need for further death while our homes are safe."

She spoke loud enough for the chief to hear, ensuring that he picked up the subtle threat of her comment. There had perhaps never been a more fragile peace, but Lorus trusted Shureek to hold up their side of the promise. He only hoped the faefolk could be trusted to hold up theirs.

Lorus had reached the grove's edge when the chief fae called out to him.

"*Wait, human.*"

It turned to the fire elemental and spoke with the voice of a blazing inferno. The elemental shifted, extending a burning limb towards Lorus. Heat radiated against his face, but he detected no malice. In the corner of his eye the chief fae gave a sweeping gesture, gentle but firm. Lorus copied the motion, opening his palm.

A single lick of fire dropped into Lorus' hand, no

larger than a candle flame. It was warm, but didn't burn as a naked flame should against his unprotected flesh. The flame curled up and pressed into his hand, like a baby seeking its mother's comfort. Lorus' throat tightened. His heart fluttered, and his vision blurred.

With great care not to disturb the last living remnant of Red Lorus raised his other hand and wiped his eyes, then clutched Red to his breast. His familiar was so frail that Lorus feared he might snuff him out if he held too tightly, or lose him to a breeze if he didn't hold tightly enough.

The chief fae watched on, impassive as always.

"Thank you," Lorus breathed.

The chief nodded. Then, without any motion at all, the faefolk were gone. The fire elemental drifted back into the darkness below the stone ring, and the wood elementals lumbered away, disappearing into the trees and leaving the grove silent and empty.

After that Lorus never took his eyes off of Red, letting Shureek guide him and the surviving guards out of the grove. Red's faint ember burned against his flesh, but he didn't mind the pain; the skin would grow back. He had no notion of how long the return journey took them. It might have been an hour, or a day. By the time they reached the horses the afterburn of Red's light was seared into Lorus' eyes, and it dominated his vision long after the familiar was safely deposited into his lantern.

Lorus saddled up and fell in beside Shureek as the group set off home. His head swam, and his body seemed to suddenly remember the numerous pains and wounds it had received. His shoulders ached. His neck ached. His palm ached. He could have fallen asleep in the saddle and not even complained about the lack of four-poster bed.

After a long stretch of riding Shureek glanced at him over her shoulder.

"That's it, then?" she said. "We aren't allowed to set foot in the forest anymore?"

"I think we can come," said Lorus, "but we can't build. We can't weaken the wilds. If we do we'll lose elementals forever."

Shureek sniffed. She was, perhaps, not so upset at the prospect as Lorus was. All the same she voiced no complaint. They rode on for some time in silence, before she turned to Lorus with that cat-like expression of hers.

"Wisest Emerel will think we've gone mad," she said.

Lorus nodded. He laid a hand on Red's lantern, letting its warmth fill his being.

"I expect she will," he said, "but she doesn't know everything."

JOEL R. HUNT
ABOUT THE AUTHOR

Joel is a writer, proofreader, ex-teacher and part-time human currently residing in the UK. Among his other hobbies of eating, breathing and crouching in dark corners, Joel constantly plans stories and screenplays - a very small number of which actually get written. Most simply languish in his ever-growing 'Unfinished' folder, which is now approaching a mass capable of generating gravitational pull.

Joel's genres of choice are horror and sci-fi, although the odd bit of sentiment does manage to sneak in between the freakishness and disturbing twists. He hopes in time that he might earn a living from putting words on a dead tree in a particular order, or at least earn enough for the occasional cup of tea and vegetarian full English breakfast.

If you are so inclined, you can follow Joel's latest exploits on Twitter, where he also posts daily micro stories. But it might be simpler to cut out the middle-man and seek psychiatric help.

https://twitter.com/JoelRHunt1
https://joelrhuntauthor.wordpress.com/
www.reddit.com/r/JRHEvilInc/
www.amazon.com/Joel-R.-Hunt/e/B07SBX6G3W

THE CHILD OF FIRE

MICHAEL D. NADEAU

CHAPTER ONE: WALKING FREE

~ Hilo, Hawai'i ~

He walked through the doors of the Hilo Seaside Hotel, the fading sun at his back, and ignored the man greeting him. His dark Armani suit and Italian leather shoes were a dead giveaway that he was out of place...if they only knew how far out of place he really was. Ravar Anil was old, older than most of the cities of this fledgling world, and he had a singular purpose this day. He had short, dark hair, black eyes, and an aura that drove most animals to flee in terror with their tails between their legs.

"Excuse me, sir. Can I help you?" the man dressed in a funny red hat asked.

"Not at all. Thank you though," Ravar said, waving his hand at the man, causing his skin to harden slowly. The man backed away in horror as his feet, then knees, turned to black stone creeping ever upwards. His screams, a testament to his escaping sanity, caused people to run in fear. They tried to call for help, but in less time than it took to dial a phone the man's screams cut off and he was gone. All that was left was a crumbling statue of ash; the remains of a terrified man who asked the wrong thing at the wrong time.

The man walked calmly into an elevator as the panicked crowd fled, hitting the button and smiling as the doors closed. He hummed softly to himself, liking the instrumental piece filtering through the speakers, and watched the numbers change as he ascended. The soft ding of the bell chimed his prey's demise as the doors opened and he stepped off, ready for this to begin. He had waited fifteen long years, and finally he was ready.

"I have him on twelve," a voice said from down the hallway.

Ravar turned in a lazy manner, seeing a security guard talking into a microphone on his shoulder. The man let go and pulled his sidearm as Ravar leaned casually against the wall, looking at his nails as if bored. "You humans have absolutely no survival sense, do you?" he asked as the man approached carefully.

"Hands on your knees, mister," the guard called out as he leveled the gun at him.

Ravar sighed and put his hands up, waving one of them slightly at the guard as he did. "Goodbye then."

The guard stopped, letting go of the gun with one hand and tugging at his collar, steam coming off of him as he did. He gurgled, eyes bulging, as first his hair, then his skin, slowly turned to blackened ash. He fell to the floor, unable to even scream as ash poured from his mouth. In seconds it was like he was never there, just a pile of soot in the hall.

Ravar started walking again as the fire alarm blared

throughout the hotel. People came out of their rooms in organized chaos, flooding around him as he made his way to where his senses drew him. *The Child is just down the hallway. It's almost time*, he thought as he felt the pull grow stronger.

A door opened at the end of the hall as a man with auburn hair, wearing a white suit jacket, exited and fumbled with his keycard. The man seemed to be in a hurry, and when he turned and saw Ravar he dropped his suitcase and pulled a small rod; one made from obsidian by the looks of it. "How did you find me?!" he asked, shaking with fear. "I've been covering my trail for years."

"I've been tracking you for longer than that, Child of Fire," Ravar said, waving his hand and sending a column of ash towards the man. It engulfed him before he could use his rod to escape. "I've just been waiting until now to start this venture," he said as the ash poured down the man's throat, ears, and any other opening in his body, choking him. The man fell to his knees, flames springing to life across his body as he tried to burn away the ash before it filled him, but it was to no avail.

The Child's eyes were pure flame now, yet were slowly starting to fade as his lungs filled with the heavy soot. He suffocated slowly, eyes bursting and veins rupturing as he thrashed upon the smoldering carpet. His flames went out as his life ebbed, and Ravar whistled as he reached for the Child's rod. It vanished before he could grab it, making his eyes go wide with surprise. He shrugged and walked to the staircase, whistling a merry tune. *One down, three to go,* he thought to himself as he took the long walk down the back stairway. Now he was off to Siberia, the pull of the next child already dragging him on to destiny.

~ *Ventura, California* ~

They peddled quickly, the shadows around them making their minds leap to horrible conclusions about what lurked within them. The two children shouldn't be out riding their bikes past nine, but they had a mission. Dylan Larson, just passed his fifteenth year, was the older brother to Rae Larson, who was only twelve years old — thirteen by the time the sun came up. They may have been brother and sister, yet they looked nothing alike. He was tall and fair, blond hair and light eyes, with a stoic nature unusual to one so young. People around the neighborhood spoke of him with smiles and nods, whispering how he was just like his father, and how proud their parents must be. General things that would normally make any child beam with pride.

Rae, short for Raesa, was tan in contrast to her brother. She had short, auburn hair and eyes like pools of liquid cinnamon. Short for her age, she had a wicked temper and an unnerving stare. Rae was both curious and unforgiving towards the gossip that she was a bastard child of some forbidden tryst. They whispered things like pacts with the devil and how she was cursed, yet none of it bothered her like it should; it only made her more curious for the truth. It was Rae that found the secret door in their Victorian house, leading to a room full of scattered notes on scientific stuff. Most of it was gibberish to the two children, even though Dylan was top of his class. There were notes about underworlds and portals, as well as drawings of fantasy creatures in the footnotes.

It was in this room where she had first found the

scribbled note. The note was the reason they found themselves out this evening, on Rosebud Drive and far from home, looking into the clues they found in their parents secret room. That scribbled note, about an old friend named Kalvin Danvers, had drawn her interest. It seems that he was some sort of Wiccan, involved in black magic, and lived by Santa Clara Cemetery. The note had four words on it that made this journey necessary for young Rae. — *She must stay hidden* —

"He might be my real father," Rae said, the fear rising in her voice as the shadows danced in the scarce moonlight, the heavy clouds trying to block it out completely.

"I know Rae, we're almost there, don't worry," Dylan said, trying to keep his own worry from his voice. He knew this meant everything to her, to find her real father. Oh his parents said they were only rumors, but he was smart enough to know that there was something different about his sister. He had learned enough in class about genealogy to know that there was no way that his blond, blue-eyed parents were hers, yet he was her brother. Dylan loved her with all his heart, and would do anything for her. So here they were, in the middle of the night heading towards an old cemetery, looking for clues on who she really was. *It's a good thing I'm brave*, he thought to himself as his eyes scanned the dark, *and I'll just keep telling myself that.*

CHAPTER TWO: DESTINY REVEALED

~ Oxnard, California ~

The darkness twisted the palm trees into wicked monsters as she walked quickly down the street. "706, that's it," she exclaimed, her heart beating so fast that she thought it may leap from her chest. The house looked like all the others, yet *felt* different somehow. Rae abandoned her bike in the driveway and hurried to the door, her eagerness to learn the secrets of her past outweighing the fear.

"Rae, wait!" Dylan called after her.

She got to the front door and tried it, rattling the handle. Locked. She ran around the side of the house to the back, hoping that she could see inside, and stopped when she heard someone crying. It was a soft sob, little more than a couple of sniffles, yet was unmistakable. She would know; she did that all the time when she was alone. "Hello?" she asked, slowing down and looking about. She could see no one on the porch or grass, yet heard it still. "Is anyone there?"

"You can hear me?" a tiny voice asked through the sobs. A light scraping followed the voice as the small table shook on the porch. It came from a little creature, no bigger than a house cat, who came out from under the table, its claws scraping along the cement. It had red skin and tiny wings with a long, thin tail. Its skin was covered in scales, similar to a fish, and smoke billowed from its tiny nostrils as it wept. It held an obsidian rod in one clawed hand.

"Of course I can hear you. Why are you cryi...wait.

You can talk?" Rae asked, shocked at what she was seeing. At first she thought it was a cat, but then it spoke. Her
mind couldn't wrap around the problem.

"Rae, there you are. Who are you talking to?" Dylan
asked, trying to catch his breath as he looked around the
dark porch, the moon just starting to shed its pale light
across the yard.

"That thing talked to me," she said, backing away
slowly.

"I'm a draclet, not a *thing*," the creature said as
Dylan walked right over it.

"What thing?" Dylan went to the back sliding door
and looked in, like he was searching for someone.

"He can't see me, and, quite frankly, I'm shocked
that you can. You must be special," the draclet said, walking over towards Rae and sniffing her feet.

"He says you can't see him," Rae said, bending down
to pet it. The minute she touched it flames came from her
outstretched fingers and bathed the tiny creature, making
it purr.

"Holy shit!" Dylan swore, backing up against the
glass door in fear. "Where...what did you..." He just stood
there, staring in shock at both of them. "What is that?"

Rae had never seen her brother at a loss for words
before. "I think I did that..." she began, but was cut off by
excited rambling from the draclet.

"You must be the new Child of Fire," the draclet
said, a kind of reverence in its voice. "I felt my master die
a little while ago, that's why I was so sad. Now you're here
and you can see me." It flapped its tiny wings and flew up
to her shoulder, then cocked its head to one side, looking at

her. "But why? These things usually don't work like that."

"What's your name?" Rae asked, not sure how she felt about any of this.

"Driscolanilvarian," the draclet said, "but you can call me Dris."

"Rae...It said it felt its master die," Dylan said slowly, like he was trying to work through something. "What if that was Kalvin Danvers? What if that *was* your real dad?"

"Oh, *that's* why you can see me!" Dris exclaimed, flying off Rae's shoulder and hovering in the air right in front of her face. "You're the one he never talked about, because he had to keep you safe." Dris handed the obsidian rod to Rae. "This is for you then. It came to me when he died."

Rae felt the invisible punch to her stomach, almost bending over with the feeling that just sank into her. She had never been kicked by anyone before, but she imagined that this is what it felt like. Tears slid down her cheeks as she shut her eyes against the truth, shaking her head in denial. *No. It can't be...I just got here. He can't be dead!* she thought as her brother came to her side and hugged her.

~ *Somewhere over the Pacific Ocean* ~

He sipped his drink slowly, savoring the flavor of this thing called alcohol, though it would have no effect on him. Ravar was feeling quite good about how it had gone so far, despite the loss of the rod, and he was looking forward to the forests of Siberia. He was about to ask for another drink when his head throbbed with a pain so intense that he cried out. The empty glass shattered in his hand as he lurched forward, tendrils of flame snaking their way through his skull. Then, as if someone flipped a switch, it was gone.

"Are you all right, sir?" the stewardess asked, waving the other people back to their seats as they started to crowd around.

"Yes, I'm fine now," Ravar said as he started to get up. "I just realized I forgot something back home. Excuse me." He pushed past the girl, smiling at the other passengers, and tried to figure out what he had missed. *The Child of Fire died and left no progeny...so why did another Child of Fire just awaken?* he thought as he neared the door to the plane. *Was that why the rod vanished?* Ravar shook the shards of broken glass out of his hand, the wounds already healing, and pushed the door to the plane off its hinges with one hand, blowing the pressurized cabin. He was sucked out quickly amid blaring alarms, barely missing the massive engine. Ravar turned in mid air to see more bodies, the stewardess one of them, being sucked out of the plane as it angled down towards the ground.

The cold, night air seemed peaceful to him as he watched the plane lose altitude, but he had business to attend to. He drew his own rod, made of hollowed bone with tiny holes in it, and closed his eyes, focusing his will into it and thinking of the airport he was just at. He didn't *need* to fly to travel, he just enjoyed it, but he needed to be outside to initiate this kind of travel. The roaring wind in his ears was replaced with silence as he appeared among people walking to and from their dreary lives. He had materialized right where he pictured, the main terminal, and no one around him even noticed. Shaking his head at the blindness of the mortals he despised, he went out and worked his way back to the hotel to finish what he started.

~ Hilo, Hawai'i ~

As Ravar walked out of the Hilo International Airport he realized that the strong pull towards the Child of Fire wasn't there. He turned and oriented on the now-slight pull, very faint and weak, and felt it tug east. The Child was on the mainland. Ravar swore and gripped his rod, closing his eyes. He stopped when he realized that he didn't have anywhere to picture. He opened his eyes, looking up at the moon the clouds tried to hide. *Well, I* am *in an airport*, he thought, *and I do so love to fly*. Soon he was back on another plane, this time headed towards Los Angeles. It was another five hour flight, but what was he going to do? He had never been to California.

He boarded amid the confusion of him already boarding a plane three hours ago, yet still being here, and left the confused humans to figure it out. Ravar smiled as he sipped his drink. He would soon track down this new progeny and then head towards the other Children. Nothing would stop him from setting his brothers and sisters free, and having their revenge.

CHAPTER THREE: COMPLICATIONS

~ Ventura, California ~

Rae peddled her bike numbly, following her brother on instinct. They had left quickly, knowing it was an hour ride back home and well past ten. Dris babbled all the way home, talking to Rae as she peddled after her brother. He talked about a realm named Lyria, a place where elemental creatures like his kind lived. It was just under this world — or between if you will — like a step sideways. If you were from there then you could just shift there, slipping from this world to Lyria like waking from a dream. The Children of the Elements could do that with their Shards, which were small, wand-like rods of power attuned to their element.

"Wait," Rae said, cutting off the little creature as he babbled away. Something the draclet said finally pierced her melancholy mood. "Wait, why hasn't anyone found this before? Surely grownups know about all of this if it's right under us?"

"Nope, none of the humans know. It can't be seen or felt by them, and their gadgets don't see it either," Dris said, flying along beside them. "Besides, humans tend to not want to see things that they can't understand, even if it happens right in front of them."

"Are you talking to that thing again?" Dylan asked as they turned off of the bridge and onto the main road.

"I'm not a thing!"

"He says he is not a thing," Rae said, finally chuckling for the first time in a while. "And yes, I'm asking him stuff."

"I wish you would wait until we get home so no one hears you," Dylan said as he watched the cars go by. Even though it was late there was still a lot of traffic.

She knew she should wait, but something told her that she needed to know this stuff very soon. It was like an anxiety creeping up her spine. "So how did your master... my father...die?" Rae asked, knowing that it was going to hurt to hear this.

"Oh, well, the Jinn probably caught him. Kalvin was covering his trail for years, but he had a bad feeling when he left for Hawai'i. I told him to take me, but he wanted to check on a few things and make sure The Dragon was all right."

"Dylan, you were right," Rae admitted, hearing those words. She didn't even know where to begin with any of that. "Let's wait until we get home."

"Oh, you can't go back home. The Jinn will probably be coming here next," Dris said casually, as if this was an everyday thing.

"Wait! He's coming after me now?" Rae's head started spinning. Yet, even after she said it, part of her *knew* it was true.

"Who is?" Dylan hit his brakes, spinning his bike sideways and looked at her.

Rae stopped as well, her breath coming short with the revelation. "Something called a Jinn. It's what killed Kalvin, I guess."

"Dad will know what to do," Dylan started, but the minute he said it his face fell.

"No he won't, and you know it," Rae said, turning to Dris. "Where can we go Dris? Where will I be safe?"

"Well...you could try going to The Dragon, but if the Jinn was just there that might not be the greatest strategy."

"Just for a minute let's try and remember that I have *no* idea what you're talking about," she said, frustrated at the lack of knowledge on her part.

"I thought we were waiting..."

"Not *now* Dylan! Things just got more complicated, so I'm winging it," Rae said, her temper flaring. "Go on Dris."

Dris took a deep breath and closed his eyes. When he opened them he seemed calmer. "All right. The elements are ruled by lords, one for each element. The Dragon rules over fire, the Leviathan rules water. Then there is Pegasus who controls air, and finally the lonely Giant ruling over earth." He landed on her handlebar and coiled his tail around it for support so she could continue peddling as he talked. "These lords exist in both your world and Lyria at the same time, and their Children guard them."

"If they are so powerful, how can humans guard them, let alone children?" she asked, not understanding this at all.

"Child is a title; to them all of humanity are children. They are powerful in this world, but in Lyria they slumber, so are vulnerable to attack. The Children of the Elements keep the portals to Lyria sealed so the Jinn can't get there. If they do they will slay the lords, and then your world is pretty much gone."

"Gone? What do you mean by that exactly?"

"Picture the molten core of the world going cold, or the atmosphere dissipating. That would be what would happen if the lords of fire and air were killed."

"What about earth and water?" Rae asked, her morbid curiosity overwhelming her good sense.

"Gravity would disappear, and the tides would rage wild."

"Oh."

"Yeah. Oh."

"So what are these Jinn?" Rae asked as Dylan led them into their neighborhood, still grumbling about invisible creatures and wild fantasies. His ability to see the draclet had faded after a few minutes.

"The Jinn are six ancient beings that fought against the lords in the very beginning. They were the in-betweens, the lesser of the elements, and hated that they were looked down upon. Ash, mud, dust, steam, ice, and smoke; they all were stripped of their connection to Lyria and locked away in the Lost Realm eons ago."

"If they were locked away..." Rae knew where this was going.

"The elements were betrayed fifteen years ago. The Child of Fire, Kalvin's father, let the Jinn of ash out."

"Just him? He didn't let the others out?"

"Just him, but that was enough. The Jinn killed him, and has been searching for a way to release the others ever since. Kalvin had hidden himself pretty well, but something must've given him away."

"Why did he let him out?" Rae asked, horrified someone she could be related to could do that.

"No one knows. He took that little secret to his grave." The draclet looked sad at that piece of knowledge.

"So where can we go?" she asked, her head spinning at all the information coming at her right now. She needed a shower, a nap, and food; not necessarily in that order.

"Right now," Dylan said as they turned onto their street, "we're going home to eat and rest. I'll leave it up to you what we tell mom and dad. Hell, I wouldn't even know where to begin."

CHAPTER FOUR: ESCAPE PLANS

~ Ventura, California ~

The first rays of light broke through her eyelids as she fought against the urge to open them. Rae woke up to the smell of pancakes and breathed a sigh of relief. *It was just a dream,* she thought as she dressed and went downstairs. She ran into the dining room and hugged her mother tight. "I love you Mom."

"Whoa, looks like I'm making pancakes more often," her mother said, patting her on the head. She was a tall woman, long blond hair cascading down to her slim waist.

"Was that you taking a shower last night, Raesa?" her father asked, coming into the room. Tall and blond, with short hair cut above the collar, he adjusted his glasses and smiled at her.

A cold fear gripped her stomach, and she felt her knees go weak. Pulling out a chair she all but fell into it, crying. "It wasn't a dream...Oh no...It really happened."

Her mother and father exchanged grave looks and sat down, not seeming bothered by the outburst at all. "Where did you go last night, Raesa?" her father asked, concern on his normally serene visage.

"We went across the river to Oxford, Dad," Dylan said, coming into the room. "We went to see Kalvin Danvers." The name hung in the air as everyone seemed to hold their breath, the secret out for all to know, though no one was ready for it; no one but Dris.

"Flames above, I miss him," the little draclet said,

coming in behind the oblivious Dylan. He stopped as he saw the light coming through the windows. "Rae...is it your birthday?" he asked.

Rae turned to look at him, not knowing how he would know that, and noticed her parents staring at her as well. "What? Did I grow wings or something?" she asked, standing up into the morning light. She looked up as she did and saw her reflection in the mirror. Her hair was outlined in flame, her eyes alight. "Mom? Dad?"

"*Now* I can feel you!" Dris said, dancing around the dining room, ignored by the rest of Rae's family. "You hadn't come into your powers last night, that's why it was so weird."

Before either of her parents could comment on her appearance the front door blew off of its hinges, black ash falling all over the rug. A man dressed in black walked in, brushing flakes of ash off his shoulder as he looked around. He had dangerous black eyes and a smile that never quite touched his eyes as he oriented on Rae. "Ah there you are, Child of Fire," he began, walking over the fallen door.

"Rae, Dylan, run!" her father said, stepping up and crossing his arms. "*Malen tor avan!*" he yelled, his voice deeper than usual. A wave of force threw the stranger against the far wall as her mother ushered the kids into the kitchen.

"Mom what the Hell?!" Dylan screamed, trying to go back in.

"Kids, go to the secret room and grab the notes there, you'll need them to figure this entire thing out." She put her hand over Rae's mouth and shushed Dylan. "Yes, we know you found it. No, we don't care. We should've told you sooner, but now we're out of time," she said, pushing them towards the back hallway off of the kitchen. "Know that we love you, and we'll give you time to get out the back door. Now go!" With a final push she shoved them forward, then turned back to the kitchen as the door blew in, her husband's body falling to the floor like some broken thing cast aside. His limbs were at unnatural angles, and there was no life in his eyes.

"Daddy!" Rae screamed as Dylan dragged her back down the hall.

"*Malen ar Vanir*!" her mother yelled, crossing her arms as her father had done. The air around her was swirling, lifting her mass of blond hair in its grasp.

The man in black lifted off of the ground, struggling to breathe, yet eyeing them coldly. "I...see you are....aeromancers," he said as he lifted his arms up.

Rae missed the conclusion as they opened the secret door and closed it behind them, Dris right on their heels. Tears falling, and her breath coming in short gasps, she gathered all of the notes and stuffed them in a bag while Dylan watched the door.

"Hurry," Dylan said as a massive crash shook the entire house. His tears fell now too as he realized his parents were likely both dead.

"I think I have it all," she said, checking all the drawers and cabinets in the small room. She found one more book, its contents unreadable, and stuffed it in as well. "Okay, let's go."

"Too late!" Dylan yelled, closing the door and throwing his weight against it as it shook from an impact they couldn't see. Ash filtered from under the crack in the door and the lights flickered.

"Dris, what can we do?" Rae asked the draclet. That was the only door out of the room, and that meant they were trapped.

"There's only one thing left to do, but you're *not* going to like it," Dris said, hanging his head. "You can shift with me to Lyria and escape. The Jinn won't be able to follow since he was locked out of that realm."

"That's a great plan! Why wouldn't I like it?" Rae asked as she backed up against the far wall. They could both hear the man chuckling now, taunting them.

"Because you can't take him," Dris said pointing to Dylan with a tone of finality. "No human can go to Lyria, except the Children of the Elements."

"No..." Rae said, her voice barely a whisper. "I can't leave my brother."

Dylan turned to look at her, knowledge clear in his face. "Rae...I know you won't leave me, that's why I have to do this. I love you sis," Dylan smiled at her, then opened the door and rushed out screaming. Tears mixed with rage as he ran right into the man, catching him off guard. They tumbled to the ground, Dylan's flailing fists and legs doing absolutely nothing.

"Dylan!"

"Rae, just..." whatever Dylan was going to say was cut off with a gurgling noise, ash streaming out of his mouth and eyes. He held onto the man though, keeping him from chasing his sister.

"I'll kill you!" Rae screamed, her temper replacing her fear. Flames erupted from her eyes and hands, washing over the man and her brother, burning the ash away. She felt something on her leg and looked down to see Dris, the little creature's eyes closed and smoke coming from his nostrils. The room started to fade as the man came through the fire, his clothes and skin burned away to reveal the being he truly was. He was hideous to behold; his charred skin was a mixture of ash and blood, with black eyes of liquid tar. He reached out, sending a stream of ash at her, but it passed right through her.

"No matter, Child of Fire. There are three more to hunt down, and you can't stay in there forever."

◇━○━─━○━◇

Ravar walked around the ruined house, waiting for his second skin to grow back. His kind couldn't go out among the humans without it; the level of panic was truly catastrophic when they did, so he spent his time playing over the battle once more and trying to figure out how he had gotten it so wrong. First the parents, who were not her parents, just *happened* to be aeromancers.

Then the girl obviously just came into her powers *and* had a draclet protecting her. Lastly the boy had fought him off *and* struggled to keep him from her with strength beholden to his family heritage. *It's a shame they all died,* he thought, *it would've been fun finding out what they were doing raising a progeny in secret.* He shook his head and looked over the maps he had found in the closet, unfolding them and finding where he needed to go. The closest city to the Siberian taiga would be Krasnoyarsk, and they had an airport. Things were looking up.

CHAPTER FIVE: STRANGE LAND

~ Shyi, Lyria ~

Rae stood among the most breathtaking landscape she had ever seen. Massive rock formations reached towards the sky, and were surrounded by the most magnificent purple-leaf trees. Water cascaded down a river, then flowed upwards towards the top of the rock formations — like a kind of reverse waterfall — and smaller rock pedestals sprouted three foot flames to light the way. As Rae walked towards the river in a daze of wonderment the wind picked up a bunch of the purple pedals that had fallen and created a bridge of them, streaming across the water before it moved upwards. "Where the Hell am I?" Rae asked no one in particular.

"This is Lyria. We're in the region called Shyi," Dris said as he waved to a group of multi-colored draclet. There were three of them, one blue and yellow and two that were a mixture of green and purple. "Shyi is the home of the Council, and is a place for all of the elements to mix and have fun."

As they approached the water the sounds of both the rushing river and the constant wind was almost deafening. Rae walked across the wind bridge hesitantly, running when she got halfway across. Once she got to the other side she stopped dead as a giant snake of flame rose out of the ground in front of her. It had no features, per se, but still seemed like it was looking at her. "Dris?"

"Oh, that's just a flamethread. They like to check out newcomers." Dris flew over and patted the thing on the head. "Easy boy, she's really new. Give her a minute, will you?"

It dove back into the ground at this and didn't even leave a mark on the dirt. "I am definitely out of my element," Rae said as she turned around and looked at everything once more. "Where are the people?"

"Well, there really are no 'people', as you call them. Just elemental creatures and such exist in Lyria." Dris did a lazy circle in the air and flapped his wings. "It feels so good to be back!"

"Dylan would've loved it here," Rae said, fresh tears starting to fall. "He was always into that fantasy stuff like dragons, faeries and such."

"Who do we have here," a voice purred loudly over the wind and water. It belonged to a figure that was made up of rock, but in such a way that it seemed almost human; and female at that. It had such a voluptuous figure that Rae was almost embarrassed looking at her. The figure wore no clothing and the stone was rough hewn, like it was broken off instead of carved. Her face held only a mouth, like it had no need of the rest of the features. Rae had never seen rough stone look so...sexual before.

"I...I'm Raesa Larson...I mean Danvers," she stumbled out, wiping the tears from her face and trying to compose herself. "You can just call me Rae."

"Driscolanilvarian, why did you bring the Child of Fire into Lyria?" the figure asked, her tone implying that this wasn't a good thing. "I thought we agreed that, after the last...*oops*...we were going to keep the Children away?"

"Sorry, Sonnel, but it was a matter of ending. We were attacked by the Jinn." Dris bowed to the figure and puffed smoke out of his nostrils.

"Is this true, child?" the figure called Sonnel asked Rae, inclining her head towards her. More features were beginning to form on her face: eyes of the color of metal, and a nose shaped like a heart.

"Yes Ma'am," Rae said, imitating the bow that Dris had given.

"Well, then it seems that he has started at least. Come. Let us gather in the council hall and inform the others. The rest of the Children will be in danger, and we need to figure out what to do." Sonnel wrapped her arm around Rae as they walked, almost like she was trying to comfort her.

Rae walked along, still staring in wonder at the alien landscape. The colors were vastly different than in her world, and the places she could see just seemed so fantastic. Her mind had a hard time even registering some of them. There were blue bushes, tiny fairies made of fire and water, and animals that resembled turtles made of rock. They walked up a path to one of the rock formations, a climb that seemed to take forever, and Rae looked out across a vast world of elements and saw clear borders to some of the realms.

Yonder was a massive stretch of flames, the tiny fires licking the top of the molten lava. In the distance huge chunks of dirt and rock hung in the air, drifting across the dark sky. Behind them they could see a huge ocean, multiple whirlpools spinning here and there. Rae was drawn back to the flames, her heart thumping in her chest the longer she stared at it.

"You feel his pull, don't you Child?" Sonnel asked in a quiet voice. "That's where the Dragon slumbers. In your world it is called Hawai'i, I believe."

Rae shook her head, as if that could help, and continued on. "I also have a bunch of notes and stuff from my parents...well, they were...It's complicated."

"It's all right, Rae. You will have time to look through them before we meet. I am just bringing you somewhere to freshen up first." Sonnel walked ahead as they neared the top of the rock structure.

Rae could see now that the rock formed a kind of tower or structure for living. Here, at the top, there were stairs down inside of the rock where strange creatures bustled to and from the egress. Faeries, birds of flame and even a satyr came up the stairs and walked by her. The sound of a sweet pan flute echoed as they passed. One of the creatures, a strange, insect-like being covered in tiny flames, stopped and bowed to her. He was orange and red in coloration, with a multitude of eyes in a pleasant, round face. If it weren't for the hundreds of legs he would've seemed funny. He bounced when he was done, leaving a small flame burning behind where it had rested, and moved on.

"They revere you, Child of Fire. You are among the highest ranks here in Lyria, and most will give you the respect your station deserves," Sonnel explained as the creature passed.

"Most?"

"Heh, well, the Groundlings don't like you very much, but the animals do at least," Dris replied, flying next to them. "They are still mad at the Child that betrayed us all."

"That is going to haunt me, isn't it?

"Probably."

"Great." They went down the stairs into the rock, where the only light was from tiny fire bugs flying around glowing rocks scattered at intervals down the stairs. Soon they were at a door of rock, which opened at their approach.

"Rest awhile Child, and I will return for you. Then we will meet you officially to see what can be done to stop the Jinn." Sonnel left, and finally they were alone and not being chased.

"He's dead, Dris...they're all dead," Rae said, falling onto the pile of straw that looked like a bed. Dris just landed next to her and stroked her head with his wing, not knowing anything else that would help.

CHAPTER SIX: THE COUNCIL

~ Shyi, Lyria ~

Rae sat up a few minutes later and pulled out her bag. She dumped the contents on the makeshift bed and sifted through them, looking for anything named Lyria or Child. After a few minutes she did find something, but it was vague with a lot of guesswork on her parent's part; mostly about where this mysterious land was. There was also a recent letter to them from Kalvin, saying he was going on vacation to Mauna Loa. Then she spied the journal. Opening it and looking at the weird writing, Rae was amazed to see it start to reform into actual words.

"Dris, look, the words are changing!" she said, showing the draclet the writing in hopes he knew what was going on.

"Oh, he must've written it in Elemental. Now that you're here the book is trying to help you. The elemental language is almost alive, so using it can help disguise or reveal certain things." The draclet flew over and started reading. "It's the journal of Gareth Danvers!"

"Is that the guy that betrayed the lords?"

"Yes. It says he thought he had a way to kill the Jinn, but to prove it he needed to release one." Dris jumped up and flapped his wings, clearly excited. "This means he wasn't in league with them, he was just stupid!"

Rae took the journal and read it through, seeing the plan that Gareth had written down. From what she had been told, there was some merit to the plan...she just needed some more information. Luckily she knew just the place to get it. "Dris, don't say anything about the journal. I have a plan, but if they know what it is they might ruin it."

"Well...I guess," Dris said somewhat reluctantly... "You're kind of new at this. You sure you know what you're doing?"

"I'm new at being a Child or whatever, but I'm not new at getting revenge," Rae said, a cold smile on her tear stained face. "You should've seen what I did to Susie Summers last year in the locker room when she told everyone I was adopted...I got suspended for three days. Totes worth it."

A knock at the door startled them both and they gathered the notes up into the bag and went out. Hovering there silently was a blue snake with brilliant wings, an impatient look on its tiny face. "You're summoned, let's go."

They followed the snake-bird-thing up the stairs in silence, the creature's mood clearly not happy at this task he was assigned. They got to the top again and saw a huge bird waiting at the edge for them, Sonnel standing at its side. "Greetings, Child of fire. Are you rested?"

"Good as I'm going to be. Are we flying on that?" Rae asked, anxiety setting in quickly at the thought of riding that thing in the air.

"Oh, elements no! He is going to carry you," Sonnel said, as if that happened every day.

"What?!" she asked, turning to Dris to ask what other ways there were to travel. Too late; huge claws wrapped around her waist as she was lifted up into the air. Her screams were ignored as the great bird flew off towards a larger structure towering above the others. Halfway there Rae stopped screaming and tried to enjoy the ride.

A little while later they were inside of a massive chamber of rock, dozens of seats sitting on a dais arranged in a semi circle. The creatures there resembled their elements more keenly than some of the strange creatures she had seen so far, most of them resembling Sonnel in that they were humanoid versions of the elements.

There was even a unicorn.

"Welcome, Child of Fire. We all mourn the passing of Kalvin, and we hear that the people that raised you also lost their lives to this evil. Truly it is a dire time for us to meet, but, alas, the elements choose at their whimsy." It was a woman of water that spoke, her form thankfully less sexual than Sonnel's.

"Thank you great...elders," she started, at a loss for the right words. *Dylan would've been much better at this,* she thought as she searched for what to say. "If I could, I have a couple of questions for you if you wouldn't mind?"

"By all means Child, speak them." This from a short man made of flames and cinder.

"How were the Jinn locked away, and how could my ancestor break such a lock?"

The unicorn stepped up, lowering its head. Its horn glowed briefly as a distant static filtered into her mind. *The Jinn were sealed away by the lords, each by a parent of their form. Only a dual Shard, of both parents, could unlock them. For example, the obsidian rod you hold is of both fire and earth, though some could argue it is also fire and water.*

The thoughts came fluidly, without accent, and she nodded, knowing that was the easy question. "How does one use a portal to enter Lyria?" she asked, seeing their heads turn in shock at that. "I've heard I can shift here, but if I need to get back here without Dris then what could I do if I didn't know how?"

A regal faerie, all of three feet tall with wings of gossamer, stood. There was a grim expression on her small face. "They are never to be used unless it is dire. That being said, they are located by the elemental lords' domain in your world, often resembling a door of some kind made of natural elements." The faerie cleared her throat and nodded to the others on the dais. "Now, a question for you, Child. Is it true that the Jinn was seen by you? Are you certain of what he was?"

"Well, Dris said it was a Jinn, but he kind of looked funny when I burned off his skin," she said as the crowd rose to their feet in shock, murmuring instantly about her power.

"Order!" a man that looked like a cross between an eagle and a man said, banging his fists on the table. "Now, young lady," he went on as the rest of them settled down. "The council would very much like to know if this Jinn said anything to you."

"Not really, other than the 'kill you slowly' stuff," she said, trying to look innocent. She had a devious plan, one that they would hate her for, but it would get her revenge; that was all that mattered right now. They fell to arguing about what to ask her and what they should do to protect the next child. They seemed to think the Child of Earth was next, for reasons she couldn't understand. This was the only part she was unsure of, but they had handed it to her on a platter. "Where is the Earth Lord? Maybe the Child is going there, like Kalvin had done."

"How do you know he was going to the Dragon?" a woman covered in purple scales asked, her bright yellow horns a little distracting.

"The notes I found said that he was vacationing there recently." She was almost there, now she just needed to distract them.

"The Earth Lord resides in what you would call the Siberian Taiga. In Russia, I believe." The speaker was a very tall woman, covered in bright blue scales and constantly dripping water. The woman's face contorted into a sneer then. "How do we know you didn't kill Kalvin in the first place?" The rest of the board erupted in chaos at the accusation.

Rae had everything she needed now. She leaned down and whispered to the draclet so that no one would hear. "Dris, how do I shift?"

"Oh, that's easy. Just picture where you want to be, or who you want to find, and you will go there. Why?"

"Grab on, little buddy, we're going hunting." With that she closed her eyes, picturing the house where she had first found the draclet.

"Wait, we can't go yet! Oh, forget it," Dris said, climbing on as she started to fade. They left the council room amid the confusion, and weren't missed for at least an hour. They never saw the unicorn stare at them the entire time with something akin to a smile on his lips.

CHAPTER SEVEN: BEST LAID PLANS

~ Oxford, California ~

Rae appeared on the back porch, bright sunlight bearing down on her from above. It was just like she remembered it, except she could see more now that it wasn't dark out. She took only a second to get her head to stop swirling in circles and headed for the back door. She pulled, but it was still locked. Smirking now that she had some tricks up her sleeve, she thought of the fire again and tried to melt the door open. It worked a little too well. The door itself started to smolder, and soon the fire alarm was going off inside.

"Rae! What did you do?" Dris asked, flying over. Once the door was open he flew up and ripped the alarm off the wall, its obnoxious noise ending.

"Hey, we're in, aren't we?" she asked, shaking her hands as if that would put the fire out. She closed her eyes again and tried to picture the flames dying. It worked, and soon she was off searching the house for what she needed. Rae prayed that the man who was her real father was a hoarder like she was, and sure enough she found what she was looking for. In almost the same place as her own house she found a switch opening a secret door. Inside were maps and scrolls that seemed to be hundreds of years old, and the map pinned on the wall had places marked with red and black pins. The red pins seemed to be for lords, as some of the spots matched the areas she knew two of them rested.

"What are we looking for, and what are you planning?" Dris asked, watching her from the side of the room.

"I need a picture of where the Child of Earth is, or a city that's close. If I can find a name on this map..." Rae said, sifting through the stacks of papers and notes.

"How about this one?" Dris asked, looking at a picture of a mining town on the wall next to him. "Mirny?"

"Got it," she said, rushing out and opening her phone. She hit the internet and put the name into the search bar, then hit images. Rae studied the pictures for a long while, looking for just the right spot. After a good ten minutes she turned to an anxious-looking draclet and smiled. "You ready for some danger?"

"I don't have a choice, do I?' he asked, flying over and landing on her shoulder. "We have to be outside though to travel this way."

"Why? Is it different than shifting?"

"Yes, quite. I'm not sure exactly why, but if you don't you may splatter us on the ceiling."

Rae went outside and closed her eyes, picturing the place she had studied over and over. She felt something, then screamed as she faded and shot straight up. In a second she hit the ground with a thump and opened her eyes slowly.

"Кто ты," a man asked in another language.

Great, I don't speak Russian, she thought as she looked around for a way to get out of sight. Rae ran off towards the back row of houses, hoping to avoid further contact until she could find a way to the lonely Giant and hopefully the Child of Earth. Once she could sense them she hoped that she could shift or travel right to them, but it was still a working theory. She was running out of time.

~ Krasnoyarsk, Russia ~

Ravar walked through the empty airport and hurried outside, anxious to get this over with. He had killed one Child, only to have its progeny avoid his grasp. Now here he was in the frigid cold of Siberia looking for the Child of Earth, and then it was off to the deepest ocean. He waited until he was outside before he concentrated on the link to the Child; a faint, pulsing pull to the northeast. This one was a bit more dangerous, as the child wasn't entirely human anymore. When the lords chose their Child that human was supposed to mate and birth offspring to be progeny, to carry on the title along a bloodline, but the first Child wasn't entirely human.

The first Child of Earth was actually the offspring of the lonely giant and a human woman. Their offspring, the oldest creature known to man this very day, was none other than what humans call Bigfoot. The race had no name of their own, and always paired with a mortal woman — or man in one case — and their offspring was always the same. They looked like an upright, humanoid covered in thick fur with powerful arms and legs, along with tearing teeth and excellent eyesight.

~ Somewhere in the Siberian Taiga, Russia ~

Ravar closed his eyes and gripped his rod, concentrating on the pull. It would take too long to walk the Siberian Taiga looking for the camouflaged creature. He travelled the distance quickly, landing in a clearing of snow and fallen leaves. A great roar went up at his appearance and he stepped forward with his hands ready, scanning the trees. The ground shook slightly as heavy footsteps sounded through the trees, snow falling from the intrusion.

Ravar spun at the last moment, flinging his hand out and sending ash hurtling at the massive creature as it charged him. Too late. The wind was knocked out of him as he was smashed to the ground, rolling over with snow and hair clouding his vision. He punched and kicked, trying to focus his ash into a weapon, but the creature kept him off balance and disoriented. As they slowed down in their tumble he focused his strength and heaved up, kicking the creature off of him.

Ravar spun to his knees, ash already spiraling towards the creature and entwining it. The ash violated the Bigfoot's eyes and mouth, filling him with death. "Valiant fight, Child of Earth, but you are no match for..." The ground heaved as the Child stomped his foot, sending Ravar sprawling on his back, his concentration momentarily lost. He rolled over and clenched his fist, bringing the ash back under control. "My fault...I underestimated you. Never again." He stood slowly, brushing off his suit as he choked the Child. He smiled to himself as he saw the beast fall to his knees, his eyes going white, then black with ash. "Now I can..." His words cut off as pain exploded in his back, a burning sensation so intense that he knew his skin was burning off of his very bones.

"I told you that I would kill you, and I meant it!" Rae called out from the opposite tree line, the little draclet hovering near her.

"You!" Ravar screamed, turning to see the little girl in her stained clothes standing with flaming fists at her sides. He clenched both fists, snapping the Child of Earth's bones and leaving him broken so he could deal with the more powerful threat. The Child of Earth was alive, but helpless. "I will kill you at last, then head to the ocean and finish this quest." He sent ash flying out at her and she screamed, running for the woods.

"You can't escape from me!" he called, running now after her. He followed through the woods, sensing a powerful presence up ahead. The pulse eerily felt like the Child of Earth, but stronger. If that was a lord then he was out of his depth while in this realm. He saw the girl stop at a door made of branches and dirt, hesitating as though afraid. The portal to Lyria...That was why the Child of Earth was here, intentionally protecting the portals from him. He ran as the girl went through, her naivety bringing him to the goal well before it was time.

~ Lhana, Lyria ~

He passed through the portal, the old, familiar feeling of euphoria slamming into him. It was the feeling of coming home. He took two steps towards the beautiful, earthen River Lysaril and almost forgot why he was here. That was his downfall. He fell to his knees as fire engulfed his entire being. He tossed ash up all around him as a shield, but that was only going to buy him time. It hurt so bad, but he still had some strength yet. Standing he threw off her fire with a wave of ash, blanketing her as she hit the ground. "You think you can beat me? You? A mere Child take on one of the Jinn?"

"Actually, I don't think anything," she said, sending fire out to burn away the ash. Her flames seemed even stronger here, which was something he hadn't counted on. "I plan on killing you, right here and now, for the death

of my family!" Her eyes blazed with liquid fire, a pure
hatred giving the flame inside of her strength it hadn't felt
in centuries.

Ravar turned back towards the portal, his breathing
frantic. She was right; she could kill him here in this realm.
How had he fallen for this trap so easily? He felt the pain
again, his second skin now burning off in great blasts of
fire. He looked back and saw her take a step for each blast,
like she was walking towards his death with purpose. "You
can't...please!" Yet he could see that she was beyond appeal, her anger fueling the flames of the element past their
tolerance. They were loving this, no doubt. Ravar Anil
died screaming on the banks of the Lysiaril River, great
currents of dirt swirling amidst the banks of high grass.

EPILOGUE: APOLOGIES

~ Lhana, Lyria ~

Rae sunk to her knees as she heard distant horns blare. *Now* she was going to get it. A host of guards, all human-oids with vibrant petals swirling around them, rode great cats of fire, and at their head was the unicorn from the council meeting.

Child of Fire, you have broken the most sacred law and led a Jinn into Lyria. Before you are consumed by the very element you were sworn to protect, you have the right to explain yourself to your lord. The majestic creature nod-ded to the guards, and they bound her hands in front of her. He lowered his head as she was led across the river and followed slowly behind as they walked. It took hours to travel to what resembled a pier, with stone boats floating on a sea of flame, their bright yellow and orange sails flail-ing in the hot winds.

The trip was the greatest experience of her young life, sailing over the serene ocean of fire, yet it held with it a sense of oncoming dread. Would the Dragon consume her for this? Would he understand her plan? In time they reached a solitary isle, no life moving across its burnt rock. The only thing visible was a great, red mountain of scales moving with a steady beat of breath. The Dragon.

One guard stepped forward with her in tow. "Great lord, though you slumber a travesty has happened that re-quires your attention," he said, his swirling petals of blue and teal seeming wilted in the heat.

I hear all within the flame, a deep voice said to all of

their minds, the booming tone a throbbing pain.

Rae was pushed down to her knees on the volcanic rock. "Well, Lord Dragon, I brought the Jinn here for a reason. The notes I found from my grandfather talked about his plan to slay the Jinn. He believed that they could only be killed here in Lyria, their original home," she said, trying not to cry in front of the massive being. "He never figured out how to get him here though, before he was killed. When I knew the Jinn was after me I lured him here to kill him, and to avenge the death of the former Child along with my entire family."

Your revenge is understood. You have done well, Raesa Danvers. Stand, and be the Child that guards me in this realm. With that the Dragon went silent, and Rae was dismissed.

Rae stayed a couple of days in Lyria, resting to regain her strength and balance after all that had transpired. She had to go back, she knew that, yet what would be waiting for her? With her family dead, and house destroyed, she would be taken away by strangers. In the end she let Dris show her the proper way to travel, mastering it before taking that final leap home.

~ Ventura, California ~

Rae landed in the backyard of her house, if you could call it that. Police tape wrapped around every door of the broken home, the windows smashed and the yard blackened with ash. Tears fell silently, weaving a path down her cheeks as she walked tentatively forward. She ducked under the yellow caution tape and walked into the only place she had known as home. Her footsteps crunched on broken glass as she crept in to looked at the scene in the kitchen. There on the floor was where her father had been thrown, and where her mother made her last stand. Following it down the charred hallway, she could see where her brother had fallen as well, remembering the fire she ignited to destroy the foul Jinn.

"Excuse me, miss, can I help you?" A heavy, accented male voice said from the far end of the hall.

Rae jumped, despite herself. Dris chuckled, knowing that the man couldn't see him anyway. "Oh, sorry. I was just looking. I'll go." Rae turned and walked quickly away, trying to get out of the house before questions were asked.

Too late.

"Are you related to the family that lived here?" The man walked after her, intent on catching her by his pace. "You see, I've been investigating the deaths of the parents, and you look like the little girl in some of the photos."

Rae stopped in her tracks, his words dropping a rock into the pit of her stomach. Then the rest of his words seeped through her anxious mind. *He said parents, not family*, she thought as she turned towards him. "Who are you?"

"Forgive me, ma'am, my name is Detective Asamoa, Ventura police department." The man showed his badge as he smiled. "The son, Dylan, can't tell us much about what happened, since he is still in recovery, so I'm hoping..."

"Dylan's alive?" Rae rushed the man, fire igniting in her eyes. "Where is he?"

Detective Asamoa backed up, reaching for his side-arm. He pulled it and trained the gun on her, but dropped it almost immediately, as he screamed in pain. The gun hit the ground, already melting.

"Tell me where he is." Rae said, her voice almost a growl.

"He...he's in Community Memorial," the detective said as he backed away, his eyes wide with fear.

Rae ran out the back door, the way she came in, her tears still falling but this time for another reason. Dylan was alive! Her life seemed brighter then, knowing that she wouldn't be alone after all. "Let's go get him, Dris."

MICHAEL D. NADEAU
ABOUT THE AUTHOR

Born in the usual way, author Michael D. Nadeau found fantasy at the age of eight with Dungeons & Dragons. He loved being different people as well as casting magic. By High school he discovered his love for reading thanks to a teacher. She fed his thirst for books by bringing her own books from home and lending them to him, even buying one towards the end of her class. He has now read hundreds of fantasy books, living in each of their worlds along with the characters. After awhile he started creating his own worlds for his games with friends. Cities, gods, ancient and terrible beings and histories...then he would burn them all down.

He is the author of the Lythinall series: The Darkness Returns book 1, The Darkness Within book 2, The Darkness Falls (coming soon), Dragon Caller; Rise of the archmage book 1, and Tales from Lythinall — an anthology (coming soon). He also has several stories in Kyanite Press's Journal of speculative fiction and Eerie River Publishing anthologies, as well as writing for Gestalt Media's monthly contest regularly.

https://www.amazon.com/Michael-D. Nadeau/e/B07L3Z-JXCL/ref=ntt_dp_epwbk_0
https://karsisthebard.wordpress.com/

What We Were Made

Crystal Lynn Hilbert

Crows carried word through the forest, bloodshed in each beat of their wings.

"*The Keeper bore twins*," they called. "Doomed, doomed. Trapped forever! One may break, but two? *Two*?"

Darkness wept. Shadows rent spruces from their moorings and set them burning an unholy autumn. Screaming filled the empty canopy, "*Twins, twins...*" the omen howling through the smoke and mist and undergrowth, battering the remnants of the broken kingdom littered between the trees.

I woke in one such fallen stonework.

A fingernail moon lighting my path I sank my claws into the earth. Each gashing strike dragged the wretched shade of my once-bright self from my bed of bones. With much effort I struggled to the lip of a stagnant pool.

There I whispered a curse, a command, and unraveled an insignificant, blood-worn memory into my hand. One of many, worth little, but in its sacrifice, its ghostly entrails an oil-slick on dark water, I spied the Keeper. Sweated and laughing before the chill of an open window, she held two newborn babes. One child howled, red-faced and hands fisted; the other only watched.

Two mouthfuls, I thought. Perhaps three. A morsel more tender than their mother's insolent offerings.

My forest mourned around me, but I smiled.

I would savor these.

◇━◦━◦━━◦━◦◼◇

It took time for enemy babes to grow, for me to regain some semblance of my strength. Years I waited, hunting what I could and gutting memories to fuel the magic.

I lost much of myself this way: maps of my outer-most kingdoms studded the mud of my scrying pool, dead enemies sinking beneath my silt, the names of their mothers and grandmothers bearing them down. I carved out whatever piece of myself I could bear to lose, portioning away my memories, my hurt, my history. Through it all I sketched battle plans in the dirt of the forest floor.

And then, at long last, my prey entered the forest.

Low and unseen, I met them at the border.

Their mother — the ward-keeper, one more daughter in a heritage of enemies — strode tall through the over-grown paths, scything back shadows and briars with magic on her blade and fire in an ancient, glass jar. Her daughters followed in line, ducklings still growing into their long-legged strides, entrail-ropes of sausages dangling through tender elbows —

And I saw warriors in them. I saw flesh parting, fields not yet soaked with blood. My vision burned. I hated — gods, I *hated...*

Drawing as close as I dared to the wall of their ward-lantern light I searched their faces, read what I could from their eyes. I settled my claws into the old spells woven to trap me and carefully frayed the smallest opening, the planning and placement of which had taken me years to devise.

For an instant I hung in my enemy's unguarded flank, perched between my forest prison and my freedom, and found myself torn between choices. Which body to steal? Which child to devour, and which to wear?

But then, unaware of me entirely, the girls...laughed.

I stopped. The break in the ward-line yawned open, shivered, and then snapped shut. Years of planning lost, but I barely saw it. Instead, unbidden, I remembered my sister.

At a look from their mother the girls quieted. They stacked the offerings carefully in a broken pile of stonework, a bitter mockery they called a shrine. More dried and ancient meat to call the scavengers, for my Feral would never bend their heads to such a paltry sacrifice.

Stricken, I watched. I — I *hurt*. Low, keen wanting rang hollow in my chest. I saw my sister in them. Watching the girls hide humor behind their hands I saw *myself*, my long-ago face remembered in theirs.

Oh, I thought, *to have a sister again.*

To have two.

And watching their retreating backs — letting them go — I changed my plan.

The girls returned and returned again, months spent training at their mother's heels. I waited. Soon — soon enough, at least — the girls crept into the forest on their own, stacking offerings and strengthening the wards from within. When they came I followed, pooling in the indentations of their footprints, deepening their shadows. Where they walked I seeped behind them, my spindled claws leaving furrows in the earth, drawing runes of claiming for the Feral to read.

Though monsters slept between these trees, in my wake none slept easy. My girls passed unhindered and unaware, the worst of the forest a mantle on their broadening shoulders. Over time they became accustomed to the pressure of me beside them, until they noticed my absence with trepidation and felt safety only in my shadow. I trained them to long for me.

And then I chose a shape.

Lingering at the mouth of a shattered well I molded the mist of my body into the suggestion of a long-legged wolf. I wandered in scant patches of sun, pelt glimmering starlight, sad and lost and ancient — the kind of creature girls teetering on the cusp of womanhood flattered themselves into thinking they could tame.

Drawn by my glow, by my quiet familiarity, within a week they crept from their safe-worn paths and into my clearing.

"Hello?" one ventured, and I smiled to hear the girl's voice.

Lifting my massive head from my paws, I replied, "Hail. Who comes?"

The girls shared a glance. The second took her sister's hand.

"We are the Keeper's daughters," she said, jaw hard and voice harder. "Who are you?"

Warm in her unsteady sunlight, I watched them and considered. Already so strong, so tall. I saw herself in the wary one, my sister in the brave. But for the lack of stories painted beneath their skin they could be my kin. Memory and need seized me. In a moment of incaution, I spoke a name unheard since before the trees.

"I am called Saga. What does your mother call you?"

Another heavy glance passed between the girls. The brave one let her furred hood fall, stole a tentative step forward, but the wary one knew the power of a name. She said, "She calls us *her daughters*," with force enough to draw her sister back. "We should go."

I retreated, also — every hesitant footfall calculated to make me seem small — withdrawing for the well, for the unsteady dark.

"You could stay," I offered, the soft slope of my shoulders urging *trust, trust me*. "I could tell you stories?"

The girls stopped. The warier bit her lip, pressing the sharp edge of a tooth into her flesh. Those that knew the price of names knew the value of stories. She saw the bones scattered through the blankets of dried needles and sensed the battles sleeping here.

"No," the braver snapped, jaw firm as she held tight to her sister. "Respectfully, no."

Hesitant, the warier nodded. "We should go."

And, hands locked, the two slipped back the way they came.

They *left me* — and I almost leapt, almost damned the plan and called the hunt. But my sister's face hung in my mind, and I forced myself still.

I let them go. And though their bodies bent to run… the girls glanced back. They wanted me, even as they fled from me.

Smiling in my shadows, I swallowed my discontent and settled.

I would wait.

I did not wait long.

When the sun tumbled from the sky and into its grave, the Feral woke. I felt them hunting, straining at the runes I'd carved in my girls' footprints, snapping at my name written in their shadow.

Rising from my needles and moss I thundered a command. I sent my voice where I could not send myself — crows and beetles coughing, *"No,"* foxes barking, *"mine,"* — until the trees fell silent in the echo of my claim. Snarling still, the Feral withdrew.

And, through the trees, my girls came walking, uneven ward-light dancing in their path. A badly tethered beast, their fire blackened the jar a little more with each unsteady step between furrowed roots and fallen towers.

From the depths of my well I peered up at them, darker than the absence of light. I watched the braver swallow, steel her jaw and lift the guttering light a little higher.

"Saga," she breathed into the gaping mouth of stone.

A summoning, an invitation.

Uncoiling, I billowed out. I scattered into their watery ward-light, a wave of shadow sprawled amongst the pine needles and wild thorns. There I stole a moment, reading their eyes, their backs, their unbent heads.

I measured the space between their shoulders, weighed their shadows, gauged the strength in their arms and the span of their strides. I slipped into their frosting breath, took from their tongues the taste of boar and honey, vinegar and hearty cheese. I learned them. From the lines between their eyes, the berry-stains of recent magic on their fingers and the scent of spent mistletoe still clinging to their cloaks, I *knew* them.

And so, when I rose again, I rose as a woman, re-claiming as much as I could of the shape I'd worn before the trees.

"Fair night, Keeper's daughters," I greeted, my hands open, my palms empty in peace and welcome. "What brings you?"

The two retreated a half-step back. I felt their eyes rake my form, the shifting mass of my face. The warier wove a simple ward between the cage of her fingers — a cat's cradle for snarling pursuers. The braver lifted her lantern high, curses ready beneath her tongue.

Charmed, I smiled.

"You've nothing to fear," I told them, mimicking their mother's tender cadence. "I won't hurt you."

The warier shook her head, jaw hard. She bit down on the single spell she held between her teeth. Some small protection against fairy charms, I guessed by its scent — mint and attorlaðe, icicles in rain. It comforted the girl, though the wanting never left the curve of her spine.

"Why us?" she asked, fingers white around her spell-work. "The Feral speak to no one. Mother says they cannot speak at all."

I smiled, soothing. *Love me,* my eyes whispered. *Trust me,* read my open hands, even as I lied, "Your birth left omens on the belly of the full moon that shone to greet you. Why wouldn't I speak?"

The girls shifted. They glanced at each other, a battle of hope and disbelief.

"Omens?" the braver asked.

"Skill and legend," I offered. "The shadow of war."

"War hasn't come to Gróa since before a forest grew here."

Curling my shoulders I drifted backwards, carefully choosing my reply.

"Some shadows fade in sunlight," I said. "Time will tell us."

The warier kept on building wards between her fingers, unaffected, but her war-born sister watched my shifting form, rapt and ravenous.

"Mother never said," she murmured, her words at once hope and accusation.

Their mother. I had to force my gentle smile.

"Ah, your wise and well-trained mother. I imagine she was too busy giving birth to speak with the moon. I am a queen of fallen kingdoms; I have the leisure of stargazing."

The warier stopped her weaving, dropped threads fraying from her fingers. "A queen?"

"Long ago, before the forest."

In its lantern the ward-light guttered and choked, raw power burning without the shaping blade of skill. Relaxing her grip on its handle the braver bent and let it drop.

She said, "My name is Verja."

The warier followed, "I am called Kenna."

An offering.

A gift.

The trees howled. Smiling, victorious, I opened my arms to them.

◇━◉━◦━━◦━◉━◇

The girls came when they could. Spending stories like breadcrumbs, I drew them deep into my trees and away from the reaching, warding arms of their mother. I left a trail of words behind me, little gifts painlessly given.

For Kenna, wise and wanting, I shared a tongue common amongst the hunting hawks. I taught her how to pluck a mind from the branches, how to ride its wings and borrow its eyes. I taught her raven spells for luck and whistles for wind.

For Verja, wild as my long-ago sister, I gave her words for lightning. I taught her how to build a storm on the back of Kenna's summoned wind. Taught her to speak the tides sideways, to bring fish or to shatter a ship against the ice-strewn rocks.

In return they gave me songs. Kenna pounded the rhythms for births and harvests on the belly of a hollow log. Laughing, growing into her long legs, Verja danced. They brought me the deeds of heroes and monsters, their faces pressed in gold, coins rattling against the marbles in their pockets. They taught me riddles and rhymes, games for dim firesides I found I excelled at.

And, in this way, months passed. My girls grew, filling into their shoulders and hands, until the lantern they carried through the trees no longer shuddered. My girls grew, tall and fearless, until they no longer carried a lantern at all.

"You remind me of my sister," I told them one night, seated amongst the wreckage of my own charred and brittle bones. "You remind me of us both."

Verja grinned, white-toothed and wild, but Kenna paused in her idle collection of wrist bones and knuckles. She looked up. A spell lay half-finished on the ground beside her, a pattern woven from my fingers.

"Your sister?"

And so, in the darkness of fallen towers and tangled thorns, I spun legend from my history. I spoke to them of building kingdoms, of my army rolling across the landscape with the spring rain, of cities rising in our footsteps. With every careful word I wove a tapestry of inventors and spell-singers, a net bright and strong enough to snare a Keeper's daughters.

I told them of my long-ago home at the mouth of a distant ocean, built the fish of my childhood for them out of pine needles and set them swimming in the air. I painted their scales with stories — mine, my sister's, my ancestors' — until each flick of their sharpened tails scattered shards of light through the wreckage in which we sat.

At last they asked about the forest. I'd known they would eventually. And so, as they grinned at me through flashing tails and fallen needles, I spoke of war.

"We thought this coastland abandoned when we came," I told them. "We saw no marks otherwise, so we stayed. We built our towers in a night, singing stones from the earth in the shapes we needed. By sunrise a plague of ships pockmarked the water."

I let the fish fall. In their dying light I parsed my girls' faces, picking interest from the purse of Verja's lip, trepidation from the narrowing of Kenna's eyes. They bent their bodies towards me, leaning into every word. And so, flattered, I offered another gift.

Beneath the jagged eaves of a fallen arch I found a small puddle and with the edge of a twig, flicked a burnt shard of bone inside.

A small sacrifice, I thought. Means to meet her ends and nothing I didn't mind losing.

The water boiled. Warriors and trees rose through the shadows, but unlike the smooth-worn memories I shaved away to scry, this bone — some insignificant portion of my ankle — brought no cool and empty relief, only pain. Standing amongst my own body and ashes, I burned once again.

Birds beat at my ribcage from within, beaks and claws rasping me raw. Choking on feathers, on falling stones, I forced myself to continue.

"They summoned the forest," I said. I heard my own voice from a far distance, strained beneath the drum-song swelling from the water. "They pulled living matter from the ground as we pulled stones, called the memory of an ancient forest from the mud. They unsung the heaving ground around us, vines and branches dragging our towers to the earth. And archers — archers gathered at the edges of the trees, firing fragments of their wards shaped to fly. Arrows we could dodge, but *thoughts…*"

I saw the faces of my enemies in the water, still painted with ships' runes. Each word, each charm beneath their eyes, spelled safety even as the Feral staggered and fell, choking on blood.

I knew these faces too, each twisted form mutilated and falling. I remembered every name.

Snatching at bracken I tossed handfuls of needles and uprooted ferns into the pool. The screams faded, but the drums and smoke remained, billowing behind my eyes, and the scent, the *stench* —

"We still fought," I snarled, watching golems in my head as women crashed through each new thicket of flailing trees. "For days we fought, and when we gathered our strength and spells, when we took up shields of our own and charged the line, they trapped us in a net of ward-spells and set the trees aflame."

Outside their fallen tower shadows shifted in the unsteady dark. A breath of feathers rustled overhead. For a long moment no one spoke and nothing called. The forest hung, waiting.

Until, like an exhale, Kenna reached forward and caught my hand.

Warm and silent she held me, offering comfort — of all things, *comfort* — but I couldn't stop watching my sister running in my mind's eye. I saw Vefa grinning, spear lifted.

I saw her mouth, open and empty, a shard of light jutting from her breast. No sound, no final word, no warcry—just a wheeze of air from spoilt lungs and crumpling limbs. My sister, ferocious and cunning, taken in a whimper.

And across from me — seated amongst needles and the remains of my own body — were my enemy's daughters, offering *comfort*.

"We were warriors," I growled, an old monster with my jaws clenched on the throat of an ancient war. "Wherever we walked we left queens in our wake, and the world opened for us. We were wild and we feared *nothing*."

At something in my voice — or the words, perhaps, passed down in one of their threadbare tales — Kenna rocked backwards as if struck. Her eyes closed. Slowly, she retrieved her hand.

Low and broken, she breathed, "You were the Unafraid."

Mouth filled with long-ago flame, I bared my teeth — something like a grin, something like pain. I whispered, "Yes."

"*No*," Verja said, and then again, "No. *No*."

Wild-eyed the girl jumped to her feet. She paced backwards, hands picking and clawing at the air, moving in the patterns I had taught her, calling lightning and killing it. She shook her head, body twisting on itself.

"In our stories you were a terrible evil. You were the worst of all the Feral — fearless and mad with it. Everything you touched you changed or destroyed," she said, her voice sick with disbelief and accusation. She started, "They built these wards for *you*. Your sister — " but could not finish.

Pained, I smiled. I remembered running barefoot with my sister along weed-bitten beaches, racing to hide in our secret sea-coast caves. I remembered salt stinging the cuts on her knees, remembered Vefa singing to the sirens in the waves, her voice badly pitched and breaking as the seal-toothed women laughed from their shoals.

I remembered braiding warrior's knots and dandelions into each other's hair.

I remembered the first time we killed a man.

I did not remember the second.

I could not count the last.

"Oh, my little warriors," I said. "You have so much left to learn."

Verja spun. The storm in her hands raged brighter, lapping at her fingers. Outside wind howled, battering against the tower's cracked stones. The scent of salt filled the space between them.

"So *teach us*!" she insisted. "Tell me they're wrong. Saga, tell me they *lied*."

I said nothing. In my silence Verja raged, rattling between the stones strewn throughout the wreckage. Through it all her sister remained still. Seated in the bones and needles Kenna traced patterns in debris. Her fingers trailed the shards of my hands.

Eyes quiet in the shadows, she asked, "Are you what they say you are?"

Long ago, if asked such a question, I would have laughed. A decade ago I might have still.

How could I speak to them of my sister? How could I explain the paths we'd walked, the change welling in our footprints? How could I show them success and failure and have them understand either, warped as they were now by years and blackened trees?

But for all that I tried. Meeting their eyes through the unsteady dark, I told them, "The dead have no stories the living do not give them."

"But *are* you dead?" Verja demanded. Still so young and untrained, wild in her loves and losses, she could not hold her storm. It billowed around her forearms, whirling up her shoulders, lightning flashing at her temples. Rain clouds gathered up above. "What of *your* stories, Saga? Are they not yours to tell? Are you not alive?"

An ill-considered blow. Nevertheless, it found a target. Anger swelled in the absence of my chest, blistering and raw.

"Alive?"

Rising, I looked at the daughters of my enemy, warm and young and full of promise. They were nursed on my sister's *slaughter,* fatted on the spoils of a long-ago war.

So righteous. *So helpless.*

I could take one. I could take *both.* As I'd planned so long ago, I could choose a body and slip inside. I could walk from these trees in *flesh,* let the mask of these bodies break the imprisonment enchanted on the remnant of my soul. With living hands, with Keeper's blood running through her stolen veins, I could *shatter* the ward-line. I could free the Feral, finish my war. And what spell could my ancient enemies weave to greet me? They'd have nothing—nothing, save a ward-smith and the *wreckage* of her daughters.

But I looked at the girls — *my* girls — and even while furious couldn't hurt them. I loved them, insofar as I loved at all, and I would swallow every monster in the forest before I let them come to harm.

At last I managed, "I suppose this is a kind of life. I sing the stories of my people so the trees remember what we were. Rain still falls when I dance for clouds, but I sing to silence and outside the forest, no one feels the rain. Am I alive? Oh, my wise and well-fed children, only you would know."

Blackened and embittered, I shed my shape. With a flick of my mind I broke Verja's storm, let the water wash away my features.

Kenna rose, frowning as she reached for me. "Saga — "

But looking at them, tonight, I saw only my sister, spear slipping from her upraised hand, a flower blooming on her chest.

I saw myself, hands full of promise and potential, leaking like a broken cup.

I turned my back. Sliding through wind and earth, I melted into my bones. Away from their gaze, from the sound of my name, I closed my eyes on them both.

◈━◉━◇━━◇━◉◎━◈

When I woke, I woke to a new season. A toothy wind roamed the high branches of the snow fir. Through the cracks in the tower walls I smelled the threat of snow. But beside me, their presence a winter fire, I felt my girls.

"I don't *care*," Verja snapped. Her boots crunched in needles as she paced.

"She knows this forest, though," Kenna insisted.

Blind, quiet in my bones, I kept still and listened. I could hear their breathing. Kenna's sword held steady some small distance past the remaining pattern of her ankles. Verja's jumped and seethed, keeping time with her steps as she walked the walls, fingers picking pockmarks in the stones.

Shaping, I realized after a beat, reclaiming the intricate whorls and spirals they'd long ago carved into the gneiss.

"She knows the same tattered old stories we do, year after year of the same ghost tales. Who's to say how much they're true?"

"I'm not saying they're *fact,* Verja, only that Mother tended these trees before we were born. She may well know more of them than we do."

"Are you worried she'll come looking? She'd never walk this far into the trees. Not after us, anyway. Maybe a lost cow. Something *valuable.*"

For a long moment, truth ringing them hollow, neither spoke.

At last Verja whispered into the silence, "Saga would come. If we needed her Saga would go anywhere."

Cloth rustled as Kenna shook her head. "We can't know that."

The hands on the stonework stilled, needles crunching beneath new-shod boots.

Verja said, "I do."

Smiling, I closed my eyes, blind though they were beneath the earth.

I could wait. Until they called me — until they *needed me* — I'd wait.

Let them want me. Let them earn my forgiveness.

Not much longer now.

◈━◦━━◦━◈

I woke wearing armor, the pattern of the leather distinct and separate from the skin of my arms. For the first time since the trees I traced the carved dragon on my breast and found not only shape, but the shadow of color. Once again stories spilled from my shoulders, behemoths of woad and gold flowing to pool in the shallows of my palms.

Carefully I stepped from my bones. The fringe of my cuirass whispered around my thighs, braids of beaded troll pelt chiming against hard-won scales. Turning, I found Kenna seated at the shards of my skull.

The girl held her wool-wrapped hands splayed over the pattern she'd woven from the wreckage, her face tight with concentration. I watched her. As my form steadied, I eyed my bones.

Heavy, blue-dyed yarn spun my body together. Copper wire looped the knives of my arms, the spears of my thighs. Sun-shard ribs danced around my skull. Alabaster and obsidian glittered in my mouth, gold spiraling my spine.

For a long moment, stricken, I could not speak.

At last I breathed, "You wove a tapestry from me."

Birds fluttered in my throat, beaks sharp as I swallowed. In the doorway Verja grinned, remnants of summer sun still freckling her nose.

Releasing her hold on thread and bones, Kenna sat back. Slowly, she smiled. "Is it better? I thought you might like it."

Without meaning to, I laughed. My joy sent nightjar reeling in the sky, toads burrowing into mud. Deer fled, crushing underbrush. Lynx scattered into the rocks and trees.

"Such a gift — *thank you*," I told them, admiring my hands, my feet, the *odal* runes swimming my thighs like salmon. "I almost feel as though I have a body again."

Beaming, I held out my arms to my girls, the memory of my rings catching sunlight through the tree limbs. While Verja strode to meet me — long ready to be forgiven — Kenna remained where she sat. She held her spine hard, shoulders low and ready. In her eyes I saw the remnants of a long battle, love and distrust tangled in debris.

No longer a girl, I realized, but a grown woman.

"Is there a spell for that? To build a body?"

Verja pulled away, mouth pursed. She stared at her sister, a warning in the line of her jaw, but I offered, "Possibly? None that I learned. But then, the dead are notoriously jealous teachers."

"You share freely enough." Kenna met my eyes, her face almost an accusation.

I weathered her stare unflinching, lifting a brow. "What are you asking me?"

"Why us?" Kenna said, and the words, the look on her face — despite her bravery, her poise, I saw the child behind the woman, the girl I lured from the path, fingers clenched and pale, facing down an ancient beast.

I smiled as though I did not understand. "Why you?"

The line of Verja's mouth grew harder, her shoulders tight. "*Kenna,*" she warned, but as sisters do, Kenna ignored it.

"No," she said, low and insistent. "There were others. Other girls — other Keeper's daughters, even — lost to the trees."

I shrugged.

Certainly there had been others. Simpering, honor-bound creatures staggering in the footsteps of a duty they did not understand. Some played at keeping house, some played at killing monsters. In the end they'd all waded through thorns and streams at the glimmer of something beckoning.

Of course there had been others. Some came with offerings, others with demands. Cunning girls, sweet girls — on occasion *my* girls had played amongst their bones, picking flowers from the remnants of their ribcages, losing marbles in the empty sockets of their eyes.

But of all those others none had ever *laughed*.

A little thing, perhaps, but not all monsters required elaborate traps.

"Yes," I said, her voice sharp. "Incautious creatures, stumbling through ditches and into dens. Should I have saved them? Would that have pleased you?"

Kenna's hands clenched. She rose.

"But you saved *us*! You walked in our shadows long before we were old enough to hold a light. Saga, your trees feel safer to us than our own mother's hearth. *Why*?"

I snarled, "Because you're *mine.*"

The tower trembled in its moorings. Outside loose stonework shattered down. The trees grew close. Without meaning to, I laughed. My joy sent nightjar reeling in the sky, toads burrowing into mud. Deer fled, crushing underbrush. Lynx scattered into the rocks and trees. The sky darkened.

Verja stepped away. She moved to her sister's side, placed an arm around her shoulder and looked at me, mouth tight, a question in her eyes.

Faced with the two of them closing ranks, I softened. I *salvaged*. My shoulders dropping, I turned away. "My darling girls, my dearest kin made flesh again, how could I allow *anything* to harm you? How could you even think it?

After all I've taught you, all I've done…"

Kenna's face fell. She sighed, a long exhale that left her spent, her face drained and tired. "You're right," she said, shaking her head. "Saga, you're right. I'm sorry."

Head bent I shrugged, drifting away. I put her back to them, stepped outside the wreckage of my tower and into the unsteady shadows of the trees.

"I understand. War leaves such a long memory. I'm outside of time, trapped in this forest. I forget you're a Keeper's daughters."

Verja followed, close at her elbow. "Kenna didn't mean it. Only, Mother dusted off her ghost stories. Every night she tells us some new horror."

Slowly I looked up. I turned, meaning to look interested and forgiving, but my eyes fell instead on the ward lines.

Where once I'd sensed only suggestions of boundaries I now saw every burning thread. Uneven gold wove walls between the trees, magic briar-snarled through spruce and pine like glittering shields on a battlefield.

"She's afraid," Kenna said at my opposite elbow. "She has only the stories. She doesn't know this place like we do. She doesn't understand."

For hundreds of years I had slipped like mist between snarls and loopholes, making my way as I wished. But looking at my familiar paths, the wards threaded wire-sharp, I knew my rabbit holes and warrens could not contain me now. Shaped by the strength of my girls' wanting, I stood too strong—too nearly *living*—to pass unhindered.

Inconvenient, but amongst the trappings of my prison, I spied an opportunity.

"Oh, she understands," Verja snapped. "She doesn't *care*."

Slowly I smiled. I turned to Kenna, opened my mouth as if to speak, and strode into the warded snarl.

Generations of binding magic savaged me. The lines coiled, burning, sinking jagged teeth into the tattoos and braids that named me. It reached for my mind as I reached for it, throwing myself further into its grasp. Sharp claws skittered over my history, groping for purchase.

Holding the names of my girls, the memory of my sister like a talisman, I waded further. I tangled my legs, wore the wards as oath-bands down my arms until their weight brought me to my knees. Some distance away my bones began to smoke, tossing in the protection of copper and quartz.

I could hear my girls behind me, frantic. Over my own screaming I could not make out the words.

And then, suddenly, the lines snapped free.

I fell backwards, my form ringing like a plucked string. When the searing light faded from my vision I blinked up at a spinning sky. Slowly, language returned to me.

"I'm done. I don't care, I'm *done*," Verja snarled, pacing, feral. From where I lay I could see her teeth bared, her fingers clawed. I heard tearing silk — the wards shredding. "I wash my hands of this inherited madness."

Above me I watched the lights dance and die. I watched Verja rip her mother's work to tatters, watched her biting holes in her grandmother's careful edging as she savaged lines knitted and darned several ancestors thick.

At last I came to realize Kenna crouched at my side.

I felt a hand hovering above my hair, heard her ask, "Saga, are you — can I touch you without it hurting worse?"

And oh, I hurt. Hurt like I hadn't since the fire. Lying on my back amongst the roots and needles, I watched a hole bloom in the thickest patch of wards the forest knew. Forcing down a smile, I watched the silvery dome of ward-lines crack open and saw, for the first time since my death, the aching beauty of the sky beyond.

Wincing I pushed myself upright. "I'm dead, my dears," I managed. "Very little else can be done to me."

Aching, every inch throbbing, I climbed to my feet. Beyond my girls' hearing I sent my voice through the trees. Speaking the words of *my* mothers, *my* grandmothers — a language unknown to my enemy and my daughters — I marked this place.

Throughout the forest the Feral stirred, eyes opening in the dark.

And, balanced on Kenna's shoulder, I watched a handful of crows take to the sky.

"Can we bring you somewhere?" Kenna asked, quiet as a coming storm, breaking my reverie. "Is there a place where Mother's meddling can't reach?"

Blinking, my form hazing, I returned my attention to my girls. I weighed my options, planning paths and future battles as I hadn't in many years. At last I decided.

"The shrine."

Verja shook her head. "Mother has bear traps with fewer teeth."

"No. Not the storehouse wreckage your mother fre-quents with her marching rations. The true shrine. The heart of the forest."

For a moment the sisters said nothing. A glance passed between them, a wordless conversation. At last Kenna nodded. Verja grinned. Both stood so tall, carrying the shadow of future spears.

"In the deepest dark?" Kenna asked. "Where no ward-smith has ever walked?"

Slowly, my fingers almost solid, sharp as her rings, I reached up to stroke a loose braid back from the girl's face. "I'll protect you, if you walk with me," I said, gentle as a rain. "I will *always* protect you if you walk with me."

Fox-like in the half-dark, Kenna smiled.

"I trust you," she said. "Lead the way."

Feral watched as we wound through the deepening trees, travelling the broken roads of our last city. Where once the Feral waited, hunting, today my girls passed through their midst as kin. Those that stirred shared their silent trek, dead heroes marking an old path.

Our hands twined I led my girls through the darkest belly of the forest and into moonlight again.

I brought them to a clearing, still bright despite the swiftly-approaching winter. Here, empty of trees and the broken teeth of towers, grass rose knee-high. Wild flowers studded the ground. Carved stone basins lifted their heads above the sea of greenery — some large and cracked, some small and shattered — all holding at least a residue of water and memory.

"Scrying pools," Verja said, glowing, blinking darkness from her eyes. "They're real."

I nodded, drifting through the clearing, trailing my fingers over the lips of still-standing bowls. "Yes."

"Can you teach us?"

I walked to the fallen standing stone at the far edge of the clearing, deep-green granite glittering with captured fragments of moonlight. I ran her fingers over the runes, worn nearly illegible — words of protection for a new city, the names of long-forgotten gods.

"I can."

Looking up from her inspection of a wide, uneven chalice, Kenna smiled. She opened her mouth to speak and stopped, her eyes falling to the stone at my side, to the moon-bitten bones on their byre. As though she'd been struck, she breathed, *"Vefa."*

At the sound of my sister's name both girls fell suddenly still. And I knew my girls. I'd witnessed their birth and every year since. I'd taught them to hunt, to cast, to learn from watching. Even now they wore the braids of my mothers in their hair, careful knots and spirals weaving a story of family — of *history.*

But just the same, the reverence on their faces caught me like a boot to the back.

These bones…these bones meant little to me. Though the skull yet smiled it retained none of Vefa's charm. But watching my children —

I felt distant, a thousand years younger and an old ache in a hollow pit.

"Yes," I whispered. "This is my sister."

Quietly my girls crept to the stonework. Kenna found my side, close enough to reach if I wanted — yet another small offering of *comfort.* Verja met my eyes but kept a distance, fingers playing in the whorls of the byre-stone. Though they understood me differently I found I appreciated both.

Gentle as moths, Kenna settled Vefa's bones in order, arranging wrists and ankles around their fallen decorations. Verja soothed the stonework, sharpening the runes and faces of lost gods.

Standing at my sister's grave I watched them work. The wide spoons of Vefa's shoulders resettled. The tower of her spine straightened against the stone. The runes she'd carved so many years ago shone bright and new in the deep granite, clear as the day she'd called them.

And suddenly I knew — these were no longer my enemy's daughters.

They were *mine*.

◇━●━◇━━◇━●━◇

I felt the moment the Keeper entered my domain. Hunting her was not difficult, not with so many of the wards that should have held me ripped and fraying. In a moment, the breath of a spell, I spun through the trees on the backs of bats and night birds until I crossed the woman's path.

Around me the Feral laughed. They called thorns to snarl the Keeper's steps, fouled paths with fallen trees, but still she walked on. Curious, I followed her.

She walked deep into the forest, away from the paths. Lantern held aloft, her ward-light guttering, she pressed on into the full dark.

What did she hope to achieve, I wondered? What war could be waged by one woman alone? But the Keeper lay no wards and spat no spells. She only walked, forcing herself further and further into the trees.

At last, she said, "I know you're there," low and quiet, a prayer at a fallen alter. "Release my girls."

Uncoiling from the branch of a nearby spruce I slipped into a raven's skin. "I do not hold them," I croaked in the creature's borrowed voice.

The Keeper turned her head, but blind outside the circle of her light she found nothing on which to rest her eyes. Still, she tried. She steeled her jaw, straightened her spine.

"You must. The *years* they've spent in this forest — learning the wards, they said. With you I take it."

Raven's beaks weren't built for smiling. I cocked my head instead, hopping into watery ward-light. "Yes. I told them stories."

"Stories?" she asked, knuckles white on the grip of her lantern.

Like shedding clothing I slid from the body of the bird. I puddled into mist, slipping down the tree and into the outlines of the woman I once was.

"I miss my sister," I said. "It helps to speak of her."

Cold and dark, the woman stared me through. "Name yourself."

I met the eyes of my old enemy, reading her face. I picked fear from her dark circles, determination from the folds around her mouth. I saw this woman loved her daughters.

But I loved them more.

"Of all the many names I've worn, does one mean more than another?"

Fingers twisting threats in the remnants of her wards, the Keeper snarled, "*Who are you*?"

"What I was made," I answered. "Unafraid."

I watched the woman go pale. A tremor started in her hands, the wards spinning loose like spider threads. Around us my Feral laughed. Here and there, I caught fragments of songs I used to know.

The Keeper stepped back. Her boots broke branches, loud in the waiting silence of the trees.

"Release my daughters," she breathed.

Sharp-toothed and hungry, I smiled at her.

I whispered, "*No*."

Winter trudged onward. With every passing day, to my ravenous delight, my girls unwove more and more of the warding that trapped me. Where they walked Feral slipped through the snarls.

Soon. I felt it like a heartbeat in my teeth, like the first thrum of a war drum — *soon, soon.*

If the girls noticed it didn't stop them.

"You're already *dead*," Verja snarled, weaving wards that climbed their kin and dragged whole masses down. "I don't know what more Mother wants."

"Control," Kenna said, eyes dark. "She likes owning *monsters*."

I didn't tell them their mother had no power here, or that she had come to beg me for their freedom with terror in her eyes and ran from my trees with Feral nipping at her heels.

I did not tell them, but then they did not ask.

They bent to their work with fervor. They came at night, when they could, when their mother worked elsewhere. My Feral followed at their sides, and behind them, shadows danced in the fires that burned throughout their village — as if *fire* could keep the Feral away now.

Trapped yet, I watched from my trees, listening to the stories the Feral sent back on the wind. They spoke of deep, ugly houses and wind-scored caverns, frost-bitten outside and smoke-black within. They told of toads souring the wells, lurking at every mouth of the damp earth. They laughed as deer kicked in retaining walls and danced in the wet rivers of mud. I heard their smiles in every lynx waiting behind a barred door, screaming in the unclaimed territory of early morning.

Small triumphs, yes, but every battle began somewhere small.

Soon — soon enough, at least, with winter raging hard — the oldest wards began to fray. A little of my power crept between the failing seams. I waited, forcing back the tides until the ships headed out. And, when their many oars touched water, I shattered every vessel against the rocks. From a long distance I heard the sirens laughing, heard them sing my name.

More and more the girls stayed with me. Kenna washed the walls of my tower with ice-water and hung my tapestry of bones there. Verja built a fire pit into the floor, adding to the chill-ward that circled the tower to stave off wind and snow. Along the walls dried haunches waited in oiled sacks, ropes of sausages hanging from outcrops in the stone.

"The elders are speaking of raiding the forest," Verja told me one night.

Seated between my girls I considered this. I weighed options against opportunity, pitted consequence against reward. At last, at a small risk, I asked, "The elders, or your warriors?"

Settling a small pot into the coals, Verja shrugged. "Either. Both. Does it matter? It means war regardless."

War. Wistful, I rolled the word in my mouth, sun-warmed and sweet. When the time came, I wondered, would the girls fight for their mother? Or would they take to the trees, shoulder-to-shoulder with all the wild things?

Carefully, I said, "Wars depend on their beginnings."

For a long moment neither sister spoke. Eyes low and considering, Verja stared into her pot. Kenna wove patterns of light between her fingers, building the suggestion of spear-points and knives.

In the flickering light I looked between them. My eyes caught on their hair. High in their braids, four knots in a series of coils reserved for family, I found the pattern of my name.

Throat tight, birds battering my ribcage, I reached out. My fingers fell on Kenna's hair, Verja's name woven strong beside mine — *mine* — and for a brief instant, I saw my long-ago family around this fire. My mothers, my grandmothers, their names woven together as sturdy as shields and blood.

I had her answer then.

Heart swollen, fierce, I chose my path.

"Tell me," I murmured, "do they welcome Keepers, or do they fear you?"

Kenna swallowed. Her eyes danced away before returning. "We're not…*un*welcome."

"But this isn't the first occasion they've met to solve the problem of the forest, is it?" I asked. "And odd, but I wager all their solutions speak of Keepers without Keeps."

Verja leaned back from her fire as if startled, a bundle of turnips and tubers forgotten in her hands. Mouth tight, she glanced at her sister. "They do, don't they? War, curses, fire…in the end they're always rid of us."

Reaching forward I gathered their hands. My girls — *my* girls — *nothing* in this world could touch them.

"They want your skill, your power," I said, "and if they cannot learn your weapons then they will make your weapons useless. Be wary, my girls, that when the forest burns you do not burn with it."

"Would they?" Kenna asked, meeting her eyes.

I spread my arms to the trees, to my own mist-formed body and my bones hanging on the wall. "Would they not?"

"They say we're a bandage on a split belly," Verja said, her jaw hard enough to carve. "That the only way of saving the hold is to raze the forest."

I shrugged. With all my sharpened teeth, I smiled.

"Oh, my warrior girls," I said. "Why not let them try?"

I haunted my sister's grove. Passing from stone to stone I stirred memories into water, exchanging songs and faces for enemy plans. In those cloudy visions old men crouched and crowded around a table, thunder in their faces and weapons useless in arthritic hands.

Time held little meaning. Days passed, marked only by changing faces at the war tables. Until, at last, my girls returned.

"Be careful," I told them. "Please, be careful. If I had a body — a form, *any* form — I could stop every spell and flame from ever touching you, but without flesh my power is sorely limited. Please, my girls, be careful. I cannot lose you too."

Grim, my girls agreed.

They joined me, walking the circle of my scrying bowls, learning at my side. Peering into the council session, Verja asked a hundred questions. She learned the meanings of the words they used, the marks on their maps, what paths they knew between the trees. She disassembled their advantages and pieced together weakness. Watching and counting, she numbered their warriors and their skills.

Kenna said little. Mouth hard, eyes keen, she considered individuals. Private coups unearthed beneath her fingers, discontent spilling ever-outward. Where angry warriors found each other in darkened corners she watched. Where they spoke of their suspicions she listened. Even in the face of her own name, her sister's name, she listened.

Sinking to her elbows in the water, Kenna wove. She flicked fear like unseen horseflies to buzz around their heads, unease lingering in their mead. Every fire brought shadows, cold fingers coiling around unwary ankles in the quiet edges of the night, until no one slept easy in their beds.

I taught them what I could — watched in deafening pride as they learned the rest. My girls, her warriors, grown so clever, so blindingly strong…

Still, I urged them caution. "Take care that when war finds you, so can I." Hands spread and empty, I murmured, "Without flesh, and over such a distance…"

As I expected, Verja nodded. "We'll stay close to the forest."

But Kenna surprised me. Weaving in the ripples of a shattered scrying bowl, she shook her head. Beneath her fingers a man screamed, trapped within a web of night-mares.

"If war is coming," she said, "then let us go to it."

⟡━○━◇━━━◇━�»◆◇

And so it began — my revenge, at last.

In the bowl of a scrying pool I watched men crash in a wave against the trees. Some rode horses, some their own two feet. All came armed, talismans for luck and safety jangling against their cuirasses.

The Keeper stood statue-still at the mouth of the forest, rooted in the center of its only road. My girls stood a distance behind, one on either side.

"Turn back!" she cried, arms spread wide. "We cannot protect you all in there!"

The passing warriors sneered, shouting war cries into the thunder of swords on shields.

I saw my girls exchange a look. Their eyes met, laughing in the last strip of sunlight that reached between the trees. Kenna smiled. Verja nodded.

Their mother steeled her jaw. She sank her feet into the earth, twisting her fingers in the remnants of her wards.

Though she could do nothing, regardless, she tried.

And as her eyes fell white with other sight, her daughters — *my* daughters — turned and slipped into the trees.

◇━━◦━━◦━━◇

Wards frayed and broke, shattering in sun spirals as the Feral slipped their chains. The ground shook. Stones rattled in their moorings. Howling filled the trees.

Though I longed to join them I remained in Vefa's shrine, solemn in her sacred place. Woman-shaped, I bent my head over bones.

Let them come to me. Let them defile my sister's grave. Let them give me *reason*, so as not to frighten my warrior girls.

Soon approaching footsteps shattered through the bracken. I lifted my head.

My girls ran into the clearing, spells for safety clotting in their mouths.

A moment later a man broke through the underbrush behind them. Tall, spruce-heavy, he carried a serviceable sword, chipped along the blade from other battles. This he held in front of him, the sunlight of the clearing catching the oath bands of his arms.

"Demon spawn," he snarled. "You brought this on us! Bastard children of elves and ghosts — "

"They are *my* children," I said, and where my voice fell silence grew.

I stepped away from my sister's grave, placing myself between my girls and harm. Meeting the man's eyes, nightmares reflecting in my own, I lifted my hands. Palms upwards, unarmed, I greeted him.

The man struck.

I parted around his blade like the ocean against teeth. I dissolved my form, rising as moths and enveloping him.

The man screamed. His sword fell amongst the needles as I pressed inside him, invading, sliding through his eyes, nose, mouth, dipping my fingers into every pore. He beat at his face, struggling against my flame-heat, but I sank into the cuts on his hands, gnawed my way into his veins.

I scooped the soul from his body and spat him into the trees — a weak, trembling morsel for the Feral. Finally, a proper sacrifice.

And standing in flesh, suddenly, my magic held shape and form again. I flexed human arms, feeling spells pool into my hands, not so unlike taking up an old spear after many years away.

"Saga?" Kenna asked. Not shy or frightened, but intent. Both girls watched me with the eyes of foxes — the eyes of mages, battles raging in their hands.

They'd brought me a body.

An offering. A gift.

"Oh, my warrior girls," I whispered and fierce pride clenched like a fist around my unfamiliar lungs.

◆━◦━━◦━◆

Together they stood amongst the trees and watched their battle rage.

Crows screamed war-cries with bloodied beaks. Moon-silver bears charged through the underbrush, their paws stained red. Laughter rang even in the highest bows of the trees.

And all around us the Feral took up shapes left rusted and forgotten for years. Here and there I recognized the faces of my warriors — my vicious, bright-limbed women, berserkers draped in oaths and teeth. Wild as wolves they careened through the trees.

"They were human," Verja breathed.

Tucking my girls beneath the man's two-bear cloak I held them tight, an arm over both.

"We were something close," I said, and watched my long ago kingdom rising like a bird from ash, the glimmer of the future sprawled panting at our feet. "Something older."

Kenna surprised me by grinning, eyes bright in the flame-lit trees. "Unafraid."

I laughed, holding my warriors, my future queens.

"Yes," I said. "So we are."

CRYSTAL LYNN HILBERT
ABOUT THE AUTHOR

Crystal Lynn Hilbert haunts the forgotten backwaters of Western Pennsylvania. She lives with her husband, a clutter of cats, and a towering pile of books that may consume the house any day now.

She can be found at https://clhilbert.wordpress.com/ or on Twitter @cl_hilbert

The Hounds of Everspire

T.M. Brown

The sagging beam exploded into cinders in front of him, and it was all Raimund Plesner could do to leap out of the way. There had been no time to save his fellow Sentinel Aaron; the supports buckled, and the loft crashed down moments later. There was nothing left where Aaron had stood but a plume of unsettled dust and shattered crates of dried squalfish. Raimund couldn't think about it. There was no time, and he was the only member of his Septem remaining. That damn Sorcerer had to be nearly depleted, since her attacks had been relentless. *This is why you had to kill them young.*

Raimund rushed toward the old hag. He had to close the distance between them as fast as possible, as sorcerers were always the most dangerous at a distance. He could make out the faint flicker of light in her bone-thin fingers, and he threw his shield in front of himself just in time to be driven back several steps by an immense force. Searing heat burned narrow bits of his exposed flesh and licked at his plate armor. *Good.* The shield had taken the brunt of the impact, and the blast was decidedly weaker than the last. *She couldn't keep this up forever.*

He resumed his attack and closed the distance on the old woman. She gasped for breath, looking as if she might collapse on her own. Capturing a Sorcerer as powerful as her would have been a huge boon for the Adellum Order, and had the rest of his Septum still been alive he may have even tried it. Unfortunately they were all dead, and this abomination was far too dangerous to be left alive. He brought down his longsword with equal parts rehearsed precision and innate savagery. The blade should have struck her brittle neck, but an unseen force repelled it. He continued to press downward with all his strength, the blade holding firm nearly a foot from its target.

Raimund had been ordered to secure the back door to the warehouse in case the Sorcerer tried to flee. He'd waited there dutifully, until the screams and sounds of combat drew him inside. He should have come quicker. Raimund had never before seen arcane power like the old woman possessed, and she'd cast over a dozen spells from multiple disciplines in what couldn't have been more than a minute. She had wiped out his entire team of Sentinels - the best in Torsstrand - as if they'd been little more than conscripts. None of this should have been possible. This... *thing* was exactly what the Order had warned him about for all these years; no wonder the Obsidian Coven had refused to provide their usual assistance. He'd deal with them later, if he survived this.

The old crone looked up at Raimund, who was a good foot and a half taller than her. Her eyes were crimson red, with streaks of blood running from every facial orifice and following the wrinkled contours of her wizened face.

She didn't have much left in her - he had to keep pressing. She spoke in a strained whisper. "You've been blinded, Sentinel." Blood dribbled from her mouth as she spoke. "You're a dog on a chain."

Raimund could feel something twist deep within his bowel, the pain so excruciating that he nearly keeled over. He continued to exert force on the blade. It inched closer to the Sorcerer, but the burning pain spread; first through his chest, then into his legs and arms. It felt as if molten steel coursed through his veins. If he relented for just a moment he'd be dead; he had to keep pressing the blade downward. The pain diminished elsewhere in his body, concentrating itself in his wrist. He felt as if something under his flesh was trying to tear its way out.

The seven-pointed star branded on his wrist - the symbol of his holy order - began to move. One-by-one the seven tines peeled away from his skin, each becoming an insectoid leg. The scar pulled itself from his seared flesh and animated into a spindly, spider-like creature that scurried down his leg and across the damp wood floor. Raimund looked at the crone in astonishment. He'd never seen magic like that before, had never even heard of magic like that before.

"No more leash," the haggard old woman whispered. She smiled through blood-stained, rotten teeth. A concussive blast rang out from across the room, and the old crone's face winced in pain. The force holding Raimond's sword at bay was suddenly released, and his blade cut deep into the Sorcerer's paper-thin flesh. Crimson blood sprayed from the wound and painted the Sentinel's helm. The old woman collapsed to the ground and Raimund stood frozen, not knowing exactly what to do. His mind was reeling - it had all unfolded so quickly.

He looked down at his wrist. The brand of the seven-pointed star looked the same as it always had. He didn't feel any different, so the spindly little creature had to have been some sort of illusion. Sorcerers relied on such trickery all the time; it was how they survived. If that old hag had managed to elude the Adellum Order for a lifetime, then she was almost certainly adept at manipulating the minds of others. Still, it had felt so real, and there had been something about her words…

There would be no further answers from the Sorcerer, who lay motionless in a bloody heap in front of him. Aaron hobbled from the wreckage of the collapsed loft, covered in dust with his smoking flintlock still in hand. "Raimund, are you alright?" He asked. Raimund should have been asking Aaron that question. His fellow Sentinel looked terrible. Unfortunately, he was having trouble placing his thoughts into some semblance of order.

"I'm fine…" Raimund responded absently. He removed his helm and held his branded wrist in his hand. It still burned. He muttered softly to himself, "No more leash…"

◈━◦━━◦━◈

Two decades later and Raimund had never been able to purge the old Sorcerer's words from his mind. His weary eyes strained in the dim candlelight as he pored over maps of Torsstrand and the surrounding countryside. Small marks indicating rumored sightings, confirmed sightings, and expiations of Sorcerers dotted the weathered parchment. There had to be another powerful Sorcerer out there, as the pattern was much the same as it had been two decades before. They hadn't realized it then, and it had cost the Order dearly. This time Raimund would ensure his Sentinels were prepared for the threat they faced.

It seemed as if every power in the city was working against him. The Governing Council downplayed his claims, the Ruling Council remained characteristically aloof, and the Obsidian Coven deliberately dragged their feet. *Bureaucrats will be bureaucrats*, there was no changing that. They disliked anything that raised even the faintest spectre of alarm. The Ruling Council wouldn't take an interest in chasing Sorcerers until their own interests were at risk, and as he'd heard on numerous occasions, 'That's what they paid him for.'

The Obsidian Coven was another matter entirely. Raimund had begun to suspect they had their own motivations for obstructing his investigations, but had yet to determine what, exactly, they may have been. His quiet resentment of the Coven had begun on that fateful day at the warehouse. They had known something that they weren't telling the Order, and they should have been there. The antipathy between Raimund and the Coven's leadership only grew after they exploited the incident to expand their own power in Torsstrand. The old crone had called him a 'dog on a chain.' *My chain has never felt tighter.*

"Lord Keeper, First Sister Coretha is here. She's requested an audience with you," a young Sentinel addressed Raimund from the threshold of his study. The lad was dedicated, strong, and disciplined. He'd taken quickly to the Order's training, and he reminded Raimund of himself when he was younger - before the bitterness and resentment had taken hold.

"Did you tell her to choke on slagtooth piss?"

"I did not, Lord Keeper," he responded with a straight face. The kid really needed to lighten up. "If you would like me to, I'd - "

"Thank you, Berin, but that won't be necessary." Raimund stood painfully from his chair. Everything ached these days. "I don't think that would do anything to improve our current situation."

"No, Lord Keeper," the young Sentinel agreed with a humorless expression. Raimund sighed.

"Bring the old vulture in…" Berin nodded in response and departed, returning several minutes later with the First Sister. The acolyte was no younger than the Lord Keeper, but had aged much more gracefully. *No doubt the result of avoiding all the hard jobs.* She wore an elegant, flowing robe and a fitted leather jerkin trimmed in delicate steel accents. They'd do nothing for her in combat, but they gave her a vaguely menacing appearance. It was the costume she wore when she was planning some sort of power play, and none of her usual entourage was in attendance. *Neither could be a good sign.*

"Lord Keeper," the acolyte threw her arms open as if she was greeting an old friend. *We aren't friends.*

"First Sister…" Raimund showed no sign of reciprocating the feigned warmth of the greeting. He leaned against his desk and rested his right hand on the pommel of his longsword. The First Sister broke off her approach and smiled politely. "I'm quite busy with the ongoing in-

vestigation, if you would please make this meeting quick."
Coretha's smile disappeared.

"That's exactly what I'm here to talk to you about,
Raimund."

"I don't think we're on a first name basis, Sister."

"Raimund, I refer to all of my subordinates by the
first names…" Her devilish smile returned, highlighting
her wrinkles. "There's no reason to be so combative." The
Lord Keeper gritted his teeth.

"I'm not your subordinate, Sister. The Adellum
Order remains an independent institution…despite your
machinations." Raimund could feel years of resentment
welling up inside him as First Sister Coretha sighed.

"It does…for now." She examined him with a look
of cruel satisfaction. "Nonetheless, you are now directly
subordinate to me."

"On whose authority?" Raimund scoffed. He'd like
to believe she was bluffing, but the look in her eyes said
otherwise. "I wasn't informed of this."

"I'm informing you now, aren't I?" She shrugged her
slender shoulders. "I thought you'd want to hear it from a
friend." Raimund's grip tightened around the hilt of his
sword. "You went too far with this ghost hunt, Raimund.
What was it you called your mystery Sorcerer?" The Lord
Keeper said nothing in response. "Oh, yes…a 'Matron', I
believe it was. Well, it was certainly clever terminology.
You managed to get High Counselor Joffridus so worked
up that he felt compelled to intervene."

So that's how Coretha had managed to outmaneuver
him…She'd finally spurred the intransigent Ruling Council into action. It'd been years since they'd done anything

substantive, so it seemed fitting that their first order of business would be to dig his grave. Whatever role Councilor Joffridus may have played, First Sister Coretha was almost certainly behind this reversal of fortunes. Raimund had come to associate her with bad news in general.

"As of this morning, the position of Lord Keeper falls under the direct supervision of the Obsidian Coven. It's critical that our two institutions work hand-in-hand... Don't you agree?"

"I couldn't agree more..." Raimund's voice was seething.

"Good. The transition in authorities is specifically designed to help facilitate this relationship." Her tone grew progressively more condescending with each word she spoke. "I feel as if our relationship has been strained for some time."

"I can't imagine why..." Raimund couldn't take much more of this. The First Sister looked him directly in the eyes and cocked her head slightly. "You look like you want to say something, Sister. If you have something to say then say it, otherwise leave me to my work."

"The Managing Council still trusts you...for some reason. I'm inclined to let you retain your position..."

"If..."

"If you call off the fruitless search for this Matron and resume your Order's primary function."

"No." He refused to accept the old hag's authority. "She's out there. I think you know it just as well as I do. If she's anywhere as powerful as the one I faced, she's the real threat to everyone in Torsstrand."

"They're all threats, Raimund."

"They're children!" The Lord Keeper snapped. The First Sister shook her head, her expression turning to one of disappointment.

"You really have gone soft, Raimund. Commander Nicolai was right."

"Stay your tongue, woman. I've killed more of those kids than any Sentinel in the city." That fact was well documented in the Order's archives, and the faces of their grief-stricken families still haunted him.

"Torsstrand thanks you for your service... As a reminder Raimund, you expiated them. You didn't kill them. You cannot kill that which does not have a soul."

"And how many children have you expiated, Sister? It always felt a lot like killing to me." The two glared at one another.

"You're out, Raimund. I'll be recommending to the Managing Council that you be replaced by Nicolai." She forced a mocking smile. "It's time for some fresh thinking in the Adellum Order."

"Nicolai is a fop. Neither the Managing Council nor the rank-and-file will support this."

"It doesn't matter, since the Ruling Council will. They've already been advised that your removal may be necessary in order to ensure a more... harmonious integration of our institutions."

"You're cashing in a lot of crim on this one, Coretha. There is something about this investigation you must really want to see buried."

The First Sister brushed a lock of hair away from her eyes. "The only thing I want to see buried, Lord Keeper, is you." She departed the study without saying another word.

Raimund relaxed his grip on the pommel of his longsword.

First Sister Coretha got her wish. Less than a week later, Raimund Plesner was unceremoniously removed from his post after three decades of service.

◆━◦━━◦━◆

There were two types of magic-users in the world: Acolytes and Sorcerers. The primary difference between the two derived from the very source of their magic, but differences also extended well beyond that. While Acolytes received their arcane power as a gift from the Seven Divines, Sorcerers derived magic from within their own dark hearts. Acolytes enjoyed an elevated status across the Sunspring Empire as members of the Obsidian Coven, while the Sorcerers lived a life in constant fear of being discovered, captured, and expiated. Raimund spent the better part of his years relentlessly hunting the latter of the two, but he had ultimately come to hate them both. In the end they were both rats; one was just better fed than the other, though either one would chew right through you if you got in their way.

One of those rats was seated right in front him. She was a Third Sister - the lowest of the fully initiated Acolytes - with a slightly pudgy, petulant face. He didn't recall her name; there wasn't any point. A week ago Raimund couldn't have been bothered to speak to such a lowly rank, but now that he'd been forcibly retired he'd been assigned a Third Sister to escort him safely to Ignir's Rest.

Raimund's new home was far away from the bustling streets of Torsstrand, conveniently tucked in a bucolic valley at least two days' travel from anywhere of significance. It was said to be a place of peaceful reflection and rest for Sentinels wounded in combat, or who were no longer capable of discharging their duties. Many looked forward to it, but to a man like Raimund, who had spent his entire life within the walls of one of the Empire's most populous cities, it felt like a death sentence.

On the previous day of travel the buildings and vendor stalls had grown less and less dense until they disappeared entirely, soon being replaced by shifting seas of golden grain. After a night's stay at the small crossroads town of Sebina, they left the bustling Inner Way and turned into the Hundgård Wood. The roadway narrowed, and the sweeping sunny vistas gave way to a seemingly endless expanse of trees.

The view from the coach's dusty windows grew tedious, but Raimund nonetheless preferred it to staring silently at the Third Sister or at young Berin, the sole Sentinel accompanying him on the journey. He felt both ashamed of himself and slightly envious of his escorts; they were both so young. They didn't yet see the world in the diminished manner he did - the way anyone did if they lived long enough. Raimund fought his whole life, but in the end everything he'd built had been taken away. He tried to reassure himself that, even if he'd cut down First Sister Coretha in his study that day, it would have changed nothing. Either way, his time in Torsstrand was up.

Raimund was long familiar with regret. He regretted times that he had acted in haste or anger, and he regretted times that he'd failed to act at all, but this was different. He felt powerless. As the coach continued toward Ignir's

Rest he couldn't help but to imagine it was a feeling with which he was about to become well acquainted. Raimund rested his head against the iron latticework of the coach's window and watched the trees pass by.

The Third Sister knocked at the back of the cab, signaling the driver to halt. Moments later the carriage slowed, and the rocking ceased. "I'll only be a moment." She glanced between the young Sentinel and the former Lord Keeper. "Stay put," she said firmly. The Third Sister stepped out of the carriage and departed into the surrounding trees.

"I'm trusting you to continue the search for the Matron while I'm gone," Raimund said in a low voice. He didn't take his eyes off the forest.

"I understand, Lord Keeper." Berin paused. "You can rely on me."

"I know I can…" Raimund replied. The kid may have lacked a personality, but he was loyal to a fault. "Just try to keep a low profile. I don't want you, or any of the other Sentinels, taking unnecessary risks. I'll be back before the frost." He turned from the window and looked Berin directly in the eyes. "Ensure the Order is prepared."

"Of course, Lord Keeper." The young Sentinel nodded. "We await your return." Raimund placed his gloved hand on Berin's firm shoulder and squeezed it reassuringly.

"As do I," he whispered. Rustling in the nearby brush indicated the Third Sister's return. "Remember, no unnecessary risks." Berin nodded. The Third Sister reemerged in the coach's doorway, her eyes darting between Raimund, Berin, and the surrounding woods.

"Sentinels, there… there is something you need to

see," she said shakily. Raimund furrowed his brow.

"What is it?" He asked skeptically. "Are we in danger?" He didn't trust a word coming out of the Acolyte's mouth. Still, her anxiety appeared real enough.

"Just follow. You'll see." The Third Sister stepped back out of the doorway, Raimund and Berin exchanging concerned glances. Before Raimund could exit the coach the young Sentinel grabbed his cloak, unsheathing a dagger and presenting it to the former Lord Keeper. Neither man said a word, though Raimund smiled faintly and took the blade. *The kid was right to suspect something was off.*

Raimund stepped out of the coach and onto the roadway, Berin following close behind. Colorful birds chirped and flitted about in the branches of the nearby trees. The Third Sister stood in the roadway and faced away from them. The carriage driver perched atop the coach and packed a long-stemmed pipe. Raimund gripped the hilt of the loaned dagger. He carried no other armament.

"Sister!" Raimund called out as he approached the Acolyte. "What is it that you insist so fervently on showing us!?" He scanned the surrounding forest for signs of movement and continued to close the distance with the Third Sister. He could make out the sounds of Berin's footsteps following close behind him, and Raimund was uncomfortable with their distance from the Acolyte.

The Third Sister turned back toward the Sentinels, her obsidian cowl fluttering softly in the light breeze. The nervous look in her face was gone - replaced by a hardened expression. "Zhog'dren Gakuras, expiate the former Lord Keeper." The tattoos on her face emitted a soft, blue glow as she spoke.

That bitch! I should have known First Sister Coretha wouldn't just let me walk away. The Third Sister didn't try to cast any additional spells. There was no movement in the woods; she simply stood there with a smug expression. *What does she think she is doing?* Raimund answered his own question, but did so too late. By the time he spun to face Berin the blade of a longsword was already flashing downward.

Raimund's quick movement saved his head, but the sword still caught his shoulder. The honed blade cut to the bone, though it struck nothing vital. Berin moved to withdraw the sword from his victim's shoulder, but Raimund grabbed the blade and pressed it into his own flesh. The pain was immense, even though he'd trained for it. If Raimund permitted the young Sentinel a second strike then he would have been as good as dead.

There was nothing the old Sentinel could do to keep Berin from withdrawing his blade. The steel slid through his grasp, severing flesh and ligaments as it passed. It didn't matter; Raimund had bought himself the time required to thrust the loaned dagger up and into the young man's exposed neck. Berin's longsword fell to the soft, leaf-covered roadway as the young Sentinel choked on the blade. Berin tried to wrest the dagger away, but it was already too late. The wound was fatal.

As Berin fumbled desperately at the dagger lodged in his throat, Raimund caught a glimpse of the seven-pointed star branded onto his opponent's wrist. It glowed blue, the same glow as the Third Sister's tattoos. Raimund released the hilt of the dagger and backed away from Berin. Gore spouted from the young man's neck, covering his chest.

The glowing in his wrist faded, and he looked at Raimund with wide, terrified eyes. He tried to speak, but choked on his own blood. The young man collapsed to the ground shortly thereafter, and there was nothing Raimund could do.

The old Sentinel turned slowly back towards the Third Sister. Her pudgy face was fixed in a mocking smile, and her eyes were cold. She couldn't have been more than twenty years old. At that moment Raimund hated the nameless young woman with a passion he'd previously thought impossible. *They were all rats.*

"Not the order I'd expected, but... it's just as well." The Third Sister's smile widened. "I think First Sister Coretha would be very pleased with the result. The look on your face..." She shook her head. "Oh, come on, don't act so surprised. You're an old dog that refused to hunt! What's worse... you growled at your masters."

Raimund had no interest in carrying on a conversation with vermin, as it would only inflate their ego further. The Acolyte may have been cocky, but she'd been smart enough to back away while he was distracted. That was bad news for Raimund. If she wanted to kill him, however, she'd have to do it quickly. Raimund couldn't listen to another word; he charged at the Third Sister as quickly as his old legs could carry him. His only plan: *close the distance, kill the rat.*

"Taz'gonal Almok, halt and expiate yourself!" The Third Sister commanded. The tattoos on her face glowed as she spoke. Raimund felt nothing beyond burning hatred and familiar pain. The Acolyte's eyes widened, her smile fading. *No more leash.*

Every one of the Third Sister's tattoos lit in bright unison. Roots burst from the ground and wrapped around Raimund's legs, pulling him downward and coiling their way around his body. There was no muscling his way out of this one; the grasping roots were far too strong. The Third Sister couldn't have been more than thirty feet away. He threw the gore-spattered dagger and struck his target, the blade lodging in the Acolyte's abdomen before she keeled over in pain.

The roots loosened momentarily, and Raimund slipped free. He approached the Third Sister just as she regained her composure. She attempted to resume the spell, her tattoos flickering and the surrounding roots twitching to life. *Too slow.* When Acolytes were frightened their magic was not particularly reliable, so the girl was clearly scared. *Good. She should be.*

The Third Sister recoiled, her hand still grasping the dagger lodged in her abdomen. "W-Wait," she stammered. Raimund grabbed the hilt of the dagger, ripping it from her gut, and thrust it into her heart. He withdrew the blade as the Acolyte collapsed to the ground, dark blood spurting from the wound. The former Lord Keeper stood over her as she writhed and gasped for air.

Before she expired the intense hatred Raimund felt for the girl had already dissipated. She was so young... They were all so young. No more than a child, really. Raimund Plesner had made a career killing children, but he'd really thought he had been serving a righteous cause. Now…he wasn't so sure. He knelt beside the Third Sister as she drew her last, labored breaths and brushed the hair away from her eyes.

When the crone and the Third Sister had called him a dog the words had stung. Long ago, an old Sentinel told him that words that stung were barbed with truth and the recollection made Raimund sick to his stomach. That Sentinel had been right, of course. He was certainly a dog in at least one sense; a dog knew no morals but those of his master. Raimund felt used, tired, and old. *No more kids.* He wouldn't let himself, or his Sentinels, be used any longer.

The Third Sister ceased breathing. Raimund closed her eyes and stood back to his feet, contemplating his next course of action as he bandaged his ruined hand. He'd been close to something back in Torsstrand, enough so that some aspect of his investigation into the Matron had First Sister Coretha spooked into deposing him as Lord Keeper and arranging his murder. Raimund considered going directly to Everspire, but reconsidered. Accusing the Obsidian Coven of treachery was a serious matter, and if he was going to appeal to the Addelum Order then he needed more than the body of a Third Sister and wild accusations.

No more leash. He couldn't shake the old crone's words from his mind. He needed to revisit that fateful day at the warehouse. Everything stemmed from the events of that day; there had to have been something he missed. Only one other man had survived the encounter - one he'd not spoken to since that very day. Raimund resolved to visit Sentinel Aaron Naeworth.

He turned back toward the coach. The driver still sat with the reins in hand, and upon meeting Raimund's glaze, the man threw up his hands. "I wasn't involved in none o' this!" He declared. "Honest!" His eyes were nearly as wide as the Acolyte's had been when her spells had failed her. Raimund believed him.

"I know," the Sentinel growled. "Now get off of that carriage and help me with these bodies." The driver nodded several times and scrambled to join him. Raimund picked up the dead Acolyte's legs and waited for the driver to grab her arms, his bandaged hand making the lift more difficult than it should have been.

"Lord Keeper, where would you like me to take ya?" The driver asked. They lifted the body in unison. She was hefty for such a young girl.

"No need to change course now," Raimund responded. "We're going to Ignir's Rest."

When Raimund imagined what the Sentinel's retirement community looked like he had always pictured it as an austere monastery, walled and tucked away into some sort of rugged terrain. The image could scarcely have been more different than the village that spread out before him. Small cottages followed the contours of low, rolling hills, and a crystal-clear brook trickled through the village center as wisps of chimney smoke hung in the air.

There were no banners emblazoned with the sword and shield of Ignir, no sheer stone walls or heavily armed patrols. There were few stone structures at all, and even Raimund may have been capable of finding peace amongst the pleasant green. Unfortunately, the events of the last few days precluded such a happy ending for the old Sentinel. Raimund now doubted such a peaceful retirement had ever truly been an option for him and he couldn't help but to sigh as he peered through the curtains of the small carriage.

The dirt road was replaced by cobblestone. The coach halted, and Raimund stepped into the village square. His shoulder ached. His hand ached. Come to think of it, so did most of his body; he couldn't recover as quickly as he once did. Raimund took in his surroundings. Some of the village residents eyed him with vague curiosity, but most carried on with their daily activities. The population skewed expectedly towards older males, though not quite as much as one might expect. There were younger lads, and even a few women, among them. The only real contrast between Ignir's Rest and any other village was a weathered, stone statue of Ignir the Guardian, along with a complete absence of children.

Raimund knew exactly where to look for his old comrade. He turned back towards the driver. "Where's the tavern?"

"There's two, Lord Keeper. The Sword and Shield is right across from you and the Ornery Ox is up the street." Heads turned when the hapless driver addressed him by his former title. Raimund should have cautioned him not to do that. *Too late now*. "Which is cheaper?"

The driver cocked his head. "Well, they're both free to Sentinels. An allotment from the Order, Lord Keeper." Raimund should have known that. It was a stupid question, but he was growing frustrated nonetheless.

"Fine. Which has more...*buxom* servers?"

"The Ornery Ox," the driver replied with a heretofore undemonstrated certainty.

"Take me," Raimund commanded. The pair arrived

at the tavern minutes later. It was an old, but sturdy, structure. A fire crackled in the hearth, warding off the crisp air. The taproom was surprisingly full, given the moon had not yet slipped below the horizon. The customers were almost exclusively old men, their skin colors representing the full scope of the Sunspring Empire - coal black from the Verdant Coast, bronze from the Heartlands and the Triveza Accord, smokey grey from the misty shores of Shorn Coast and pale white from the gloomy East. The driver pointed towards two serving girls behind the bar.

Sure enough, bountiful cleavage spilled over the top of their bodices like over-poured ale. The driver nodded in their direction and smiled suggestively. "Yes, yes…good work." Raimund humored the man and scanned the taproom for his old friend. It didn't take long. He took the driver by the shoulder. "What's your name?"

"Günther, Lord Keeper. Günther Schatz."

"Günther, that's not my title any more." The driver nodded his head in agreement. "Good. When are you expected back in Torrstrand?"

"In two days, Lord K - I mean, erm… Sentinel." Raimund tried his best not to smile. It was important Günther took this seriously.

"Do you report directly to anyone associated with the Obsidian Coven?"

"No, Sentinel. It's just a job - honest."

"Good. Stay at the other inn. You can drink, but don't get drunk. I'll meet you at moonrise." Raimund spoke slowly and deliberately. When he finished, he slipped Günther a small pouch of coins. "I'm trusting you because I can tell that you're an honorable man. Sentinels can always tell an honorable man." That wasn't entirely true - Raimund had no idea who to trust. It didn't really matter in this particular instance, however, whether he trusted the driver or not. He needed to get back to Torsstrand and returning with the coach seemed a sufficiently inconspicuous way to do it. Besides, he'd be long gone by the time Günther and his carriage actually entered the city gates.

"Don't forget - moonrise tomorrow. Now go." Günther turned and departed, Raimund waiting a moment to ensure the driver had gone before making his way over to Aaron Naeworth.

His old comrade had grown fat and grey. They greeted one another in accordance with tradition. Aaron introduced his companions: a Cothelian named Yacobe, and a Leton named Thucer. Raimund had no desire to reminisce and lacked the time for pleasantries; he'd never been a skilled liar, and didn't want to involve anyone in his increasingly dangerous game unnecessarily. He joined them for an ale to avoid appearing impolite, then requested a more private audience with his old friend. Aaron agreed and the two departed towards his small cottage.

The two entered a cozy sitting room. Aaron lit several tallow candles and closed the door behind them, seating himself across from Raimund and pouring himself an ale. Aaron offered his guest a pewter flagon. Raimond declined, but Aaron filled it anyway. "I didn't ask you about your hand back at the tavern. Figured it might not be something you wanted to talk about in public...Why are you here, Raimund? Don't tell me it's retirement."

"I'm here about the day you ruined your leg…the day we killed that old Sorcerer."

Aaron's expression grew serious. He took a sloppy gulp from one of the two flagons. "You're late, you know. I thought for certain you'd have sought me out years ago." Ale dribbled down his stubbled chin.

"What do you mean? Why would you think that?" Raimund was puzzled by his old friend's words. Aaron looked thoughtfully into the flame of a nearby candle before he exhaled and swallowed deeply.

"At first I thought you were just keeping it to yourself…It made sense. I certainly wasn't going to tell anyone about it. I didn't blame you for that. I really thought you would ask me about it, though. Then…when you were given your own Septem, I thought you'd just been willing to sweep it all under the rug. I did blame you for that, you know, I really did." He took another long drink of his ale. "I thought you'd been bought and paid for…" Raimund wanted to speak, but couldn't seem to find the words.

"It wasn't until I heard that you'd been appointed Lord Keeper that I realized you really didn't remember… Everspire only appoints true believers, Raimund. Either you suddenly became the Empire's best liar - which I really doubt - or you clearly don't remember what happened." Aaron paused, looking his guest directly in the eyes. "So which is it, Raimund? Are you still a true believer?" Raimund didn't know exactly what to say.

"I…I remember everything, or at least I thought I did. Recent events have…well, they've led me to question everything. What did you see there? What am I missing?" Aaron finished off the contents of his first flagon, pushed it away, and slid over the next.

"I can't tell you what you didn't see, Raimund...our

Sorcerer was an Acolyte and a powerful one at that…a First Sister, maybe? I don't know. We were set up. She knew we were coming. There were supposed to be two Obsidian Acolytes with us. You know what they sent us? Illusions. We weren't supposed to kill her, we were supposed to die…" Aaron's voice trailed off. Raimund struggled to take in what he was hearing.

"What do you mean she was an Acolyte? She didn't have the tattoos…she cast spells like a Sorcerer…"

"She did have the tattoos, Raimund, and she cast both. She'd exhausted her Acolyte spells before you ever even entered the warehouse."

"But her tattoos…they should have glowed. They always glow…"

"They did, while you were still guarding the back entrance. Like I said, she used those first. She killed Bernd, Vincent, and Tristan before she transitioned over to the Sorcerer shite. How else do you think she was able to cast so much in so little time?"

"It's impossible. A caster can't be both." Aaron shrugged.

"So we've been led to believe…"

Raimund tried his best to collect his thoughts. It was possible he'd missed the tattoos if they hadn't glowed. She had been wrinkled and wrapped in robes. The only image he could clearly recall of the old crone was her cold, milky eyes and blood-stained teeth. "You said something about illusions. What illusions?"

Aaron sighed. "Two Acolytes…I think a Second Sister and a Third. They waited across the street from us. Never said a word, but gave us the nod for the raid. They faded to mist afterwards." Aaron took another drink, his hand shaking. "I saw it with my own eyes."

Much of what his old friend was telling him made sense. He'd been one of the most junior Sentinels in the Septem at the time, and hadn't been privy to much of the raid's planning. Moving forward without an Obsidian Acolyte's presence was against protocol; they rarely contributed in any meaningful way, but they were always expected to be there. The Acolytes had been quick to separate the two surviving Sentinels after they arrived and insisted on keeping them apart. There had been so many questions and divination spells afterwards that it hadn't seemed particularly out of place at the time given the climatic events of the day, but now…Now it felt different.

You're a dog on a chain. The old crone's words echoed once more in Raimund's mind. Even if it had all been a setup why would the Sorcerer, or Acolyte or Matron or whatever she was, have released him from his 'leash'? Why would she have spoken to him the way she did? Why would the Obsidian Coven have even wanted them dead in the first place? It didn't make any sense, and Raimund considered telling Aaron about his experience. It was clearly a missing piece in the puzzle. As he watched his old comrade finish the dregs of his second ale, however, Raimund decided otherwise. *Better to play my cards close to my chest.*

Aaron got up to refill the flagons. "So…what now?" Aaron asked.

"For you, nothing," Raimund replied.

"I see…I suppose I wouldn't be of much use to you anyway."

"No, you wouldn't."

"Right." Aaron slouched in his chair, apparently hurt by the remark.

"It's not your fault. You've gone and gotten yourself fat on me."

Aaron smiled. "Well, I gave up on you ever coming back there for a while…"

"That's fair…" Raimund paused for a moment and considered the question he was about to ask. "Aaron…do you…do you ever feel like your life is at risk?"

"For a long time, yes. I had dreams about them coming for me in my sleep. Too big of a liability, you know?" He shrugged. "These days…not so much. I mean, look at me." He took yet another big swig from his flagon. "I'm no threat to anyone." Raimund couldn't help but to agree with his friend's assessment. He required a cane to walk, and looked as if he might run out of breath just from traveling to the privy. Still, after the events of the day the Coven may very well find renewed interest in tying up loose ends.

"It certainly doesn't seem like a bad life. Do you mind if I stay the night here?"

"Of course not."

"Thanks." Raimund stood up from his seat. "I'll likely be gone by the time you wake. Be careful, Aaron. Things are changing quickly."

<hr />

Raimund spent the duration of the ride back to Torsstrand struggling to formulate some semblance of a plan. It didn't come to him as easily as he'd hoped; every potential course of action he considered seemed to end in some variation of his own horrible death, or, at best, a hollow vengeance against the First Sister with no real answers to a growing number of questions. If you wanted to remove a weed you pulled it up by the root, but the trouble was that Raimund was not convinced First Sister Coretha was the root he sought to pull.

He needed to separate his old nemesis from her entourage. He didn't just need to assassinate her, he needed to interrogate her. That particular requirement made the task far more dangerous. Raimund's best opportunity would be to act quickly, before she came to suspect that Raimund had survived the attempt on his life. He had an idea; he wasn't especially excited about it, but it was the best he could come up with under the circumstances.

The plan would require Günther's assistance.

The trees gradually gave way to fields, then the fields to scattered settlements. Raimund had Günther stop in one of Torsstrand's outlying towns, where the old Sentinel took his driver by the shoulder and glanced around the nearby outbuildings. There didn't seem to be anyone around. "Günther, I have a request to make of you. It is a simple one, but the repercussions are great."

"Whatever you request, Sentinel," the driver agreed without even listening to what it was. He clearly didn't understand the gravity of what was being asked of him. "You've already paid me a great deal…" Raimund tightened his grip on the man's thin shoulder.

"This is serious, Günther. Do you have a family?"

"I-I've got a dog, and my mum's still alive…" the driver stammered in response.

"Nobody else? Children? A wife?"

"No, no...nothing like that. Never could afford 'em, really."

"Good."

"W-what do you mean good? I - "

Raimund cut him off. "You'll need to leave Torsstrand and never come back."

"I, erm...alright. As long as I can keep the coach and horses..."

"You'll need to get rid of the coach. We'll see about the horses, but you won't have to worry about money. I'll take care of that."

"Alright, Sentinel. I trust your word. What do you ask of me?" Raimund withdrew a small, steel pendant shaped like a tree. He'd taken it off the Third Sister's body, and all Acolytes wore some variation of them. They conveyed each Acolyte's standing, discipline and Coven. In this particular case steel indicated a Third Sister, the tree indicated the primalist discipline and the outer filigree indicated membership in the Torsstrand Coven. First Sister Coretha should recognize it immediately. Raimund placed the pendant in Günther's open palm.

"Get in contact with whoever usually hires you for work associated with the Coven. Tell them that the Third Sister, whatever her name was, wishes to speak with her in private at the Ramshead Tavern. Tell them that the job is done, but that I had some very concerning things to say about several members of the Obsidian Coven. Tell them that I revealed the identity of the Matron." Raimund paused to ensure that Günther was taking in everything that he was being instructed to do. "After you've said what you need to say, give them the pendant."

'What - what if they ask to see her?"

"She is afraid for her life. She'll *only* speak to the
First Sister. Nobody else." Raimund looked the carriage
driver in the eyes. "Got it?"

"Yeah, yeah. Of course…Sister Kuechler won't
speak to anyone but the First Sister…she knows about the
erm…"

"The Matron, she knows about the Matron."

"Right. The Matron, got it."

"I'll meet you in the taproom downstairs, then we'll
get in the carriage and depart from there. Bring any supplies you feel are absolutely necessary. You…ugh…you
can bring your dog if you like."

"Alright." Günther glanced at an approaching ox-
cart. "What are we going to do once we've got her there?"
Raimund owed his accomplice an honest answer. He saw
little point in withholding further information at this point;
if Günther decided to betray him he was already as good
as dead.

"I am going to kill the First Sister of Torsstrand, and
you are going to help me."

Raimund waited in a cramped bedroom above the Ramshead taproom. The tavern was in one of the seedier parts
of the city - far from the breezy halls of the Obsidian Coven. It hadn't stopped raining since well before the last
moonrise, so the roof leaked and water pooled on the sagging floorboards. The smell of sewage wafted through

the room's single, narrow window. His injured hand was showing signs of infection; it had swollen, and Raimund could scarcely move it without causing himself considerable pain.

The worst part was the waiting, as Raimund didn't have any way of knowing exactly when the First Sister would arrive. She could open the door at any moment, so he had to stay on continuous alert. He hadn't really considered the problem when he'd initially concocted the plan, and after nearly two days alone and awake in the tiny room he felt as if he might pass out at any moment. It had been at least a week since he'd had a decent sleep; the scheming, running and continuous vigil had all taken their toll, while the injuries only made it worse. Raimund was in no condition for a fight. He hoped he wouldn't have to.

Getting into Torsstrand had been easy enough, since Raimund knew several inconspicuous approaches, and once within the city walls he'd gone on a quick shopping spree. He purchased enough food for several days, bitterweed oil to keep himself awake, and - most importantly - two small vials of wyvern bile. The bile was potent enough to corrode a human's flesh to the bone, making it a particularly effective tool against magic-users.

Virtually all Sorcerers and Acolyte's alike were capable of casting basic defensive spells, and one of the most frequently used was the stoneflesh ward. As its name suggested the ward protected the casters' flesh against minor, non-catastrophic injuries. It didn't do much good against a sword or a musket ball, but it was quite useful in protecting against burns, insect bites and corrosive substances. The thing about wards - even simple ones - is that they're terribly inefficient spells for all but skilled abjurerationists. Toss a bit of wyvern bile on a magic-user and, nine times out of ten, they'd exhaust every bit of magic they had trying to keep their flesh from melting to the bone. It was particularly useful for interrogations.

Raimund sat on the edge of the straw bed and gazed absently at the vial he held in his functional hand, his eyelids feeling as if they were supporting the weight of Everspire. The bitterweed oil was depleted, though it didn't seem to work anyway. Raimund couldn't remember a time he'd felt more exhausted. He closed his eyes for just a moment, knowing that he'd be able to hear the First Sister coming up the stairs. He'd listen and give his weary eyes a rest.

◇━◦━━◦━◇◇

Floorboards creaked and Raimund's eyes opened at the sound. He must have fallen asleep. Raimund sat up in the bed to find First Sister Coretha standing in the open doorway. She wore a floor-length coat, still wet from the rain, and her eyes were narrowed. Her mouth hung open as the two stared at one another for a moment, each taken aback. When they finally took action, they did so simultaneously. The First Sister drew a stiletto knife from beneath her cloak, while the Sentinel fumbled for the wyvern bile that had slipped from his grasp as he slept.

By the time Raimund grabbed the vial the First Sister was already nearly upon him. He uncorked the vial and splashed its contents on the Acolyte, who shrieked and recoiled back toward the doorway. He'd been too close when he used the bile and inadvertently splashed a small amount on himself; it began to dissolve bits of his clothing as it worked its way towards his flesh. There was no time to disrobe when he had the First Sister right where he wanted her.

The Acolyte's form flickered and shifted. The stern, gracefully aging woman was replaced by a girl no older than the Third Sister who'd tried to assassinate him days earlier. *Damn illusionists.* Of all the magic-users Raimund had always hated them the most; he should have known the First Sister couldn't be bothered to get her own hands dirty. Despite the trickery, the bile had still worked as he'd hoped. The young Acolyte's tattoos glowed as she struggled to protect her pretty features. He had no interest in killing the kid.

"I'm not here for you," Raimund told the girl. "First Sister Coretha wouldn't send you here all alone. Where is she?" He hoped the first statement was true, but couldn't be sure. He was surprised she'd been so willing to delegate murder within her own Coven. The young Acolyte didn't respond, instead focusing on her stoneskin ward and kept the stiletto pointed toward Raimund. She looked at him with pure contempt. "Listen, I think -" Raimund was thrown back into the room's aging wardrobe by an immense, concussive force. The wardrobe shattered and splintered wood cut into his exposed flesh.

The suddenness of the blast left Raimund disoriented. The young illusionist rushed forward, brandishing the knife as her flesh smoldered. Raimund threw up his ruined hand in an attempt to stop the blade. She plunged the stiletto through his swollen palm and excruciating pain flared up his arm. He wrenched his hand away with the blade still embedded inside, the illusionist losing her grip on the weapon. Raimund drew Berin's dagger from his belt and thrust it into her slender ribcage. He repeated the action twice more and the Acolyte collapsed into rainwater pooled on the sagging floor.

The wyvern bile continued to work its way to her bones, and the Sentinel's own flesh was starting to burn. He removed his outer garments and did his best to wipe away the bile. Those wounds would remain superficial, though he couldn't say the same for his hand. There was no time to waste; that Acolyte's spell was almost certain to have alerted everyone on the entire street. He didn't bother checking the illusionist for anything useful, as First Sister Coretha wouldn't have sent her on such a sensitive assignment with anything incriminating. He did, however, keep the stiletto after removing it from his infected hand.

Raimund made his way down the narrow stairway to the taproom. There were only a handful of customers present, but everyone there looked directly at him as he walked into the room. He tried his best to appear casual, though it was hard when blood dribbled from his hastily-bandaged hand. Günther didn't help matters. He approached Raimund from a small table against a nearby wall. "So... did you, you know...do it?" the carriage driver asked. Raimund continued walking toward the taproom doors, Günther following.

"No...not exactly. We need to go."

"W-What do you mean? What happened?"

"She wasn't there!" Raimund snapped. He'd spoken far louder than he should have.

"I think I might have seen her," Günther said. The Sentinel stopped.

"Why do you say that?"

"Well, you told me to keep an eye out. This old lady came hobblin' in here just a few seconds after the First Sister…or at least whoever looked like the First Sister. She left just after the explosion upstairs. Right about then, I saw her face change…she looked younger." Raimund's expression grew deathly serious.

"Where'd she go?"

"Right out the doors." The Sentinel took off before Günther could even finish speaking. He pushed through the doorway and looked down the street. Sure enough, there was a robed woman walking briskly away from the tavern. She was alone. Raimund reached into his pocket and pulled out a pouch of coins, tossing them to his companion as soon as Günther exited the taproom door. "Good work, Günther. You've been true to your word. Now go." Raimund began following the fleeing Acolyte.

"But you haven't - "

"Just go!" Raimund shouted over his shoulder. "Take the carriage and go! I don't want you caught up in this!" Günther said something else, but Raimund couldn't hear him over the sounds of his feet striking the cobblestones. The First Sister had taken notice of him and broke into a sprint. She ducked into an alley, Raimund following close behind. Despite her head start Raimund was considerably faster, and he gained ground quickly. After continuing into a larger boulevard lined with vendors and shaded by box-elder trees, the First Sister gave up her flight. She halted in the middle of the street and turned toward her pursuer.

"Is this...is this really how you want to die, Raimund? You want to try to murder me in front of all these people?" She gestured towards the several dozen bystanders scattered about the roadway. "I must warn you...I'll be forced to defend myself." Raimund saw no point engaging in conversation. The city watch, the Sentinels and even more Obsidian Acolytes could be closing in at any moment. The First Sister had time on her side and she knew it, so Raimund charged. *Close the distance. Kill the rat.*

The Acolyte's staff burst into flames. She thrust it outward and a tendril of pure, elemental fire unfurled. She lashed it toward him like a brutal, impossibly long whip. He narrowly avoided the first strike by ducking beneath its arc, and he could feel the heat on his neck as it passed overhead. He continued to close the distance between them. The second strike was impossible to avoid. She swept the whip low across the boulevard, taking Raimund's legs out from underneath him. He tumbled forward and his chin struck the cobblestone street.

The metallic taste of blood filled his mouth.

Raimund struggled to his feet. The whip had seared his legs and dislocated his jaw, but he was closer. He needed to get just close enough to use the wyvern bile. First Sister Coretha continued to backpedal as Raimund advanced, screams erupting as several vendor stalls burned and bystanders collapsed upon the ground. Raimund was preparing to uncork the vial when the First Sister lashed out with her whip yet again. He instinctively threw out his shield arm in defense; unfortunately there was no shield. The flame whip wrapped around his forearm and burned through his flesh, and as she pulled him forward Raimund once again collapsed to the cobblestone. The glass vial clattered to the street.

When the flame coiled around his arm disappeared, Raimund tried to stand back up. He was too slow. The fiery whip reformed, and she brought it down on his back, the flame burning through his clothing instantaneously and searing his flesh. She brought the whip down on him several more times. Raimund felt as if he were being burned alive; the smell of his own cooking muscle and fat made him nauseous. The fight was over, and he wanted nothing more than to pass out or die. He just wanted the pain to end.

First Sister Coretha knelt down, still careful to keep her distance from the Sentinel. She picked up the vial and examined it. "Really, Raimund? Wyvern bile? You always were a sick bastard." She tossed the vial across the street and glanced around at the gathering crowd. She drew closer to the fallen Sentinel, speaking in a whisper. "You know…I should have been the one to escort you to Ignir's Rest. You needed a friend and I wasn't there for you…I had big plans for that girl." She sighed. "Oh well, mistakes can be corrected..."

"Why…why all this?" Raimund asked. He accepted that he was dying. There was no fight left in him, he just wanted answers. He wanted to hear that there was some kind of purpose behind it all. Bells tolled nearby - the city watch would not be far behind. The First Sister smiled.

"We all must serve, Raimund." She caressed his singed hair. "There is no denying the Cloistered King." First Sister Coretha stood to her feet, backed away, and conjured an orb of swirling flame in her fingertips. "Goodbye, old frie - " The hooves of four heavy draft horses cut the First Sister down. Coretha's body was tossed about beneath the beasts, and she was crushed by the carriage wheels that followed. The horses and their carriage skidded to a halt a short way down the shady boulevard. Raimund staggered to his feet, his seared flesh screaming at every movement.

"Sentinel, we must go!" Günther called from his seat atop the carriage. Raimund ignored his pleas and shuffled toward the vial he had dropped. He picked it up off the cobblestone roadway and examined it; the glass remained intact. He then proceeded to make his way toward First Sister Coretha. She was badly mangled: exposed bone protruded through the flesh of her arm, and her ribcage had collapsed. She sucked desperately at the air.

Two Sentinels in plate armor pushed their way through the gathering crowd and rushed toward Raimund. He ignored them, continuing his task. The First Sister's tattoos flickered into life as the former Lord Keeper approached, and she struggled to speak. "Taz...gonal..." She coughed up dark, viscous blood. "Taz'gonal Almok, ex-expiate yourself!" She smiled broadly and waited. Raimund uncorked the bottle. Her smile faded and her eyes grew wide. "Taz'gonal Almok-" The Sentinel poured the vial's contents onto the First Sister's panicked face. She shrieked as her flesh melted away. The wyvern bile worked its way to the bone. *No more leash.*

"Lord...Lord Keeper Plesner?" A familiar voice spoke from beneath a steel helmet. Raimund raised his eyes from the First Sister to see two Sentinels standing only feet away with their longswords drawn. Several watchmen were breaking through the crowd further behind them, and it seemed as if every bell in Torsstrand was tolling. Without saying a word Raimund turned and began hobbling towards Günther's awaiting carriage.

"What have you done? This…this could start a war." Raimund turned back towards his fellow Sentinels, nodding solemnly.

"If it's a war, whose side are you on?" The former Lord Keeper turned his back on the pair and struggled toward the carriage. He had nothing left. His legs buckled and he collapsed to the street, feeling cold steel against his burned flesh.

⸺⬥⸺◦⸺⬥⸺

You've been blinded, Sentinel. The rattling of the carriage jostled Raimund awake, and even the smallest movement sent pain coursing through his body. Two Sentinels were seated across from him. So it would be war... He hadn't wanted this. It had been thrust upon him. For a millennium the Obsidian Coven and Adellum Order had been pillars of the Sunspring Empire, serving together to ensure the peace and prosperity of millions. When had it gone so wrong, or had it always been this way?

One of the Sentinels leaned forward in his seat.

"Lord Keeper, where should we go?" Raimund considered the question as the old crone continued to whisper in his mind. *You're a dog on a leash.*

"Everspire," he responded. If the Order was being dragged into war, they needed to make their first strike decisive. Raimund had never heard of this 'Cloistered King', but he felt confident that he was the root that needed pulling. He'd find this 'King' and bring the Acolytes to heel; a hound's gifts were loyalty and savagery. The Coven had exploited their loyalty for far too long. As each bump in the road racked Raimund Plesner's body with pain, he wanted nothing more than to tear the whole Empire apart.

T.M. Brown

About the Author

Trevor Brown, who writes under the pen name T.M. Brown, serves as an officer in the U.S. Army. He currently lives in Colorado Springs, Colorado with his beautiful wife, Anna, and his two dogs, Fry and Zapp. Although Trevor has long held a passion for speculative fiction, he has only recently taken up writing for publication. His preferred genres include horror, strange fiction, and dark fantasy.

T.M. Brown's debut novella 'The Gloam' is currently available on Amazon in both paperback and Kindle formats. He also has a variety of dark fiction under contract with independent publishers including: Black Hare Press, Burial Day Books, Cosmic Horror Monthly, Eerie River Publishing, Kyanite Publishing, Nothing Ever Happens in Fox Hollow, Sinister Smile Press, and Terror Tract.

https://www.facebook.com/RavenousShadows
Twitter @TMBrown_Author

Don't Miss Out!

Looking for a FREE BOOK?

Sign up for Eerie River Publishing's monthly newsletter and get **Darkness Reclaimed** as our thank you gift!

Sign up for our newsletter
https://mailchi.mp/71e45b6d5880/welcomebook

Here at Eerie River Publishing, we are focused on providing paid writing opportunities for all indie authors. Outside of our limited drabble collections we put out each year, every single written piece that we publish -including short stories featured in this collection have been paid for.

Becoming an exclusive Patreon member gives you a chance to be a part of the action as well as giving you creative content every single month, no matter the tier. Free eBooks, monthly short stories and even paperbacks before they are released.

https://www.patreon.com/EerieRiverPub

MORE FROM EERIE RIVER PUBLISHING

WITH BONE AND IRON

COMING SOON

IT CALLS FROM THE SEA

Printed in Great Britain
by Amazon

58713867R00170